HEMLOCK GROVE

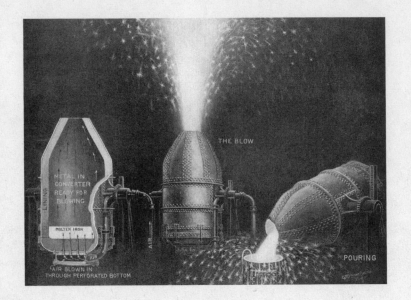

METAL IN
CONVERTER
READY FOR
BLOWING

LINING

MOLTEN IRON

AIR

AIR BLOWN IN
THROUGH PERFORATED BOTTOM

THE BLOW

AIR

POURING

HEMLOCK GROVE

or, The Wise Wolf

O

BRIAN McGREEVY

Farrar, Straus and Giroux
New York

Farrar, Straus and Giroux
18 West 18th Street, New York 10011

The Library of Congress has cataloged the first edition as follows:
McGreevy, Brian, 1983–
    Hemlock Grove : a novel / Brian McGreevy. — 1st ed.
        p.   cm.
    ISBN 978-0-374-53291-8 (pbk.)
    1. Paranormal fiction.   I. Title.

PS3613.C497245 H46 2012
813′.6—dc23

                                                    2011046352

Movie Tie-in ISBN: 978-0-374-53446-2

Designed by Jonathan D. Lippincott

www.fsgbooks.com
www.twitter.com/fsgbooks • www.facebook.com/fsgbooks

5   7   9   10   8   6   4

Frontispiece: Bessemer blow, Scientific American,
May 1924, courtesy of Rivers of Steel National Heritage Area

To Mom and to Domenica: the perennial dichotomy

Too much of the animal disfigures the civilized human being, too much culture makes a sick animal.

—C. G. Jung

Hemlock growth is usually accompanied by a "black run." This is a stream of unusual darkness in color caused by the slow decay of hemlock needles and other plant material. Periodically, high water will flush these streams and the darkening process will begin again.

—Pennsylvania Department of Conservation

PART I

ADUMBRATIO

Something Happened

The lone wolf howls to rejoin the pack from which he is separated. But why does the pack howl when no wolf is lost?

Isn't it obvious?

Because there is no other way to say it.

○

The night after the Harvest Moon, the body was discovered. It was nearing October and the sun was still hot, but the leaves were falling now with intention and every night was colder. Peter was walking home from the bus stop when he saw the flashing light of a fire truck up at Kilderry Park. He wondered if there had been an accident. Peter, who was seventeen at the time of which I'm writing, liked accidents: modern times were just so fucking structured. He saw in addition to the fire truck a few cop cars and an ambulance, but no signs of wreckage. He turned his head in passing, but there was nothing more to see beyond the norm. Two of the cops combing the area by the swings he knew; they'd hassled him a couple of times in that kind of obligatory cop way that, in Peter's experience, every uniform was an SS uniform. Probably some junkie had OD'd or something. There was that bum who hung out around here, an old black guy with yellow and black teeth and one dead eye that looked like a dirty marble who might not have been old, really. Peter had given him a light once, but no change. Better that paid for his own drugs. His interest flagged. Old black junkie kicks it it's no more news than chance of rain tomorrow. Then he heard it, one sentence. *No sign of a weapon, Sheriff.* Peter looked again but there was no more to see than a milling cluster of uniforms by the tree line and he put his hands in his pockets and went on.

He had a bad feeling.

Nicolae had always told him that he had been born with an unusually receptive Swadisthana chakra and that underneath the surfaces of things, the illusion of the illusion, there is a se-cret, sacred frequency of the universe and that the Swadisthana was the channel through which it would sing to you. And the Swadisthana being located of course just behind the balls, he should always always trust his balls. Peter did not know what it was, but something about the scene in Kilderry Park had his balls in a state of agitation.

When he got home he told his mother, "Something happened."

"Hmm?" she said. She was smoking a joint and watching a quiz show. The trailer was warm and smelled sweet, pot and baked apple. "Hummingbird!" she yelled suddenly, in response to the question *What is the only bird that can fly backwards.*

He told her what he saw. He told her he had a bad feeling.

"Why?" she said.

"I don't know, I just do," he said.

She was thoughtful. "Well, there's cobbler," she said.

He went to the kitchen. She asked if he'd been in town.

"Yeah," he said.

She emptied his backpack of items so small and modest it could hardly be considered stealing while Peter scraped the tar of sugar at the edge of the cobbler and tried to shake this feel-ing. The feeling that whatever had happened in Kilderry Park was no good. And not in some greater existential sense but no good with his number on it. There was a coffee mug on the counter with the comic strip character Cathy on it and a small chip the shape of a shark's tooth that held loose change. He dipped his hand in the mug and went to the door and scattered a handful of coins on the stone path out front.

"Why did you do that?" said Lynda.

Peter shrugged. He had done it because he wanted to hear something dissonant and beautiful.

"You are one strange customer, you know that?" said Lynda.

"Yeah," said Peter.

Nothing Weird About It

And remember: the flesh is as sacred as it is profane.

I forgot this.

Whoops.

O

The green-eyed boy sat alone in the food court and fingered the needle in his pocket. The syringe was empty and unused, he had no use for the syringe. He had use for the needle. The green-eyed boy—he was called Roman, but what you will have seen first was the eyes—wore a tailored Milanese blazer, one hand in pocket, and blue jeans. He was pale and lean and as handsome as a hatchet, and in egregious style and snobbery a hopeless contrast from the suburban mall food court where he sat and looked in the middle distance and fidgeted with the needle in his pocket. And then he saw the girl. The blond girl at the Twist in pumps and a mini-skirt, leaning in that skirt as though daring her not to, or some taunting mystic withholding revelation. Also, he saw, alone.

Roman rose and buttoned the top button of his blazer and waited for her to continue on with a cone of strawberry, and when she did he followed. Maintaining a discreet distance, he followed her through the main concourse and stopped outside a women's apparel store as she entered, and he watched through the window as she browsed the lingerie and finished the cone. She looked around and stuffed a mesh chemise down her purse and exited the store. Her tongue darted to collect crumbs from her lips. He continued following her to the parking structure. She got into the elevator, and seeing there were no other passengers, he called Hold please, and jogged to the car. She asked him what level and he told her the top, and this must have been her floor as well because it was the only button she pressed. They rode up and he stood behind her smelling her trampy perfume and thinking of the underthing in her purse and silently tapping the syringe through the fabric.

"You ever close your eyes and try real hard and trick your brain you're actually going down?" said Roman.

The girl didn't answer, and when the door opened she stepped out curtly, like he was some kind of creep when he was just trying to make friendly conversation. But so it goes. The game as it were afoot.

He took out the syringe and palmed it, stepping out of the elevator, and outpacing the clip of her heels he closed the distance between them. She was now aware beyond question of the pursuit though she neither turned back nor made any attempt to run as he came on her and jabbed in an upward thrust, the needle puncturing skirt and panty and the flesh of her ass, and just as quickly he withdrew as she gasped and he continued past her and down the row to his own car.

He repocketed the syringe and entered the front seat, putting it back all the way. He unzipped his jeans, freeing his erection, and laced his hands behind his head. He waited. After a few moments the passenger-side door opened and the girl got in and he closed his eyes as she lowered her head to his lap.

A few minutes later she opened the door and leaned over and spat. Roman's hands unlaced and his arms came down and as they did his hand fell naturally to her lower back, and just as naturally he rubbed. Nothing weird about it, or even a thing you think about, you rub a girl's back because it's there. But at the feel of his touch she recoiled abruptly and straightened. Roman was confused.

"You don't like that?" he said.

"Oh *no*, baby," she said. "I think it's totally hot."

But she was lying, and lying, he realized, about the first thing, about the needle and sucking his dick, and not what he was asking about, about her hate of the barest human-to-human gesture at the end. He was depressed suddenly and terrifically by the defeated life of this lying whore and he wanted her to be gone now, and to get out of the fucking mall.

"It'll take a hose to get the smell of prole out of my nostrils," he said.

"Poor baby," she said, neither knowing nor making any attempt to care what he meant.

He reached into the blazer and took out the money in cash and handed it to her. It looked wrong and she counted it. It was $500 over the agreed amount. She looked at him.

"You know my name?" he said.

"Yeah," she said. It would have been pointless to say otherwise, everyone knew his name.

He looked at her. "No you don't," he said.

Morbid Curiosity

Details the next day. Brooke Bluebell, a girl from Penrose, the next town, had been found. That is, most of a girl named Brooke Bluebell. Subcutaneous wounds and bite patterns consistent with some wild animal attack, but the coroner could not determine what kind—coyote, bear, mountain lion. Murder wasn't suspected but rumor was not gun-shy. Rape, devil worship, another one just like this in et cetera . . . In first-period gym class Alex Finster, knowing Peter was in hearing range, said he had heard it was Gypsies, fuckin' Gypsy cannibals, tastes like chicken.

"Well, people meat is more like bacon," said Peter.

Ashley Valentine looked at him with disgust.

"I mean, that's what they say," said Peter.

In the main building Peter ran into Vice Principal Spears coming out of the faculty restroom. Vice Principal Spears never had anything to say to Peter. Vice Principal Spears was happy to pretend Peter did not exist so long as Peter gave him no reason otherwise. Neither had anything bad to say about the arrangement. But this morning he gave Peter a thoughtful look and said, "It's just terrible, isn't it?"

Peter nodded. *Just terrible.*

"In this day and age."

Peter shook his head. *This day and age.*

"It just really makes you wonder," said Vice Principal Spears.

"It was probably a bear," said Peter. "I bet it was a bear."

Down the hall Peter could feel the man's eyes between his shoulder blades like pinpricks.

He went to his locker. On the other side of the section was some kind of hushed conversation. He paused as is irresistible when you are privy to business not your own and cocked an ear.

For the lamb which is in the midst of their throne shall feed them, and shall lead them unto living fountains of waters—

Oh. Gay. He continued on his way, passing two girls and Mrs. McCollum standing with heads bowed. Mrs. McCollum's eyes were open and eager for persecution over this commingling of church and state and they locked on Peter's and lighted indignant. Embarrassed, Peter gave a thumbs-up. Whatever peels your banana, lady. Mrs. McCollum shut her eyes, annoyed at the presumptive Satanist's blessing.

—and God shall wipe away all tears from their eyes.

In the three weeks of school before the discovery of most of Brooke Bluebell from Penrose, Peter had made no friends—and lost one.

Peter and Lynda Rumancek moved to Hemlock Grove midsummer. Lynda's cousin Vince had died of alcohol poisoning and left his trailer on the outskirts of town to another cousin, Ruby. But Ruby was newly married to the owner of a pawnshop she frequented and had no use for so plebeian a windfall. So she passed it to Lynda in exchange for half a pack of cigarettes and a hand massage. The Rumanceks preferred trade to charity out of principle and Lynda gave legendary hand massages. The timing was auspicious enough. Lynda and Peter had been living in a small apartment in the city for nearly two years and were feeling the itch. Two years was unnaturally long for a Rumancek to stay in any one place; it made a mausoleum of the brain.

Hemlock Grove was, at this writing, a town in transition. Its past: Castle Godfrey, long the colloquial name for the steelworks, which sat on the riverbank shuttered and half razed in a field speckled with gold and white, goldenrod and Queen Anne's lace. The Godfrey Steel Company, founded in 1873 by Jacob Godfrey, was at its peak an integrated steel outfit encompassing 640 acres and employing upward of 10,000 men in the endeavor of building the country on two axes—vertically in Manhattan and Chicago with high-grade steel from its open-hearth ovens, and horizontally to the west with rail from its Bessemer converters: a gauntlet dropped before heaven and earth, shrouding the sun in clouds of black dust that required the wives of steelworkers to hang whites inside and plated the teeth of livestock miles away with steel filings. But now an old dead thing that interrupted a flower bed. Its future: health care and biotechnology, the two largest employers in the Easter Valley now the Hemlock Acres Hospital, the flagship psychiatric facility of the regional university system, and over the next ridge the privately run Godfrey Institute for Biomedical Technologies. The latter the bastard successor of the steelworks, a 480-foot incongruity of steel and glass the summit of which was the highest point in the county. And known colloquially as the White Tower because it had not in twenty years of operations gone dark once. So after a century-long legacy as a mill town, much of Hemlock Grove had transmuted into middle-class blamelessness. But while the blood of industry may have run dry, the husk, like Castle Godfrey, still breached. Rail yards and strip mines and beached coal barges all fallen to some degree of disuse or decay, streaked with tears of rust in contrast to the forests of the region, the trees and the rivers and the hills day by day overtaking the rude, rotted exoskeleton of the Godfrey empire, all dotted with moldering desanctified churches that had gone the way of the working class.

So—why not?—a change of scenery. Vince Rumancek's trailer was situated in a wooded cul-de-sac at the end of Kimmel Lane, down the hill from Kilderry Park and just past the tracks—the traditional divider of workers and management and to this day a telling indicator of socioeconomic station. Still, good to get out of the city and give your thoughts some elbow room. The nearest neighbors were a retired couple, the Wendalls, who lived half a mile up in a house over a pond Peter sometimes skinny-dipped in late at night. The Wendalls were tame enough. They bore welcoming biscuits and euphemistic praise of Vince—one, one *heck* of a whistler—and hid their discomfiture over the Rumanceks' tattoos. The visible ones, at least. Or Lynda's tolerance of her son's semantic dispute with the Commonwealth of Pennsylvania's definition of "minor"—deduced by the number of Budweisers he consumed over their short visit—and yet how little provocation it took for his laziness to vex her into hurling curses at him in the old tongue, or the lung-flattening hug she pulled them both into on their departure. (The first time I experienced Lynda's embrace I have the distinct recollection of feeling like she was trying to squeeze the last drop of toothpaste from the top of my head.)

Days later they were visited by the Wendalls' granddaughter, Christina. Christina was thirteen and small for it, a girl with chipped painted nails and skinned knees and a black raven's nest bramble of hair containing a face like a single pale egg. Christina was a girl both young and old for her years; she had never shed the breathless curiosity of a child assembling a taxonomy of the known universe—what is that? where did that come from? why is that like that and not another way and what is its orientation with every other thing? why? why? why?—and the only person her own age she knew who wanted nothing more when she grew up than to be a Russian novelist. Naturally, she found it imperative to experience these unfathomables firsthand, and she was not disappointed. How perplexing and thrilling, these Rumanceks! Her own parents were both production support analysts for a firm in the city, and that this lifestyle of breezy and pantheistic irreverence existed and was somehow permissible knocked her sideways. She marveled at Peter especially, a real-life Gypsy close to her own age.

"Half-breed," he corrected her. Nicolae, his grandfather, was full-blooded Kalderash Roma from the Carpathian region but had married a *gadja* woman after emigrating.

"What does any of that mean?" said Christina.

"It means his bloodline will forever ride the earth on two horses with one ass," said Peter.

This setting the tone for their relationship: her confusion over what he was talking about and the evident pleasure it gave him. Half the time she didn't understand what he was saying, and the other half whether or not he was pulling her leg. For example, the bunch of dried milk thistle and centaury root over the door, the purpose of which he said was warding off the Evil Eye. But—whose?

"It's more like buckling your seat belt," he said. "You just never know."

And his claim that her arrival on their doorstep had been presaged by the presence of soot on a candle's wick, or the elaborate pentagram that Peter had carved in a tree trunk. (Not, he told her, a Satan thing, but because each point corresponds to an element and the topmost the soul, and because it looks fucking metal.)

Enough! She demanded of Peter how much of this business was real.

He shrugged. "Let's say it's a bunch of baloney," he said. "Then it's baloney that's been getting people through the night since we humped in caves. Now look around. Would you say the world has its shit together any better without it?"

She hadn't thought of it like that.

"And of course it's all real, numbnuts," he said. "You know it right here." He poked below her belly button.

Thus her doom was sealed.

For their part the Rumanceks received Christina's regular presence the same way they did the bone-bag black cat, all eye and ear, who started hanging around—with shrugging acceptance and one simple stipulation: eat eat eat. Lynda was a woman as cheerful as and similarly proportioned to a beach ball whose maternal inclinations tended to encompass whatever happened to fall into her immediate field of vision.

One afternoon Peter was lying in the hammock idly twirling a string for Fetchit (so named because of Nicolae's habit, owing to an immigrant's lack of sensitivity to cultural nuances, of using "Stepin Fetchit" as an umbrella designation for all black cats) and half listening to Christina explain to him that no matter how funny it sounded there was nothing funny about actually *suffering* from restless leg syndrome, when abruptly she changed the subject and asked him if he was a werewolf. Peter's hand stopped and the cat went for the kill.

Peter cursed and sucked his knuckle. "What the hell would make you say that?" he said.

"Your index and middle fingers are the same length," she said.

Peter removed the hand from his mouth and regarded his symmetrical forefingers.

"Jesus," he said, "where'd you pick that up?"

"I don't know, TV or something. Just one of those things floating around, I guess. But I was just looking at your hand and poof, there it is. So are you a werewolf or what?"

Peter shrugged. "Yeah."

"Really?" she said.

"You bet your ass," he said. "But don't tell your grandparents. It would probably make them uncomfortable."

"Were you bitten by a werewolf?"

Peter made a face at this distasteful notion. He was no fan of violence in general, and in particular when it was directed at him. "Nicolae was the seventh son of a seventh son," he said. "It's in my blood."

"Is your mom?"

"Nah. It's a recessive gene or some shit."

The implications of this revelation crowded her head and she tried to think of something intelligent to ask.

"Do you . . . like being a werewolf?" she said.

"What do you think?" he said.

"I don't know."

"Use your imagination, dipshit."

She evaluated the pros and cons. "It seems like it would be kind of neat," she said.

"Well, it's probably about the best thing in the world, for your information," he said. "So there."

"Really?" she said.

"Obviously," he said.

She was quiet but her mind was still a whirlwind. How about them apples! But in the tizzy of a thousand and one urgent questions she now had, the foremost popped out of her mouth.

"Can I be a werewolf?" she said.

"In theory," said Peter, evasive.

He dangled his arm, snapping his fingers a few times, and Fetchit came and nuzzled the back of his hand.

"Little prick," said Peter.

"Will you bite me?" said Christina.

"Don't be retarded," said Peter.

"Come on." She lifted her leg so her calf was level with him. "Look how young and tender."

"Get that skinny, sorry drumstick out of my face," said Peter. "Wouldn't do you much good anyway. You'd be way more likely to get tetanus and die than turn."

"Yeah, right. I think you're just being selfish."

He considered. "Well . . . there might be another way."

She was eager. "What?"

"Go get me a beer and stop hassling me."

After school started, Christina stopped spending days at the lane and Peter saw her only in the halls, but that was the extent of their relationship as of the first day, when she skipped over to give him a hug in view of her friends, identical twins Alexa and Alyssa Sworn, as beautiful and cruel as albino tigers, who were appalled she would have anything to do with that walking herpes factory, let alone touch him without *scouring* afterward. Though Peter did not take her distance after that personally, it was no picnic being a girl that age.

But the day after most of a girl from Penrose was found in

Kilderry Park, Peter really wished he hadn't told Christina he was a werewolf.

○

Peter made people nervous, and they did not have to know that once a month he discarded his man coat and roved in the purview of arcane and unruly gods to feel it: he was not their kind. Peter didn't mind. He had his family and infinite roads to explore and could not imagine needing more, and if this was at the expense of fitting in—whatever that meant—so what. There was so much to learn from every place. Or at least something worth watching. Who was in love with their best friend's boy- or girlfriend, who was in love with their best friend, who cut, who starved, who locked themselves in the handicapped bathroom to jerk off or cry, who was addicted to what or had been raped by whom—it was everywhere, a wonderful world of darkness and desire right under the roaring bleachers, if you had your eye out. But in the halls of HGHS the greatest concentration by far of curiosity and intrigue collected around two students, brother and sister: Roman and Shelley Godfrey.

Roman was also a senior, well within the innermost ring of privilege and popularity. The Godfrey name as sovereign as Dupont or Ramses, and he made no attempt to obscure it from hair he would think nothing of taking a half day off school to go into the city to have styled and bleached (his bone pallor suggesting a natural dark, not to mention a general indisposition to playing outside), or the small but impressive pharmacy he carried in a tin mint container. And obviously the car. The desire to be burdened by possessions was one that had in the main escaped Peter, but as a teenager of traveling blood he had no defense against anything with a combustion engine and the fact was that car was totally metal. But Roman otherwise had little in common with the other rich kids, exhibiting a nearly complete lack of regard for social expectation. His behavior not rebellious so much as entirely unmotivated to behave in any way that didn't conform exactly to the cast of his mood at the moment, his sense of entitlement as phenotypal as the green eyes. This characteristic of his dynasty dating back to its first possessor, his three times great-grandfather the legendary steel baron, Jacob Godfrey. (Green of course being the color of money.) It had made him mercurial.

But none of this was what Peter found so compelling about Roman Godfrey.

"There's an *upir* at my school," Peter told Lynda the first week. His Swadisthana made him sensitive to these things.

"Well goodness," she said. "What's he like?"

"I don't know. He seems okay."

But Peter did not attempt to strike any sort of aquaintance-ship with Roman. The *upir* were a queer breed. Nicolae had told him stories, by and large unverifiable shadows passing through the mist even for an old Gypsy with a credulous child, but Peter had only ever encountered them personally once before, when he and Lynda were living upstate. He'd wandered onto a lake-front property deep in the Lake Erie woods that Snow Moon. The snow was thick and the trees looked like tufts of frayed black thread pulled through a white comforter and there were three of them, one man and two women. They were drinking wine on a patio and speaking French, each nude except for one of the women, a statuesque mulatto, who wore a Santa hat. Peter knew immediately there was something strange about these people. Beyond the obvious. "*Loup-garou!*" exclaimed the mulatto as Peter emerged from the tree line, and they called to him with great excitement. He came up the stairs and they fawned over him in delight, patting and stroking and putting the hat on him. Making him the life of the party and he was glad to have found such merry friends. But then there was a low whimpering sound in the darkness just beyond the patio and the white woman made a sympathetic *uh-oh* sound as though hearing a baby in need and took a piece of cheese from a platter on the table and held it out to a shape hanging from a tree branch that came close to the house. Peter moved in for a closer look. His stomach became a knot. The shape was a fox with its hind leg in a snare. The leg was broken and from its pathetic, emaciated appearance it had been here awhile. The woman scratched the fox's ears and held the cheese an inch or so below its lowermost reach. The fox's snout worked vainly and she raised her hand just enough for its tongue to lap the morsel, then with a clumsy-me expression she dropped the cheese to the ground. The man smiled at Peter—wasn't this a fun game?—and handed him a piece of cheese. Peter was paralyzed. Many times later he would replay the scenario where he had the presence of mind and the courage to reach out to the fox and snap its neck, but in the vital moment he possessed neither. It was a living thing with a shine still in its eyes and he would have given anything for the bravery to take that from it. With shaking hands he placed the cheese carefully back on the platter and walked down the steps and back to the tree line, not meeting their faces. *"Très vulgaire!"* he heard the white woman say behind him and he felt a light thud against his back. Peter whirled to make sure he wasn't in some danger from their projectiles but she was simply throwing cheese. The man called out insults and turned, waving his buttocks and slapping them emphatically as the mulatto observed him with cool detachment. Peter raced now into the forest, the hat falling softly in the snow behind him.

For days he could hardly stop crying, but after Lynda finally got him to relate the incident she simply shook her head and said, "The French."

Peter could not say whether or to what degree his classmate was of similar character; nevertheless it did not seem like a bad idea to proceed with caution around Roman Godfrey.

But this policy did not prevent Peter from paying careful attention to the *upir*'s conduct the day the news about the Penrose girl was out.

Between second and third period Roman bought an ambitious amount of coke from the resident dealer, with whom he engaged in a prolonged and emphatic debate over who would win in a fight between Batman and Wolverine, then skipped fourth period to nap in his car, a 1971 Jaguar with what had every appearance of a mule cart hitched to the back. At lunch he tossed a Tater Tot into Ashley Valentine's cleavage, and recess he spent sitting on the picnic table in conversation with Letha Godfrey, also a senior and Roman's first cousin, though sharing none of his more outstanding qualities except, it goes without saying, the green Godfrey eyes. In English, Mrs. Pisarro, who took particular exception to Roman's cavalier approach to scholasticism, singled him out to read an excerpt from the poem *Goblin Market*:

> *She clipped a precious golden lock,*
> *She dropped a tear more rare than pearl,*

To Pisarro's surprise, as well as the bulk of the class, his reading was hushed and reverential, investing the dead words with, of all things, dignity.

> *Then sucked their fruit globes fair or red:*
> *Sweeter than honey from the rock,*
> *Stronger than man-rejoicing wine,*
> *Clearer than water flowed that juice;*
> *She never tasted such before,*
> *How should it cloy with length of use?*

The room was quiet. Ashley Valentine closed her eyes. Pisarro was annoyed. Though he was technically doing what he'd been called upon it seemed an all the more diabolical species of sass.

She sucked and sucked and sucked the more
Fruits which that unknown orchard bore,
She sucked until her lips were sore . . .

Alex Finster said, "Poor baby."

Duncan Fritz said he could make it all better.

Roman looked at them wearily. "Are you fucking philistines pretty proud of yourselves?"

"Mr. Godfrey!"

"Sorry, Mrs. P.," he said with expert disingenuousness. "I guess we're all a little rattled by this Kilderry Park thing."

Peter's ears perked.

After school Roman gave his sister a ride home.

If Roman Godfrey was a riddle, Shelley was the epic fornication of mystery and enigma—in all of Peter's own unlikely travels he had not encountered an unlikelier specimen. Shelley was not *upir*, and Peter was frankly at a loss what in the hell you would go about calling her; she was a blind spot for his Swadisthana. Though a freshman and at least anatomically female, Shelley was seven and a half feet tall, her head and shoulders huge and hunched, her skin the pensive gray of a late November sky. One side of her already misshapen face was paralyzed and she could produce no syllables approaching coherence. But the second strangest thing about her was her boots, for lack of a better term. She wore on her feet two hermetically sealed plastic cubes roughly the size of milk crates.

The strangest was the glowing.

Shelley climbed into the cart and Roman behind the wheel and they drove off, Roman turning his head and looking directly at Peter, meeting his eye. The other boy's face frank and impassive, dispelling any doubt he knew he was being watched. Roman tapped the side of his nose: Keep it clean. The car turned from the drive and from her cart Shelley raised one broad palm. Peter returned the wave. He had established a precedent of being friendly to the creature, passing winks or courtly bows, one time stopping her and with his foot removing a trail of toilet paper affixed to one of her cubes. The Godfreys passed from view.

Peter turned to head for his bus and discovered that he was not the only one playing I Spy today: over by the flagpole Christina was watching him; she startled on detection and she disappeared with the flux of bodies. Peter boarded his bus and sat holding one hand in front of him and regarded his symmetrical index and middle fingers together as though examining a manicure. His balls were in a state.

○

That night Peter went to the park. There was no evidence of the girl except for a warning from the police stating that anyone caught trespassing after hours would be incarcerated. He entered, drawing his fingertips in a stutter across the links of the fence, and nosed around until he found it. To say there was no evidence is an exaggeration, the land has a memory of such things. It was behind a bush, maybe ten paces from the perimeter of the woods. Fewer, you were running. The spot. He lay down where Brooke Bluebell had been killed and laced his fingers behind his head and looked up at the stars and the trees on the hilltops and a few miles to the east the halo of the White Tower. The light that never went out.

Her picture was distinct in his mind. It was not that he felt any special kinship with her apart from morbid curiosity, but that all the news agencies had gotten hold of, if not collectively willed, the Picture. You know it, the one where she's in her cheerleading uniform and smiling not for the camera, but for her sister or her best friend or a boy or any of the countless things to put one on her face, when she had one. The Picture, pornographic with tragedy.

He wondered if Roman Godfrey had done it. Peter had been in the hills that night and smelled something, a vague but forbidding malevolence. But it was nothing that coalesced at the time, and with a mental hospital down the road you could expect some funny vibrations come full moon. And it wasn't the first time he had felt some occult disturbance in this town. There was something else, a presence of some kind, dwelling underfoot, no manner of thing under the sun. Peter could not get a grasp of its horns but he knew it was down there, older than the hills it lived under. There had been a couple of times when, in a liminal state on the hammock, a vision would come to him of a snake, a Bible black serpent slowly and sensually consuming itself by the tail. But then his eyes would snap open and he would look at the sky through a lattice of boughs and irritatedly push it out of his mind. Peter had a great talent for not losing sleep over questions to which he did not know the answer, so these intrusions on that very sleep really rattled his cage. But it, whatever *it* was in some dark place underneath and older than these hills, was not the same thing that had killed Brooke Bluebell from Penrose. He knew it in his Swadisthana. The world is a body and different parts channel the frequency differently. Some *more* than others, closer to the pulse of mystery underneath the illusion of the illusion. Hemlock Grove was such a place, and the thing under the hills—if *thing* was not itself an overstatement—was part of it, fearful and unknowable, like the "thing" that superintended that animals breathe in what trees breathe out.

Could the girl have been the victim of a wild young *upir*? Possibly. It was not their traditional style, but the breed was capable of far greater transgressions. Or so old wives had it. And though Roman did not really seem the type, Peter was one to talk about how far to trust appearances.

There was a breeze and it carried the smell of grass and he held up his hands to feel it pass between his fingers when he saw something in the tree line: a gleaming—no, a twin gleaming, eyeshine: it was a pair of eyes, glowing like a cat's. Peter rose. Roman Godfrey emerged. They stood apart, looking at each other. Their clothes rustled in the breeze and the cicadas were indifferent.

"What was it like?" said Roman.

"What was what like?" said Peter.

Roman hesitated, hands together, fidgeting. Scared?

"Killing that girl."

You're Not the Only One

"I didn't kill her," said Peter. "I figured it was you."

Roman was confused. "Me? Why would I do it?"

Peter shrugged. "Why would I?"

"People are saying you're a werewolf," said Roman.

"You believe everything people say?"

Roman persisted. "Then why did you come back? Is this your territory or something?"

Peter's hackles went down, identifying no immediate threat of attack. He sat Indian-style. "Territory is so bourgeois," he said airily.

Roman eyed him. "Are you sure it wasn't you?"

"You could try to like contain your disappointment," said Peter.

"I was just asking," said Roman, chastised. He sat too and picked a leaf from a bush. "Then who was it?" he said.

"Bear," said Peter. "Cougar. Creative suicide."

Roman tore the leaf down the middle and rubbed the halves between his forefingers. "It's weird," he said. "I knew her. I mean, I didn't know her know her. But to see her. Parties and stuff. She liked my car." Tearing the leaf into quarters. "Now she's dead. How fucked is that?"

"It's a nice car," Peter said.

"I also knew your uncle or whoever," said Roman.

"Vince?" said Peter.

"Yeah. Sometimes we'd have bonfires and he'd show up with a bottle of hooch. I liked his stories. The girls would get pretty freaked out, but girls, you know?"

Peter nodded that the intrusion of an alcoholic vagrant who had grown tired of shaving by the age of fifteen was the kind of thing to put girls in a state.

"I didn't know him very well," said Peter. "He called me Petey and I didn't like that much. But he always used to slip me one last nip after Lynda cut me off and sometimes he had this way of passing out while he was still sitting at the table with his eyes open that I thought was a neat trick." He was reflective. "I guess he had a real problem."

A cloudywing moth passed close by and Peter's arm darted out to catch it. A flair for opportunistic showmanship ran in the Rumanceks' blood and he was pretty sure he could get twenty bucks from the rich kid in a dare to eat it. But his hand wasn't clever enough and the moth fluttered off.

Roman tore the leaf into eighths and let them sprinkle to the ground. "I remember coming here with my dad," he said. "I don't have too many memories of him, but I remember when I was pretty young and being here and getting stung on like the webbing between my toes and the look on his face. How helpless he was. Because there was no way for him to figure out why I was crying like that. Until my foot swelled up like a tit with toes."

"What happened to him?" said Peter.

Roman made a gun out of his hand and blew his own brains out.

"Shee-it," said Peter.

"Shee-it," said Roman.

"My mom says my dad is dead or something," said Peter. "She doesn't really get more specific. Ladybug."

Roman brushed a ladybug from his lapel.

"What's it like?" he said. "Living like, you know. You people."

It didn't bother Peter being referred to as "you people"—it respected the fundamental boundary of life: haves and have-nots. And Peter did not account himself the impoverished one.

"I guess there's always something over the hill I gotta see," he said. "What's in your sister's shoes?"

A pair of headlights fell on them and a police light flashed silently.

"Shit," said Peter.

"It's cool," said Roman, but Peter was already sprinting for the tree line. He stopped in the same shadows from which Roman had appeared and watched as the pair of cops he knew emerged from a sheriff's cruiser and approached Roman, who looked up into the flashlights without concern.

"Get yourself lost, buddy?" said the shorter one, who had a fat weight lifter's build and no real neck to speak of.

"I'm fine but appreciate your concern, officer," said Roman.

"It's that Godfrey kid," said the other, tall and reedy with a shrilly aggressive nose that led his stooped walk, a drawn bow waiting for release.

"You know it's a school night?" said Neck.

"I'm a night owl," said Roman.

"You know you're not supposed to be here, wiseass," said Nose. "I don't care what your name is."

"Am I disturbing anyone, officer?" said Roman.

"Who was that with you?" said Neck. "Was it that punk Gypsy? Now what could you two birdies be hatching out here that we would look upon favorably?"

"We were having a conversation," said Roman.

"What about?"

"The mysteries of mortality," said Roman.

"Okay, let's go," said Nose.

Roman looked at him, he looked into his eyes and for a fleeting moment his own candesced in that same cat's eye way that had attracted Peter's attention in the first place, and he said with a kind of rote inflection as though feeding an actor his line, "But his old lady's gonna be a pain in the balls."

Nose was quiet. His face was a whiteboard between periods.

Then his eyes blinked several times rapidly and he said, "You know, on second thought, his old lady's gonna be a pain in the balls."

"What?" said Neck.

Roman looked into his eyes. "Yeah. Beat it, kid."

"Yeah," said Neck. "Beat it, kid."

"Yes sir," said Roman.

They returned to the cruiser, Neck muttering, "Spooky little fucker."

Once they'd gone, Peter rejoined Roman.

"I bet you save a lot of money on roofies," said Peter.

"Potting soil," said Roman. "That's what's in her shoes."

Peter's tongue stood at a crossroads between silent acceptance and trying to understand any of this. He said nothing.

Roman lay down flat and put his ear to the ground like a movie Apache.

"Can you feel it?" he said.

"What?" said Peter.

"Whatever it is that's . . . down there."

"Oh," said Peter. "That."

"Good," said Roman. He stood. "It's good to know you're not going crazy."

"Or you're not the only one," said Peter.

A cloud drifted over the White Tower. There was probably the sound of a train.

○

From the archives of Dr. Norman Godfrey:

From: morningstar314@yahoo.com
To: ngodfrey@hacres.net
Subject: Let them eat croutons!

Dearest Uncle,

Another week and time again for you to indulge my incorrigible
prattle. I would suggest you've opened Pandora's (in)box, were
it not so laborious pecking at the keys with the eraser end of a
pencil—these fingertips the Almighty (with some assistance
from Dr. P.) saw fit to provide too, shall we call it, abundant,
to press one key at a time. I suppose it would be simple enough to
request Mother order me some variety of keyboard receptive
to a less dainty touch, but I've grown to appreciate that every
word I choose is the product of deliberate effort. It seems to
me so many who don't need to select their words carefully,
do not.

Now what's happened since our last correspondence worthy
of my eraser's attention? (An irony that somehow escaped me
until this moment—how wonderful!) Of course—you will be
so proud of me, Uncle, I followed your advice and asserted my
independence to Mother. We were having dinner at the club,
Mother, Roman, and I, and while orders were being taken I
noticed a salad of the most stirring medley of color pass. So
just as Mother was telling Jenny I would be having my usual I
impetuously took up a menu and pointed with great vigor.

"Is that what you want, honey?" said Jenny, my most favorite
of the club staff.

"No, no," corrected Mother, "we'll be going with her usual, I
believe."

Which is, of course, a tureen of chopped beef.

But I shook my head and gesticulated once more to my bold whim.

"Darling," said Mother, "you must have your meat."

To which Roman made an off-color remark. Jenny, with whom he regularly engages in light flirtation (and perhaps more outside her place of employment—how fatiguing it is trying to keep track of my brother's extracurricular activities), hid a smirk. Mother was cross.

"Her usual will be quite satisfactory," she said in her the-matter-is-settled voice. Which I confess would have withered my determination on the vine were it not for divine Jenny's intervention.

Resting her hand on my shoulder with no hint of repugnance, she said, "Oh now, she's just thinking of her figure. All those cute boys at the high school."

I could have kissed each of her fingers one by one but restrained myself to an absurd grin from which Roman dabbed a regrettable strand of spittle.

"Now, Shelley," said Mother, the terrifying reason of her tone reflecting her increased annoyance at this alliance, "whatever decision you make you'll have to live with. I think both of us know you'll end up wishing you'd made the more appropriate choice."

She looked at me, naturally expecting acquiescence. How it startled her when I firmly tapped the menu one final time. And though Mother was, in fact, correct—my stomach was rumbling its second guess before we'd even gotten home—I nursed that hunger all night as proof I was indeed capable of living with my decisions. But without a single instant's regret!—tasting all the while the delectable discord between the sweet of the apricot and bitter of the spinach, the effusive pepper and rakish scallion, chaste almond and concupiscent tomato: a feast if not for the belly then the spirit. And more important, I feel as though Mother took note. I am more than some living—albeit unwieldy—marionette who will dance obediently at the manipulation of her strings; as you have been so kind to suggest, I am an intelligent, autonomous individual with valid desires. I believe this encounter may have earned your nervy niece some small measure of, does she dare say it? respect.

Otherwise, I'm finding the transition to high school genial enough. My studies are coming apace; I continue to progress at a rate in defiance of standardization: while the more advanced of my classmates are occupied with Spanish subjunctives or trigonometric functions, I am at my corner—my sanctuary—in the back boning up on my classical Greek or Bohm's quantum mind hypothesis (food for thought—I am indebted for the recommendation). I am also, it shall please you to hear, racking up friends at a positively dizzying pace! Christina Wendall has taken to giving me sympathetic looks when no one is watching—working her way, I'm confident, to a proper introduction (as though words had more to offer than the plain grace of the soul's window); your own Letha remains, as I'm sure is no news to you, a positive angel; and that Gypsy boy I referred to once before continues to favor me with his charms. What a devil he is!—a few inches shorter than the other boys his age, but broader in the shoulder (of course, either way he is doll-sized relative to your affectionate authoress). He is of swarthy complexion with a black ponytail possessing the sheen that suggests petroleum jelly as his hair product of choice. Roman says he is a werewolf. Mother says he is vermin and to have no truck with him (directed, naturally, at Roman—it would not occur to her to include me in such an admonition).

I do hope he was not involved in the incident at Kilderry Park. (How I wept when I heard.) Of course, if I am to live with the decisions I make, I suppose I ought to take care with questions to which I may prefer not to know the answer.

Yours always,
    S.G.

The Angel

The virgin placed the applicator on the counter and rinsed her hands and sat on the edge of the tub, waiting. Not for the answer; the answer she knew. The test was for them, for the proof she knew they would need. Or at least a certain extent of proof, to be sure a conversation starter.

Check with your physician if you get unexpected results, it said on the box. This was one way of putting it.

The virgin looked at the pending window of the applicator. She was not unafraid, but more so she remembered the way it had shone, the halo over his head, shining not just gold but all the colors in a shimmering aurora. She stood up and inhaled deeply, puffing out her belly, and held her breath and rubbed her hands over that uncanny foundry, the ember of his perfect light inside it.

○

Olivia Godfrey met Dr. Norman Godfrey at the Penrose Hotel bar the next afternoon. Olivia was an unpleasantly beautiful woman of indeterminate age. She wore a white Hermès pantsuit in brazen Old World indifference that Labor Day had been weeks ago, with a head scarf around a head of black hair and blacker Jackie O sunglasses. She sipped a gin martini. Dr. Godfrey was a trim man in his middle age with prematurely graying hair and beard, and eyes that under normal circumstances had a certain cast of patrician magnanimity, this the favored result of the parallel character traits of a deep fundamental kindness and near complete lack of humility. But these were not normal circumstances and his stride was hard with purpose, his green Godfrey eyes bullets in extreme slow motion. She slid a scotch neat down the bar at his arrival and he ignored it.

"Did you have anything to do with it?" he said.

"Why *thank* you, Olivia," she said. Her accent was careful British with continental traces. She had been in her time an actress of some favor on the boards of the Lyceum and even at their most extemporaneous her words had the ring of her craft.

He regarded her evenly. His composure was volcanic.

"Don't think, answer. Were you or that walking God complex in any way involved?"

"Norman, you'll *really* have to be a little more goddamn specific," she said.

"Letha's pregnant," he said.

"Oh." Her lips were a perfect formation of the syllable. "Well, I'm afraid you'll find me inadequate to such a task, and as for Johann, I think we both know his . . . proclivities lie elsewhere."

"I am not fucking around here," he said. The bartender looked over.

"Lower your voice," she said. "Sit down." She patted the stool next to her. *Come come.*

He sat. "You will drop that patronizing tone right now," he said.

"Well, you have to admit that's a fairly *astonishing* accusation to respond to in a civilized fashion."

"We haven't reached the accusation stage. Right now it's just a question and you *will* give me a straight answer."

"No, Norman, I had nothing to do with it," she said. "Nor, to my knowledge, did Dr. Pryce, and frankly that you would feel compelled to ask would be beyond outrageous were it one *iota* less mystifying."

He tilted his glass one way and the other regarding the level plane of the liquor.

Her tone became delicate. "Has it occurred to you she may be . . . reluctant to share with her father the specific circumstances of conception?"

He tapped the glass on the bar top in punctuation of a private punch line and laughed bitterly. "Reluctant? No. Not reluctant," he said.

She looked at him.

"She says she's still a virgin," said Godfrey.

She was quiet. He responded to her silence.

"She says," said Godfrey, "it was an angel."

She was quiet.

"She says it visited her this summer," he said, "and she didn't say anything at the time because she didn't want us getting all bent out of shape—her words—but she felt the time had come she needed our help with the . . . child. And she took a pregnancy test, so she's not hallucinating that part."

"Has she got a boyfriend?" she said.

"None lately."

"Has she been going to church?"

"When have you known this family to go to church when someone hasn't died?"

"What's your . . . professional evaluation?"

He looked at her. Was that a real question.

"Rape," he said. "She was raped and her mind bricked it over with this fantasy. The clinical term is *psychogenic amnesia*."

"Have you contacted the police?"

"With what? My suspicion of something that would have happened in July that she won't corroborate? At this point my hope is to talk her out of keeping it."

Her eyebrows arched. "Is that for the best?"

"As opposed to encouraging her to carry to term a child she's convinced is a product of immaculate conception, at seventeen, when at any minute the actual event could come back to her after an irrevocable decision has been made?"

She nodded the point.

"Now might I ask what could possibly give you the notion I could have any involvement in this?" she said.

He regarded his reflection in the wall mirror across the bar. He had found that when his hair had begun to silver, maintaining a neat beard conferred on him a certain archetypal authority: I have things under control. The fact was he could provide no rational explanation for why he was here. Last night his crying wife had left the room and he had remained seated and his child had taken his hand across the table with the grace of the sunrise, and in that moment when there wasn't another comprehensible thing left to him he had a feeling. Darkly and obscurely and defiant of any rational analysis, he felt Olivia's hand in this. And that feeling, it had to be admitted, was not having things under control. It was in fact no more rational than his daughter's explanation. It made his beard a liar. But independent of the absurdity of this intuition, hopelessly apparent on voicing it, he understood now its true and ugly little function. It gave him something to hit back.

"Because I honestly have no fucking idea what you would be capable of if you were afraid of losing me."

He glared at her. She removed her sunglasses and met his eye.

And then the hard and angry thing sheltering him to his hot relief cracked and he covered his face and wept. A booth of half-drunk lawyers pretended not to stare. Olivia gently rubbed the back of his neck with one hand. She replaced her sunglasses with the other and pulled her olive from the toothpick and stripped it of brine with her tongue.

○

They went up to their customary room and had the customary dispassionately antagonistic sex that was the way things were done for years. Afterward Olivia lay on her stomach smoking a cigarette though smoking had not been permitted in their room for some time, but the notion of moving to another was not one they would have given any more serious thought than a bird would flying north for the winter. It was not the way things were done. There ran along Olivia's spine above the coccyx, like the mountain range of a relief map, a pale, pinkie-length scar, the remnant of some crude surgery. Dr. Godfrey was up and stuffing his shirt into his trousers. His eyes swept the floor.

"Where's my—" He saw her foot waving to and fro and his tie dangling between her toes. He reached for it but her foot darted away. He seized her ankle and took his tie and moved to the window, looping it around his neck. Visible across the river on the Hemlock Grove side was the lancing flame burning waste gas from a chimney of the coke works, now operated by a Luxembourg steel company but once a part of the Godfrey dynasty of polluting vulgarity that like so much else was lives ago.

He sat on the edge of the bed and pulled his socks on. Olivia exhaled smoke and steepled her fingers.

"I was afraid you meant it," she said. "Last time."

Last time, which had been in the spring, he had said not to expect him to call again. It was news to both of them, his saying it had surprised him maybe even more than her. The way the most obvious thing can be the least thinkable. Atlas shrugged.

"I see," she'd said eventually.

"Because I just don't have the energy anymore," he answered in explanation to himself.

"The energy for what?" she said. It was a rhetorical point, and a correct one. Their arrangement required none. It was a perpetual motion machine by now, older than the tides. He knew married men who would kill for it. Men who would kill for her. It occurred to him he had once been a man so worthy of envy and pity.

He said nothing. His face was a much-used sponge that had not actually held moisture in years.

"Please," she said. The quiet dignity with which she said this word belying how infrequently she used it. "Please . . . think about it."

He lied without charity that he would and in the interim had not. He had instead taken up drink as affective novocaine. If the point of novocaine was the numbing of a numbness. In his last loveless years Jacob Godfrey was known to spend hours on end standing in the front yard of the house he had constructed at the summit of the highest hill in the valley. He would survey the land of his sovereignty, a land he had forged into his own vision through blood and fire, and know at his life's epilogue that it was all a petty, transient thing, nothing about it transubstantial, and that here he was just a lone and useless rich man at the house on the hill, visible and still forgotten. Dr. Godfrey had spent his entire life terrified of this fate and taking every step to rebel against it by throwing himself into a vocation that was as antithetical as he could imagine: compassion. Hence his calling to psychiatry, the meeting place of matter and spirit. He had helped people, so many people, and what more can be said than that? I helped. Tell me what else there is to be said.

Presently he stood and said, "I meant it. I didn't want this to happen. This was—"

"Spiteful," she said.

"Weak," he said.

"We'll agree to agree," she said.

She held out the butt of her cigarette. He took it into the bathroom and dropped it in the toilet, then stood in front of the mirror and smoothed his hair. Olivia rested her face in her hands.

"Frightful business," she said. "This Penrose girl."

"Your daughter thinks it was a werewolf."

"My daughter has an impressive imagination." She rolled onto her back into a full-body stretch. "Still . . . it does hold a terribly erotic sort of appeal. Being hunted down and *devoured* by some savage brute. It's enough to give one the shivers."

He shut off the bathroom light and went to the door. She made no move to cover herself.

"I meant it, Olivia," he said.

She smiled wistfully. "What makes you think I don't know that?"

○

On the third Saturday of October Roman gave Letha and a few friends a ride home from the movies. By now the agitation over Brooke Bluebell had settled. There was no target to which blame could be nailed, no face to the outrage, nothing to be done except the handful of hunters who attempted to track the creature that had left a ghostly lack of trace, nothing to be said except how senseless, utterly senseless it was, and how it just went to show you. Leaving unspoken what was nonetheless agreed: at least she wasn't from here.

Once it was just the two of them left in the car Roman produced from his blazer the flask of vodka from which he had been taking slugs during the movie and helped himself to another, then held it decisively in Letha's face. She'd been waving it away all evening with what he considered an appalling lapse in manners. She made no move to take it so he gave it a shake in case it had somehow escaped her attention.

She held up her arms in an X and told him to get over it.

"Since when?" he said.

"Since get over it," she said.

Growing up, Roman and Letha had seen almost nothing of each other; there had been no formal meeting between the branches of their family since the death of Roman's father and the two of them did not have regular contact before high school. Letha had gone up till then to a private Episcopalian academy but had found that the elitism made her bones ache: Roman did not seriously consider any of the prep schools it would have been logical for someone like him to attend for the simple and unthinkable reason it would have required living away from home. So when they did finally indulge their mutual curiosity it was with the bond of blood but none of the familiarity. Letha was a small and sandy blond girl with distinctively idiosyncratic features that were as far from pretty in the conventional sense as they were from homely, and where Roman was mercurial, Letha was mystical. She possessed a kind of half-step-removed sense of discovery as though she passed through life having just woken from a successful nap. Naturally this polarity drew them only closer—a fact that filled her father with no small disquiet.

Roman made a wounded face. "Have a drink like a civilized person," he said.

"Watch the road," she said.

Roman merged left onto 443. They entered the mouth of a wooded passage between two hills, and dark branches from either side made a trellis overhead.

"Don't be uncivilized," he said.

"Can we drop it?" she said.

"We can drop it when you stop being a See You Next Tuesday and have a drink."

"Roman, drop it."

"What, are you pregnant or something?" he said.

She said nothing. He looked at her.

"Shut up," he said.

She nervously smoothed her hair.

"Shut your lying whore mouth," he said.

"I . . . was waiting for the right moment," she said.

He drank, and pulled suddenly onto the shoulder and stopped the car. Route 443 was a road with many dips and blind curves with regular accidents for that reason.

"Roman, start the car," said Letha.

He sat with his hands on the wheel, unmoving.

"Maybe I didn't tell you because I didn't want you to be a drama queen," she said.

"Is it Tyler?" he said.

Tyler was a boy Letha had dated briefly in the spring, an utter drip Roman held in just about the regard of a wet towel left on the bed. But now Roman sat looking ahead and in the center of his mind's eye he saw the other boy while off on the edges there was a dark flickering like a pair of taloned shadow hands slowly wrapping around his face.

"It wasn't Tyler," she said. "Now please start the car and stop being a drama queen."

Tyler left his mind but those dark fingertips continued to dance, to taunt, to close.

"Who," he said.

"I don't want to talk about it unless you start the car."

He rolled down the window and took the keys from the ignition and dropped them onto the ground outside.

"Who," he said.

"See? I knew you were going to make a federal case over it."

"Who," he said.

She folded her arms. "Well, you sound like the world's dumbest owl," she said.

He shut his eyes, wanting the shadows to go away, but they didn't care whether or not his eyes were closed. He opened his eyes and took one hand off the wheel and pressed the horn so it made one long blare.

"Who," he said.

"Stop it, Roman."

"Who," he said.

"Stop it, Roman."

He centered his vision on his hand on the horn, only distantly hearing it. This is really here, he reminded himself, growing less convinced.

"Stop it, Roman!"

The finger began to lace and he grew less convinced.

Afraid, she tore his hand from the wheel and clasped it hard between her own.

"It was an angel," she said.

The shadow evanesced from his mind's eye and he grew aware of a pressure, the pressure of her hands on his. Really here.

"It was a what," he said.

"It was an angel," she said.

He was quiet.

"Literally?" he said.

"It was an angel," she said.

He was quiet.

"Tell me about it," he said.

"How would you talk about dancing to a person without legs?" she said.

"I have legs that won't quit," said Roman. But as someone who was by nature a taker he knew when he had taken exactly as much as he was going to get. Though it had never before been so much more and so much less than what he wanted.

He opened the car door and leaned out and picked up his keys. He took a long drink from the flask and turned the ignition and pulled back onto the road.

"Told your folks?" he said.

"They're . . . adjusting," she said.

Roman raised his eyebrows. Imagine that.

"Mom is coming around to where she can even admit it. Dad . . . Dad wants me to have an abortion."

"Holy cow," said Roman.

"He thinks it's all in my head."

Roman offered no opinion.

"But I'm having this baby." Stated with a calm, nonpartisan, and immovable authority. "Deal with it," she said.

"I didn't say anything," he said.

"Deal with it," she said.

Roman rounded a curve carefully, his drunk driving always

much more conscientious when Letha was in the car. Neither spoke for a while as he dealt with it.

She let him. She had not enjoyed hiding this from everyone she loved. Liar! In fact possession of a miracle all to herself had filled her with a private thrill no less than a pack rat who had stumbled across a lost temple of fascinating refuse—it was hers, all hers! But now the time had come to share it; it was no longer hers alone. Annoyingly.

Roman did not reopen the subject, but he did pick up his iPod and put their song on the sound system. Their song was a British pop-rock ballad about a rich girl who sexually slums it with a poor boy in the interest of vacationing among the lower classes. Their mutual appreciation of this song was a private joke between them, being the only members of their own peer group who could relate to the unique position of having been born into irrational privilege. Letha began to hum along and Roman gave the volume a quarter turn up and followed shortly with another.

You'll never do what common people do

And soon enough the dial could turn no farther and both Roman and Letha sang along with it at full volume, her hair swept from side to side as she danced in the passenger seat and he steered with his knee and pretended to drum the wheel.

You'll never watch your life slide out of view

They rounded another bend where the vagrant who frequented Kilderry Park was lying in the middle of the road directly in their path. Roman slammed the brakes and the car screeched to a near perpendicular angle before humping to a crass stop. The air was bitter with hot rubber and the radio continued.

because there's nothing else to do-o-o-o-o

Roman turned off the music and asked Letha if she was okay.

She nodded, looking out at the man. The man was on his back, grimacing and mashing his palms into his temples as though trying to squeeze something out.

"We should help him," she said.

Roman nodded in disagreement. But there you had it with girls and their notions. He put on the hazard lights.

"Maybe you should stay here," he said.

They both exited but Letha stood by the car as Roman cautiously approached the man. There was on his shirt a damp bib of vomit and he smelled like the underside of a bridge. Roman asked if he was okay and the man emphatically jerked his head from side to side in indignation over what he heard in place of Roman's question.

"It's not right," said the man.

"Would you like to come with us?" said Letha.

Roman winced. "Calling the paramedics is also an option," he said.

"I don't want to see," said the man in an infantile whine. "I don't want to se-e-e-e-e tha-a-a-at."

Roman stepped to the side and dialed 911 on his phone as Letha came forward. He tried to stare her back as the call connected but she knelt over the man.

"What's your name?" she said.

"I don't know, there's a guy here on the road, I nearly hit him," said Roman into the phone. "I think he's schizophrenic or something."

The man looked at Letha with terrified incomprehension. The lid of his dead eye twitched.

"What's your name?" Letha said again, with a preternaturally supple bedside manner like a nun played by Ingrid Bergman.

"Uh, 443," said Roman, "about two miles south of the White Tower. Right before Indian Creek."

A look came over the man's face like there was suddenly something of desperate importance he needed to communicate.

"Ouroboros," the man whispered.

"Is that your name?" said Letha.

"He's just, uh, he's out here in the middle of the road freaking out. He really needs some kind of help."

His gaze fell from her face. Tears streamed from one eye.

"Today I have seen the Dragon . . ." said the man.

She held out her hand.

"Don't—" said Roman.

But the man took her hand and held it, a flower known to be extinct.

"I'm Letha," she said.

"What?" said Roman. "My name?"

He hung up and gently drew Letha away.

"Okay, boss," he said, "how about we chill out right over here where no one's gonna makes us roadkill?"

He swallowed his own antipathy and bent to lend the man a hand. The man's eye met his. The seeing eye like bloody milk, spotlit and then shadowed in the blinking hazards. Roman attempted something like a smile, it was like lifting a thousand pounds overhead. The seeing eye became a thorn that hooked into Roman and the man held up his hands protectively and they fluttered frantic and effete as he screamed with full-throat horror.

"Jesus!" said Roman, leaping back.

The man desperately crab-walked to the side of the road. *"YOU!"* he screamed. *"IT WAS YOU! IT WAS YOU! IT WAS YOU! IT WAS YOU!"*

Roman was still and quiet. He felt a tug on his arm; Letha was pulling him to the car. His eyes lingered on the man, who had backed himself into an escarpment and his legs continued pushing uselessly, like a remote control toy commanded by a cruel child.

"I don't want to see," he said pitifully to himself, and repeated this appeal in incantation long after the car had disappeared.

They sat in the car in competing silences. As they passed over Indian Creek, Letha looked at Roman. The moonlight on his affectless face like silk gliding over stone. Her hand rested over his on the shift.

A Pattern

Later that night Roman was sitting at the darkened dining room table sipping from the flask and slowly counting the number of crystals that comprised the chandelier—160, he knew well, but the product of 40 fours was considerable comfort to him and its confirmation a soothing process—when those crystals began to glitter from a faint light.

"What are you doing up?" said Roman.

Shelley was filling most of the doorway. She was wearing a shapeless nightgown and emitting a soft glow, an idiosyncrasy of hers when experiencing agitation and anxiety.

"Thirsty?" he said, offering the flask.

She did not move and in her eyes there was the justifiable apprehension over what pyrotechnics habitually erupted in Godfrey House after a period of studied silence.

"I'm fine," he said unconvincingly. "I'm . . . just thinking."

Her glow gently lapped the ceiling through the chandelier like the light in an indoor pool. He shoved back from the table.

"I'll tuck you in," he said.

They went up to the attic, where Shelley slept on a stack of king-size mattresses, with another stack of twins crosswise at the foot. Shelley did not have an auspicious relationship with bed frames. The walls were lined floor to ceiling with books and in one corner was an easel and in another an antique astrolabe consisting of concentric brass rings. The ceiling was a firmament of many dozens of glow-in-the-dark star and moon stickers.

Shelley sat on the bed. Roman stood at the astrolabe and placed his fingertip to the rim of the outermost ring and traced an orbit. He regarded the darkening of dust on his fingertip, the abstruse whorls and eddies providing a pattern but not a clue. Outside, there was an owl's low hoot and Shelley's light guttered under her gown.

He brushed his finger along his jeans and came over and sat on the edge of her bed, facing away from her. She waited for him to say something.

Softly, he began to hum. She smiled wide and joined in with him. He started the words and she kept the melody.

"This little light of mine," he sang,

"I'm gonna let it shine . . ."

He turned and ran his finger down Shelley's cheek, leaving a faint, luminous worm in its wake.

"Come on," he said. "Let's brush your teeth and change your shoes."

Peripeteia

On the afternoon of October 29, Roman surprised Peter by passing him a note in English. A month had passed; tonight was the Hunter Moon. No further relationship had developed between them since their earlier meeting, which Peter believed to be for the best. Roman was unstable, like a coin spun on a tabletop: the closer it came to rest, the greater its velocity, now one end up then the other. He was neither heads nor tails. And of all potential outcomes in their continued association nearly none fell outside Peter's extensive Hierarchy of Shit He Could Live Without.

But then, without warning albeit in keeping with his mercurial nature, Roman handed Peter a piece of folded notebook paper with a disarmingly plain request:

can i watch?

"Are we passing notes, Mr. Godfrey?" said Mrs. Pisarro.

"Wouldn't dream of it, ma'am," he said.

After the bell rang, Peter approached Roman. He had debated all period and convinced himself that indulging the other boy's curiosity was the more sensible course than evasion—discouraging him would only egg him on. But in truth his Rumancek blood would not permit him to pass up an opportunity to show off. He said, "Come by around five."

"Holy shitbird, is that Gypsy butt-pirate asking you out?" said Duncan Fritz.

"Eat a tampon, you uncouth mongoloid," said Roman.

The sky was in a hierarchy of reds when Roman arrived at the Rumanceks'. Peter let him into the trailer, a dense babel of inherited and inventively scavenged furniture and incense and healing stones and Hollywood musical collector plates and figurines of Renaissance masterworks and unreturned library books and a cabinet devoted to the Indian god Ganesh gaudily bordered with Christmas lights like the Virgin of Guadalupe. Roman stopped at the latter, confused. He asked if they were Hindu or whatever.

Peter shook his head. "He's the god of new beginnings. But I'm not sure if Nicolae ever actually knew that. He would always call him Jumbo and ask him if what he had between his legs was anything like what was on his nose. Nic was a real class act," he added.

He led Roman into the kitchen and introduced him to Lynda, who was placing a pan of peanut butter cookies in the oven. She had been delighted when Peter informed her the *upir* would be visiting them after school: since her son would be out for the evening it gave her someone to cook for. She sat the boys at the kitchen table and asked if they'd like milk.

"Sure," said Roman.

"Honey?" said Lynda.

"Lactic acid," said Peter.

"Right right," she said. She poured Roman a glass of milk and gestured at her own abdomen, spinning the finger. "It does funny things to the tummy," she explained.

Peter's eyes flitted out the window to monitor the sunset. He had, Roman now noticed, a general air of twitchy distraction, rubbing both his biceps like he had a case of the mean reds after smoking his last cigarette.

"So," said Lynda, "what are your plans after graduation?"

Roman shrugged like it was a question of commensurate

49

consequence to his agenda for the weekend. "I guess my mom'll bribe my way into somewhere decent."

"That's nice," said Lynda.

Peter's hand clacked a butter knife on the table independent of any conscious motor command on his part. She laid her hand over his.

"He gets nervous beforehand," she said. "Hormones."

"I have Xanax," said Roman.

Peter declined.

"Maybe just enough to wet my whistle," said Lynda.

Roman took out his tin mint container–cum–apothecary and produced two Xanax, giving one to Lynda.

"Does it hurt?" he asked Peter.

Peter shook his head. "You wouldn't notice if a bus hit you."

"Are you still . . . you?" said Roman.

Peter looked at him. *Guess.*

Lynda reached and pinched her son's rough cheek. "He's a good boy," she said, tugging on the flesh between her fingertips with the brutality of perfect love. "He's his mother's handsome little honeybun."

A few minutes before five-thirty the three of them went outside. Lynda held Roman by the door as Peter went forward. He removed all his clothes. He was brown and covered in black densities of hair and his penis was uncircumcised. On the right side of his rib cage there was a tattoo of a letter, a small *g*.

"What's the *g* stand for?" said Roman.

"'Go suck an egg,'" said Peter.

He walked forward undoing his ponytail and his hair fell around his shoulders. It was as though the scent of falling night soothed his shaky nerves and he moved with a grace and authority invested by no lesser power than the earth under his feet. The air was suddenly so pregnant with anticipation of magic and its brother menace that it occurred to Roman somewhat belatedly to ask if they were safe here.

"It's fine," said Lynda. "Just stand back."

Roman then snapped his fingers and said, "Darn."

"What?" she said.

"I forgot to bring a Frisbee."

With shamanic gravity, Peter raised his middle finger. He glanced at the last of the sun puddling into the horizon like red mercury and got down on his knees, head bowed and hair hanging over his face. He was still. He waited for the calling of his secret name. Lynda clutched Roman's arm. Fetchit sauntered over and sat with one leg splayed, licking himself.

Then there was a spasm in Peter's shoulders. His toes curled and his fingers clutched the dirt. Lynda's grip tightened and Peter let out a cry like nothing Roman knew walked this earth. Peter fell to his side, his face contorted as though pulled by a thousand tiny hooks and muscles quivering in a frenzy of snakes under the skin. The cat fled into the trailer. Peter clutched at the pulsing flesh of his abdomen and raked, leaving pulpy red gashes with wet bristle poking through. He gripped the pulp and tore decisively, the flesh coming away with the slurp of a wet suit to reveal a blood-matted vest of fur. Roman put a hand over his nose as a stench of carrion filled the air and the sloppy, ramshackle operation that moments ago had been known as Peter thrashed its hind parts, the lower half kicking free of its man coat. A wet tail protracted and curled. Its howls all the while more plaintive and lupine as a snout emerged through its lips and worked open and shut, its old face bunched around it in an obsolete mask. It rolled onto all fours and rose shaking violently, spraying blood in a mist and divesting itself of the remnants of man coat in a hot mess.

Now standing before them in the gloaming was the wolf. Roman leaned against Lynda; he had lost his center of gravity. He had not actually known what to expect in coming here tonight, much less that it would reveal to him two essential truths of life: that men do become wolves and that if you have the privilege to be witness to such a transformation it is the most natural and right thing you have ever seen.

"Fuck," Roman whispered.

The wolf was a large animal, tall and sleek and regal as the moon its queen, possessing the yolk sheen of the newly born and lips curling back to reveal white fangs as it yawned and stretched out its forelegs, rump wiggling in the air. Lynda's eyes moist with ultimate maternal egotism and Roman weak-kneed with admiring envy of those fangs, white fangs gleaming, gloating over the purest dichotomy of having/not having. Of course the fangs of a werewolf are of an exaggerated length and curvature more typical of the feline family. They are the final say; once the jaws are closed nothing on earth can escape them. *Lupus sapiens*: the wise wolf. This, Roman, who had lived here all his life, finally saw, is the lord of the forest. You are a serf.

The hurly-burly settled, Fetchit reappeared and inquisitively approached the wolf, which gave the cat a peremptory and aloof sniff before turning its attention to the slop of flesh from which it had been born and burying its snout within with wet gnawing sounds soon following.

"Can I . . . pet him?" said Roman, somewhat recovered. To the extent he ever would be.

"Not while he's eating," said Lynda.

"Peter," said Roman.

The wolf finished its supper and looked over, snout comically wreathed in red pulp, but whether or not there was any recognition in those old eyes it would have been impossible to say. What, however, was with certainty absent was any conventionally canine display of interest or affection. Werewolves, unlike either species of which they are representative, are not pack animals. It defeats the whole point of being a werewolf. This was a wild thing as cosmic and inscrutable as all truly wild things, and having an entire world of smells waiting, it turned and walked intentionally to the trees and with a rustle disappeared.

○

Three days after the Hunter Moon, Christina Wendall cut through a wooded path behind her house to the Walgreens to make a secret purchase. Tyler Lane, an eleventh grader, had asked her out this Friday and not only had she defied expectation by agreeing, but she was also planning on doing something to set expectation on its head. Christina did not have that sort of reputation—really her reputation was pretty much the complete opposite—but recent inner portents suggested to her some significant changes were in the tides. People change—who says they can't? Alexa and Alyssa didn't buy it, pointing out she still blushed at the word *menses*. Christina blushed. But a person could change, and if she was to become an important writer of her time she had an obligation to broaden her horizons. So she was a late bloomer, this gave her Character—peripeteia, they called it in drama class, a turning—but now what was needed was Material. The twins had pretty much bloomed when they were ten, so they didn't understand that. They thought they knew everything, but they didn't. As far as they knew, she hadn't even had her first kiss. There were things they didn't know. At the register the cashier pursed her lips in disapproval but rang Christina's items silently. *Cunt!* trilled an outrageous voice within the reaches of Christina's mind, with such vehemence she had the momentary thrill it might have been audible outside herself.

You see! Who would have had any suspicion a girl who couldn't say the word *menses* went around calling people cunts and fat retarded cows in her head? Saucy little bitch! She caught sight of her small smile in the ceiling mirror. She paid her money but it still felt like stealing.

She returned along the same path twisting the plastic bag on her wrist clockwise and counter and saw in a furrow of earth a small rabbit hole. She stopped. It reminded her of the dream. She considered this another less welcome occult indicator of the turn inside her, the return of a recurring dream she had not had in years. It is a simple dream. She is inside the mill, as she had been once before, in that dark you can feel on both sides of your skin, and something is in here with her. The thing is the same color and smell as the dark. But she knows it's in here all the same; there's a difference between a place where you are the only living thing and where you are not, and something in here is alive. And there is only one place to hide: in the dark she can just make out the outline of that great black cauldron keeled to its side. Of course if she doesn't know what the thing in here is she can't know what it wants, if there's even any reason to hide. But it's a chance she can't take so she makes her way to the cauldron and puts her hands to the lip and peers in. But what if hiding means there is no place to run? What if there is something worse inside the cauldron? Or if there is nothing in it at all? Real bottomless nothing? But there is a dark thing in this mill with her and she can feel its nonshadow fall on her, it is right behind her now and she doesn't know what it will want if she faces it. She is paralyzed. She doesn't know whether to turn and face it or Go Down the Hole.

And then she woke up.

"You can be such a weirdo sometimes you should just tie a ribbon around your skull and walk into the Brain Barn," Alyssa said. (The Brain Barn was the common nickname for the Neuro-pathology Lab at Hemlock Acres, which housed three thousand human brain specimens and was an object of great fascination among local youths.)

Well, what of it? Some people had funny dreams. And moments where they felt that every cell in their body was made of cancer, or that when they breathed they breathed out pure oxygen and breathed in cigarette ash. And broke down into hysterical tears at that video on the Internet of the elephant that paints its own portrait, as Christina had recently in the computer lab, for no more articulable a reason than it seemed to her that all nameless sadness she had ever experienced or for that matter existed in the great ethereal matrix of which all life is part was somehow encapsulated in that video transmitted for light amusement. She was a late and mysterious bloomer with a date on

Friday with an eleventh grader and a plan to show certain some-bodies just how much it was possible for a person to change, so peripeteia and what of it!

As she passed the rabbit hole something else came to view beyond the furrow—an incongruous patch of color—fabric, a shirt. At first she thought it might be a vagrant and she tensed, but . . . did vagrants wear pink? She crept a few steps to peek. It was a girl. Lying on the dried leaves, near Christina's age, a little older. Face pretty but smeared clownishly with mascara and body glitter as though she hadn't washed off last night's makeup, and whoever she was Christina did not know her from school, though she had some inkling of recognition. The girl's eyes were open and staring at the sky with a glazed, insensate look, what Christina would imagine a person hopped up on PCP would look like if Christina knew exactly what PCP was, except the twins' dad occasionally had a cautionary story of people hopped-up on it.

Christina stepped forward and started to ask if the girl was all right but didn't finish. She dropped the bag containing one spiral notebook, one Pilot Precise pen, one diet iced tea, and one box of condoms.

The girl was on the ground, twigs and leaf bits caught up in her splayed hair, arms twisted at all the wrong angles; her pink shirt had an image of a lewdly frosted cupcake on the chest and her skin and lips similar in hue to rubber cement, and, as had been obscured from Christina's vantage: the girl's lower half was missing.

Christina sagged against a tree trunk. No sir. Obviously this was a gag, some kind of cheap prop. It didn't even look real after a second look. Halloween on its way and some guys got this from the mall and left it here for some stupid little girl just like her to stumble on and completely freak out. And she had probably seen the horrible thing on a wall display somewhere and that was where she "recognized" her from but still fell for it. Probably a camera on her as we speak. Okay, if that's your game. She was making a few changes, here was a golden opportunity.

"Oh," she said experimentally to the torso, "you gave me a real scare there." She talked in the suggestive, wide-eyed tones of pornography. Which she wasn't personally familiar with, but sometimes the twins imitated. "Ooh, you look a little pale. Do you need . . . mouth to mouth?"

She was greatly pleased with her own performance. The unseen conspirators somewhere in the trees getting a real bang for their buck. Well, hold on to your hats, fellas. She got on her knees, flushed at her own daring—what a little slut!

"Gosh," she said, "you sure have pretty lips."

She lowered her mouth to the dummy's. The dummy's mouth was moist and feculent like if you have ever had the unfortunate but irresistible impulse to smell a compost jar. Christina fell back, gagging. It was then that she caught movement in the gray-white gore of the lower abdomen, a pulsing that at first she thought was something trying to push its way out. But then it hit her it was actually lots and lots of little pulsing feeding things that were not trying to emerge; this was the last thing they wanted.

○

Who am I? What's my dog in this fight?

I'm the killer.

Boo.

PART II

NUMINOSUM

The Order of the Dragon

From the archives of Dr. Norman Godfrey:

NG: No one's used that word, Mr. Pullman.

FP: This is a fucking crazy house, it's between the *lines*. Check my record. My luck is shit, not my head.

NG: I have. There's no history of psychosis, and your MRI is clean, but that was quite a night you had on Saturday, would you agree?

FP: . . .

NG: Do you have any memory of it?

FP: Check my record. Nothing wrong with my head.

NG: Would you care to discuss it?

FP: You got a name?

NG: My name is Norman. Dr. Norman Godfrey.

FP: . . .

NG: Would you like to discuss Saturday night, Mr. Pullman?

FP: Why are you talking to me?

NG: Why do you ask?

FP: You think I don't know who you are?

NG: Does it matter what my name is?

FP: Why are *you* talking to *me*?

NG: Fair enough. Because my daughter asked me to. You met her on Saturday, do you remember?

FP: . . .

NG: Let's talk about that night, Mr. Pullman.

FP: We talk about it you're gonna lock my ass up here.

NG: Frankly, you already said more than enough the night in question to make a case for that. I'd just like to give you a chance to explain. Now, you repeatedly told the paramedics that "they" had done this to you. Who did you mean?

FP: . . .

NG: You said "they" had killed you.

FP: . . .

NG: Is "they" the government?

FP: Do I got a dick in my mouth? I ain't fucking crazy.

NG: Is it voices?

FP: . . .

NG: Do they talk to you?

FP: . . . I see things.

NG: Such as?

FP: (*inaudible*)

NG: What do you see, Mr. Pullman?

FP: Who else is gonna die.

NG: . . . Can we take a moment for you to elaborate on what you meant when you said you had been killed?

FP: The fuck it usually mean?

NG: But you're sitting here right now.

FP: They brought me back.

NG: How did they pull that off?

FP: Cardiocerebral resuscitation.

NG: I see . . . Can you tell me about Ouroboros, Mr. Pullman?

FP: Where'd you hear that?

NG: It was something else that you mentioned repeatedly. Can you tell me its significance?

FP: Where does the soul go? It's why they killed us. The plan, it's all in their plan. It's not right. It's not right that now we have to see those things. I don't want to see.

NG: "Us"?

FP: Today I have seen the Dragon . . .
NG: I'm having difficulty following, Mr. Pullman.
FP: I seen it. I seen the thing inside her.
NG: What do you mean? The thing inside who?
FP: The thing inside your little girl.

○

If Brooke Bluebell shook the hive, Lisa Willoughby was a fist straight through it. Like Brooke, Lisa was a Penrose native, but the animal responsible was still local. Because the body had been exposed several days, a species still could not be determined, but more baffling was the continuing lack of tracks. Tracks tell a story. They tell the story of who this animal is and what it wants and how this is interwoven with the fabric of its ecosystem. An animal of this size leaves tracks, it tells its story, it has no choice. But nature abhors a vacuum, and loose tongues were once more ready to fill it. Fear is a communicable disease; it comes out in the sweat and passes from host to host. Fear is an incendiary agent; it combusts with stupidity. An escaped circus animal, an escaped lunatic, Sasquatch, a secret alien experiment, a secret White Tower experiment, werewolves. Shelley Godfrey.

On November 5 Roman caught two boys tormenting his sister in the ninth-grade locker section. She was sitting on the ground with her head between her knees moaning and drooling miserably as a crowd watched the boys leaning over her. *Who tasted better—Did you do it fast or slow—Who's next—Who's next—*

Roman elbowed his way through the Sworn twins and there was a hush as he stood, his green Godfrey eyes were hard candy. The boys backed into the lockers, vainly and stupidly protesting their innocence. Roman looked at his sister on the ground. Her head was still bowed forward and her massive humped shoulders were shaking. He looked into the eyes of the second boy and in a tone striking for its reason said, "Kiss him. Kiss his pretty little mouth."

The second boy took his friend and drew their lips together. The first boy sent an indignant fist to his suitor's ear. Roman braced one foot against the lockers and helped Shelley up as the two boys wrestled on the ground, the first a flurry of knees and nails against the other's unyielding advances. Shelley and the lights above her flickered asynchronously.

As recess closed, Roman approached Peter, who stood at the side of the building humming a current R & B chart hit and carving a lewd glyph into the brick face with a razor appropriated from bio. The news of the second girl had come as no surprise to him, only the length of time it had taken to come out. He knew now what was happening, or at least enough to know how much he'd rather think about just about anything else, but of course that would now require shaking the *upir* from his tail.

"Powwow," said Roman.

The bell rang and they went to the basketball court and sat against the chain-link fence, sending several pigeons in flight.

"Are you . . . sure it wasn't you?" said Roman.

"I never go out on an empty stomach," said Peter.

"You got any grass?" said Roman.

Peter dug a joint from his pocket.

"It wasn't me either," said Roman.

"I know," said Peter.

Roman masked his dejection at not remaining a suspect. He pointed to the pavement, indicating the ground, underneath the ground. "Do you think it's—"

"No," said Peter. "That's something . . . weirder."

"Weirder how?"

Peter shrugged and lit the joint. Roman knew he knew more than what he was saying and Peter took some pleasure in allowing the moment to stretch.

"*Vargulf,*" he said.

"What?" said Roman.

"*Vargulf,*" said Peter. "A wolf will only attack if it's hungry, or provoked. If it's normal. A *vargulf* is a wolf that's gone insane."

"Insane how?" said Roman.

"Doesn't eat what it kills," said Peter. "It isn't the way. It's a disease."

"You're sure that's what this is?" said Roman.

Peter passed the joint to Roman, nodding. He had sensed it the first moon and the latest came across its scent station but could not make hide nor hair of the discovery; it was unlike anything he had ever encountered; it communicated nothing of the other wolf's sex or intentions, it just smelled . . . angry.

"Is it someone you know?" said Roman.

"I never knew any others except Nicolae. But this is a strange town. You can feel it in your balls."

Roman nodded. He tilted his head back and exhaled smoke.

"So I guess now we find him," said Roman.

Peter didn't follow. "Who?"

"The *vargulf*," said Roman.

Peter didn't follow. "Why?"

"To make him stop," said Roman.

Peter laughed.

"Do not laugh at me," said Roman, meaning it more than any other thing he could say.

"Sorry," said Peter.

"He ripped a girl in half," said Roman.

Peter was quiet. *And?*

Roman was reluctant now, how best to explain. "Have you ever heard of the Order of the Dragon?" he said.

Peter looked at him. This better be good.

"It was a group of knights from the Crusades. My mom used to tell us stories."

Peter looked at him, but more so.

"I . . . I've always wanted to be a warrior," said Roman.

Peter came to the silent conclusion that this conference was about to jump several echelons of his Hierarchy.

Roman flicked a pebble and it skittered just short of the foul line. He silently counted the parallelograms formed by the overlaying diamonds of the opposite basketball net. It was difficult for him, admitting it. He'd never talked about it, even with Letha.

"Have you ever attacked anyone?" he said. "As the wolf?"

"No," said Peter.

"Have you ever . . . wanted to?"

"I've never had a reason to."

"I've never believed in God," said Roman in the too-fast blurt of an illicit confession.

"And Nicolae to his dying day didn't believe that squirrels don't hatch from eggs," said Peter, using calculated glibness as a derailer. He was not comfortable with this degree of intimacy. He did not like where this was going. The layers of outer affectation peeled away to reveal the other boy's inner need. His need that he thought Peter could somehow meet. The only thing that scared Peter off more than other people's needs was a cage, though in the end what was the difference?

Roman continued heedless. "I see things sometimes," he said. "I see these . . . shadows that I don't always know if they're real or not."

So there you had it. Behind that aloof and mercurial façade was a battle, and he had to decide the outcome: Was he the hero or the villain? And so what could be more black-and-white than a quest to slay the monster that was terrorizing the countryside? Wow. Peter didn't want to touch that with your dick.

"Roman," said Peter, "maybe this is the kind of thing you should be talking about with the guidance counselor."

Roman didn't say anything for a while.

"Do you think you could leave me alone now?" he said.

Peter stood and walked off the court, glancing behind him once at Roman's thin back against the distended fence.

A Very Hirsute Young Man

After school Peter lay shirtless in the hammock, idly listening to his iPod and stroking the dark hair under his navel. He felt uncharacteristic stirrings of remorse. Of course it would be the nobler thing to offer the *upir* some kind of support, but Peter was generally suspicious of his nobler impulses. And though he regretted the pain this *vargulf* was causing, and would continue to in all likelihood before its inevitable self-termination, pain was as much a part of this life as the summer and the winter and the rain, and there was no greater asshole than the one who believed you can cure it. That you ought to. Peter did not consider himself a defeatist, but Nicolae had taught him not to scratch where it doesn't itch, and he had a highly evolved sense of what was and was not his problem.

He heard the sound of tires on the gravel lane and looked up to see the approach of a sheriff's cruiser. He removed the headphones and got up as it parked in the drive and Neck and Nose emerged from the car, followed by a petite black woman in jeans and a turtleneck. Not a cop. She appeared as blandly unwelcome as a juvie shrink or any of the social workers who were no stranger to the Rumanceks' door. But there are frogs deadlier than sharks and she smelled no less sweet than a brewing storm like trouble.

"Peter Rumancek?" said Nose.

"Hello, officers," said Peter in a friendly voice loud enough for Lynda to hear inside and dispose of anything better disposed of.

"Having a nice nap there, young Peter?" said Neck.

"Yes sir," said Peter.

"That's the life, nice little afternoon nappy-poo, isn't it, Pete?"

"Yes sir."

"Well, we'll try not to take up too much of your time here. Just a little word, if it's not imposing." He drew out the syllable *pose* in a faux British intonation.

"Yes sir."

The woman stepped forward and held out her hand. Peter was below average height for his age, and she barely came to his chin. She glanced at his torso.

"You're a very hirsute young man, aren't you?" she said.

"You'd have to tell me what *hirsute* means, ma'am," said Peter.

There was a flush inside and then Lynda appeared in the doorway. Peter glanced over and gave a discreet head shake not to worry. Yet.

"It means, forgive me for saying so, furry," she said.

"Oh. Guilty, ma'am. We Rumanceks generate very healthy amounts of testosterone."

Neck snickered.

"That's good," she said. "Peter, my name is Dr. Chasseur, and I'm a special agent with the U.S. Fish and Wildlife Service."

"Well gee, ma'am, I didn't realize I was that hairy."

Neck guffawed.

"No, no," said Chasseur. "I just . . . well, hello."

Fetchit was rubbing up against her ankles with amorous insistence. She lowered to his haunches and scratched his ears.

She looked up at Peter from the crouch. "I'm here regarding the animal attacks."

Peter's balls twitched.

"Any theories yourself on that score?" she said.

"No ma'am. But I've heard some good ones."

"I bet you have." She rose and regarded him amiably. "I suppose you aren't by any chance a werewolf, Peter?"

"Beg pardon?" said Peter. Some of the old tongue's more imaginative curses flashed behind his eyes.

"When the moon is full, do you walk in the skin of a wolf?"

"No sir," he said. "Ma'am," he said.

"Good," she said. "Now that's settled."

"Could I possibly ask . . . why, ma'am?"

"Do you know Christina Wendall?"

"Yes ma'am," he said.

"And you know she was the one who discovered Lisa Willoughby."

"Yes ma'am."

"Can you think of any reason she might have to believe you were a werewolf, Peter?"

Peter thought fast. "Because I told her. Ma'am."

"Was there a particular reason you told her?"

"Well . . . because she asked."

"Was there a particular reason she asked?"

"My middle and index fingers are the same length." He held out his hand palm forward. Neck whistled.

"And this is an attribute of werewolfism?" said Chasseur.

"I thought it meant you were a lesbian," said Neck.

"I believe you're actually referring to a greater discrepancy between the length of the index and ring fingers in homosexual women indicating higher levels of androgen," said Chasseur. Back to Peter: "So this means you're a werewolf."

"She seemed to think so, ma'am. But I'm not really an expert on your whole werewolf/lesbian situation."

"Then you continue to deny all werewolf allegations?"

"Yes ma'am. There's no such thing, ma'am."

"And you really believe that, Peter?"

"I thought it was scientific fact, ma'am."

"Proving a negative is a misuse of both the terms *science* and *fact*, Peter."

He pinched his fingers. "I thought it was just this close to scientific fact, ma'am."

She nodded. "Have you ever heard the term *clinical lycanthropy*, Peter?" she asked. Every time she used his name it was putting a pat of butter on a slice of botulism.

"No ma'am."

"It describes a condition that causes the subject to believe he or she is a werewolf—and act accordingly."

"It takes all kinds to make a world, ma'am."

"Did you know either Lisa Willoughby or Brooke Bluebell?"

"No ma'am."

"What were you and Roman Godfrey doing at Kilderry Park the night of October second?" demanded Nose.

"We were catching fireflies, sir."

Nose glowered, but a quick glance from the woman censured his natural retaliatory bullying instinct. Peter, who had been in his day a person of interest to an assortment of law enforcement agencies, wondered (among other things) what gave a specialist from the Fish and Wildlife Service such a calmly confident and dexterous technique in the questioning of a human person.

"Does Roman Godfrey think he's a werewolf?" said Chasseur.

"I don't have his power of attorney," said Peter.

"Hazard a guess."

"I would guess not."

Fetchit began toying with Nose's shoelace and Nose glared down at the sass from this quarter.

Peter scooped the cat in his arms.

"Cat person?" said Chasseur.

"All creatures great and small, ma'am." He kissed the cat to rest his case and it squirmed from his grasp, having more pressing things to do than receive freely offered affection.

After the conclusion of the interview Peter waited until the crunch of the cruiser was well up the lane before going inside, slipping on a sweater, and telling his mother not to wait up. She said to pick up some bread and some cigarettes and to watch himself. He said, "I will."

A Few Other Adjectives

Godfrey House was a massive and utilitarian Georgian Colonial that overlooked the river on the summit of the highest hill in town, the province of management, and had the appearance to those below of a squat, blunt, and obscurely disapproving tusk. The property was enclosed on three sides by a forest of red oaks containing a population of occluded and vaguely horned shapes calling a low and sporadic *hoo hoo . . . hoo hoo . . .* In the circular drive was Roman's Jaguar and a black Ford F-150 pickup truck. A light was on in the attic. Peter rang the doorbell and Roman's mother answered. She was wearing a white robe and her hair was damp and she moved and also stood still like milk being poured under the full moon, and though she would have had neither time nor purpose to apply cosmetics after bathing, her lips were a shock red that in their present purse of distaste caused within Peter's privatemost circuitry a sudden and confusing crossfiring at how arousing and simultaneously dick-shriveling this apparition was. He tried to envision Shelley Godfrey emerging from . . . that. Nicolae had told him the world of the *upir* was a strange and confusing one to a simple wolf man. Peter could think of a few other adjectives.

"Yes?" said Olivia in a tone suggesting he ought to be grateful she had not perforce closed the door on his nose. But it was not yet outside the realm of possibility.

"Is Roman here?" said Peter.

"May I ask who's calling?"

"Peter. We're in the same English class."

"May I ask in regard to what?"

"Study group," he said.

"Mm." This syllable communicating her internal debate over whether to notify her son or the authorities.

"I'll inform him," she said. A moment's consideration. "You can come in."

Peter waited in the foyer as she withdrew down the hall. On one wall was an aged and chipping painting of a grotesquely fat cherub, layered rolls of dimpled fat, wings comically small, and smiling mouth smeared with chocolate. Maybe chocolate. On the other was a large framed photograph of an engorged and multi-hued hermaphrodite's vulva. Peter's eyebrows knotted. No—it was a flower, a close-up image of the stamen and stigma of a flame tulip. Peter was still entranced by this intricate arboreal obscenity when Roman appeared alone.

"Yeah?" he said, with the cold aloofness of a scorned woman.

"Powwow," said Peter.

Roman led him to his room, which was nearly the footage of Peter's trailer. On the door was a picture of a crucifix with a serpent wrapped around it. The serpent's tail was in its mouth. Otherwise there was an almost total lack of decoration, except mounted to the wall a train car coupling link, an old oblong of warped and rusted steel. Which despite its meager appearance Peter immediately knew without being told was the most valuable thing Roman owned.

"Well?" said Roman, with the cold, aloof satisfaction of a scorned woman to whom you've come crawling back.

"Development," said Peter. He described to Roman the afternoon's encounter.

Roman evaluated the story with a noncommittal expression. "So? The Wendall girl totally flipped out. They can't be taking it seriously."

"It's not that simple," said Peter. "This woman is what she says she is like a Mexican hates fireworks."

Roman nodded, what insult he may have felt about their earlier meeting losing traction to this new intrigue.

"What is she?" he said.

"She's a digger," said Peter.

Roman shrugged. *What of it?* "The only people who really know what you are are your mom and me." He grew defensive. "And I know how to button up."

"That's not why I'm here," said Peter, lying: half his reason in coming was to keep the *upir* from running off at the mouth.

"So what are you afraid she digs up?"

"Nicolae," said Peter.

"He's still alive?"

"No. But she goes deep enough, she's gonna find out."

Roman looked at him.

"That Nicolae was a killer," said Peter.

The Taste of Fear

By nature Nicolae was a pussycat. In his later years he had individual names for every duck he fed, and musicals made him cry. More than anything he loved his Sundays with Peter. On this day he would allow Peter to help him as he went around with a hammer and a dolly looking for cars that had a dent that needed to be fixed. Peter would help by pretending to be retarded because people were happier to give business to the guy with the retarded kid, and this made him feel clever and useful. Then they would go and spend Peter's share of the proceeds immediately on ice cream or at the arcade. Nicolae would never let him save; a rich man, he said, was one who spent a million. Later, when it started in Peter, the turn, Nicolae was the one who showed him the right way to be a wolf, not brain surgery but impossible to understate the importance: Don't hunt when you're not hungry; when you do hunt, go for the flank, thus avoiding antlers in front and hooves in the rear; and when you are filled with the song of the universe, the breathing spirit that passes through and unites all things, throw your head back and close your eyes and join in.

But though Nicolae may have had a heart of gold, the substance of his brain was perhaps not as valued a commodity, and when he was young he fucked things up very badly for himself. He was part of a *kumpania* in the old country, and because he

was one of seven Rumancek boys, and the Rumancek boys being about as useful at holding in gossip as a woman with a map,
the fact that once a month he discarded his man coat and roamed
in the purview of arcane and unruly gods was not only fairly
widespread knowledge but also made the young man a more
celebrated figure than even the most accomplished dancers or
dulcimer players. How the old women clucked and the young
girls tittered as that Rumancek swaggered past. It was really living high on the hog. So it was to increase his standing that he
permitted a tradition to emerge among his brothers and their
cronies, a real gentlemen's club, to get howling drunk before the
turn, then steal a pig or a sheep and watch Nicolae have at it.
Better than the movies! Of course the older and wiser wagged
their fingers over the only possible moral of this story—children
playing with fire yields one outcome just as drunks playing with
werewolves yields one other—and so it came to pass: the night
the comedian of the cronies decided it would be a gas to snatch
a bone from the wolf's mouth.

At first the others tried sticks and rocks and finally guns,
but it was already too late. Once the wolf gets the taste of fear
all there is to do is back slowly away to avoid further provocation
and then run, run and pray someone else in the pack is slower.

So that was that. It was all over before it began. It was all
over. To kill another person, this doesn't exist in Gypsy courts.
It's unthinkable. A person who would do this, unthinkable. So
there's no punishment, no sanction to be made against a thing
so irreconcilable with the breathing spirit that passes through
and unites all things. It's just over for the one who did it, he doesn't
exist anymore. And no punishment is greater, it's having your
heart removed. The next morning Nicolae awoke alone on bare
earth where the blood of his friend had melted the snow and to
the sound of the creaking wheels of the caravan and all his brothers moving on, to the sound of his heart being removed from his
body.

"That's where this comes from," said Peter.

He patted his rib cage where there was the tattoo of a *g*.

"It stands for *gadjo*. Outsider. Nicolae stood outside all worlds and I stand next to Nicolae."

"How did he get here?" said Roman.

"There was only one way. He was invisible to all his people and would have curled up and died with his thumb up his ass except for his two oldest friends in the world: his feet. So he walked. He walked day and night in the rain and the sun and he didn't stop until he hit America. And he started again."

"You can't walk to America, there's an ocean," said Roman.

"Well, he found a way to lick it," said Peter.

Roman looked at him.

"It's in the Bible," said Peter.

"In the Bible it's a miracle, you don't lick it," said Roman.

"Well, he did," said Peter. "There it was in writing, and Nicolae didn't know how to write himself so he figured if you took the trouble it must be true. So he walked up and down the beach until in his mind he licked it, and then he went inland a ways until he found a pond, and he tied lily pads to the bottoms of his shoes. And that was how he walked to America."

Roman was not satisfied. But perceiving this line of inquiry a blind alley, he changed the subject. He asked what any of this had to with Peter.

"This is my blood," said Peter. "Blood . . . stains."

Roman picked up the coupling link and hefted it thoughtfully.

"Shee-it," said Roman.

"Shee-it," said Peter.

"Who do you think this Chasseur really is?" said Roman.

"I need to know like an extra ear on my dick to hear myself whack off," said Peter. "Let's be clear, only one thing matters here: not putting me in a cage."

Roman was quiet. "What now."

"We do what you said," said Peter. "We find the *vargulf*. And we stop him."

Roman slapped the link against his palm a couple of times. "How?"

"If there's time before the next moon, help him," said Peter. "It's possible he doesn't even know what he's doing."

"If there's not?"

"I kill him."

Roman looked at the other boy who was hiding a wolf. "You would do that?"

"I would do what was necessary," said Peter, who in a past moment of truth failed to wring the neck of a dying fox in an act of merciful necessity and could make no promises to himself what he would or would not do in a replicated scenario with so much more on the line. But he did know he needed to sell it convincingly for the benefit of the *upir*'s not insignificant resources.

"So if we went through with this," said Roman, stressing the word *if* to lend the false impression there was any question in his mind, "where would we start?"

"Lisa Willoughby," said Peter.

"Seems like a bit of a dead end," said Roman.

"What's left of her," said Peter. "We find out where they're burying her."

"Why?"

"Because we're going to dig her up."

Peter was not sure if the joyful light that suddenly shone in Roman's green Godfrey eyes was indicative of how auspicious or dumbfuck a partnership this would be.

"We're not calling ourselves the Order of the Dragon," said Peter.

"Do you . . . know what it's like?" said Roman, haltingly shifting gears. "The taste of fear?"

Peter did not know what he disliked more: the idea of formulating an appropriate response to this question or that it had been asked. So he employed a strategy he had perfected in his dealing with the opposite sex: reply naturally as if to an entirely different conversation.

"That bum who hangs out at Kilderry Park," said Peter. "We also may as well try and talk to him—who knows, maybe he saw something."

Roman was quiet.

"What bum?" he said.

○

From the archives of Norman Godfrey:

NG: You wanted to see me?
FP: . . .
NG: Mr. Pullman? Francis?
FP: I . . . seen it.
NG: What?
FP: There was another one. I didn't know there was another one.
NG: Another what?
FP: . . .
NG: You didn't know there was another what?
FP: Another girl.
NG: What did you see, Francis?

○

Letha was sleeping when some obscure tension woke her and she saw in her doorway a silhouette palpable with ill ease.

"Dad?" she said.

"I'm sorry," said Dr. Godfrey. "I didn't mean to wake you up."

"It's fine, but . . . are you all right?"

He considered his response. "No," he said.

"Why don't you come over here?" she said.

For a moment it seemed as though he hadn't heard. But then, trancelike, he went to her bed and sat. He tucked his hands into his lap. She smelled the scotch on him and in her condition it was nauseating to her, it was the smell of a man in pain. She touched his arm.

"You don't have to worry about me," she said. "I'm going to stay away from the woods. I'm not going to walk by myself. I'm going to be safe, Dad. I know your job is to worry, but my job is to be safe." Her other hand passed over her stomach.

He looked at the little hand, this little person's hand resting on his arm. Looking into Pullman's story earlier in the night entailed confirming a detail about the Bluebell killing with the sheriff's department that had not made it to the papers: though the body was disemboweled, the animal responsible had left vital organs intact while consuming only body fat. Meaning she was alive; she was alive and watching herself being eaten. When asked for a statement by the paper he had declared, in his view, a state of emergency. But does raising a child have any other name? There is a fly in the ointment peculiar to the study of the mind and it is that the subject of study is also its instrument, like a microscope under a microscope. He looked out at the dendritic network of branches cast by the streetlight in shadow puppet on her blinds.

"Dad?" she said. "Why are you crying?"

○

MYSTERY CREATURE: DEMON DOG?
Todd Palermo, Easter Valley Bugle

The currently unidentified predator responsible for the fatal maulings of Brooke Bluebell and Lisa Willoughby in Hemlock Grove has been described by an eyewitness as "a giant black dog, tall as a man, three hundred pounds, at least, with glowing yellow eyes."

Francis Pullman, 53, an inpatient at the Hemlock Acres Institute for Mental Wellness, came forward last night claiming to have seen the first attack. Pullman is a homeless veteran of the U.S. Army. He said he was sleeping at Kilderry Park the night of September 30 when he awoke to the sounds of screaming. The victim, Brooke Bluebell, came running from the woods, followed closely by the "demon dog."

"She had a ten-, fifteen-foot lead, but once they reached the open, he pounced right on her. I've seen a rabid dog before and this wasn't anything like that. This was not natural."

Pullman, who was admitted to Hemlock Acres last week in a highly agitated condition, apologized for saying nothing sooner, but it was a deeply traumatic experience for him.

When reached for comment, Dr. Norman Godfrey, psychiatrist in chief of the institute, refused to speculate on the likelihood of Pullman's account on the basis of doctor-patient confidentiality.

"All I can recommend is that all parents consider this a state of emergency," he said. "If at any time you are unsure of the location and welfare of your child, that is unacceptable."

Sheriff Thomas Sworn, however, has warned not to lend too much credence to Pullman's account.

"We are willing to entertain the possibility that Mr. Pullman was witness to the tragedy, and are grateful to him for any light he might shed," he said in an official press release. "But we are receiving expert help on this case, and though the wounds are certainly consistent with some sort of large animal, there simply isn't a species of canine on the planet that fits his description, not to mention the sort of evidence it would leave."

Sheriff Sworn noted that it was night, Pullman has a history of narcotics abuse, and additionally "sometimes the mind plays tricks. I just don't want a panic to start.

It's our job to find this thing, and as the father of twin girls myself, I promise you we will. Soon."

Until then, he recommends residents continue taking precautions, "but against a typical feral animal, not some ghost dog. Those teeth are real enough."

In Poor Taste

From the archives of Dr. Norman Godfrey:
From: morningstar314@yahoo.com
To: ngodfrey@hacres.net
Subject: A girl's best friend

Dearest Uncle,

A dreadful row this morning. I was reading my newspaper
("demon dog"? horrid, horrid . . .) when Roman came to
breakfast, upon which Mother instantly set upon him about
the guest he had entertained last night, as he was paid a quite
unexpected visit by that rascal Gypsy boy, Peter—who, I've
decided, is most certainly not our hellish hound . . . well, almost
certainly—and had a rather lengthy conversation behind closed
doors. (How I should have liked to eavesdrop!—but alas, your
charming niece's sneakier impulses are in inverse proportion
with her sheer volume; I fear I would not have much of a career
in cloak and daggery barring some conspiracy of the blind,
deaf, and dumb—but even then I suppose I would be bumped
into eventually.) Mother inquired into his business. Roman
replied they were partners on a school project. Mother was not
satisfied by this patent evasion.

"Do you want the truth?" said Roman.

"Yes," said Mother.

Roman gave a lengthy and graphic account of a homosexual affair. "But don't worry," it culminated, "it's only [EXPLETIVE DELETED]."

Needless to say, it was not long before they were trading the usual poison slings and arrows. And despite my unhappy familiarity with the phenomenon, it still eludes me: how two people whose love for each other is so great can find words of such hate. Maybe I'll understand one day, but I am not impatient for enlightenment.

I am dismayed to report that this is not the only evidence of a general decline in Mother's temper lately. I went with Roman to the mall this past weekend (I needed a replacement copy of *Beyond Good and Evil*; I had ripped mine in two in a rage but on reflection decided there were a few points that warranted—ever so tentatively, Herr Nietzsche—reevaluation), and who should we encounter but Jenny from the club! She had been absent from our most recent supper and was to my surprise ringing up a sale at the earring boutique. I poked Roman, quite accidentally bowling him over, and restrained myself from tucking him under my arm like a suitcase to hasten our salutation (I do get excited sometimes).

But at our approach Jenny looked over with a distinct lack of enthusiasm and gave the barest nod of recognition. Of course I was crushed and racked my brains for any cause I may have given to offend her. My first assumption as always was that it was my own fault.

My brother, however, with his characteristic nonchalance in the face of the vagaries of mood of the fairer sex, asked how she'd been.

"Terrific," she reported flatly. "Your psycho [EXPLETIVE DELETED] mother got me fired."

I was simultaneously horrified at Mother and to hear Jenny speak of her like that.

"Yeah, well, she's a [EXPLETIVE DELETED] on stilts," said Roman. "Stop the presses."

This was even more distressing. Of course he's hurled far worse within our walls, but to talk so in this public setting . . . I grinned like a nervous dog (the friendly household variety).

But my brother's waggishness had its reliable effect on the mademoiselle—who took apparent pleasure in the all too easily romanticized cynicism of the throne's heir presumptive.

"You think you got troubles?" continued Roman, impressed with his own performance. "At least you didn't end up with your brains gussying up the wainscoting."

My knees grew weak, and I scarcely think this recounting is any more pleasurable for you, but you are my trusted doctor in addition to dearest uncle, and I depend as much on your professional as familial compassion. I'm sure you have heard the vulgar jokes as well, implicating Mother in this family's great tragedy, and for the most part I am able to turn a deaf ear to such lurid insinuations, but to hear one cast so thoughtlessly from the lips of my brother . . . It took all my will to remain stoic—not to mention upright.

Jenny laughed, the way the fairer sex tends to around Roman. "You're *bad*," she diagnosed. But coaxed now from her initial sullenness she turned to me and graced the thoroughfare with one of those smiles that had so many times brightened our supper, and my dejection was an unmourned memory. Truly astonishing just how much of the world's trouble could be erased by the simplest smile. She tapped her ears and said, "Come to accessorize, honey?"

I returned her smile with my own inferior facsimile and shook my head.

"You know what would look fabulous on you?" she said, and then unlocked a display of the more exclusive stock and removed a pair of teardrop diamond earrings that would nearly rival some of Mother's.

"This is the fanciest thing we carry," she said. "Just waiting for the proper lady. Come here."

I bent in mad glee and glanced in the mirror as she held one to my ear, and even the juxtaposition of her fine hand with that monstrous countenance (which, though it happens to be my appearance, I will not call my reflection) did not darken my spirits once more. Rather, both of us, Jenny so fair and Shelley its antithesis, were equally delighted by the gentle farce that a thing of such delicate beauty could have a home on such a grotesque.

"*Jolie fille!*" exclaimed Jenny. "What do you think, big brother? It's not like it's outside your spending limit."

"Brilliant," said Roman. "Mom would [EXPLETIVE DELETED] a bowling ball."

"Well, I think your mom just doesn't want the competition."

It would hardly have been noticeable under the skylight, but I began lightly to shine.

But the bell will be ringing soon (eighth period, it tolls for thee). Christina is absent again today, the poor girl. One cannot imagine what toll stumbling on the demon dog's handiwork must have taken on such an innocent. I sent her a card with a humble little poem to perhaps give her courage (no! I will not repeat it here), and also mentioned your name should she desire the audience of a professional. Despite my own impediments on the elocution front, you will never have a more vocal advocate to those in need.

I know it all weighs on you, Uncle. The burden of it is there between your words. Forgive my presumption, but when I am making my own reconciliations—at least, attempting to!—I derive heart sometimes from standing apart from my fear and remembering these words:

"I cannot tell how it mounts on the winds through the clouds and flies through heaven. Today I have seen the Dragon."

Irrepressibly yours,
　　　S.G.

○

Letha was walking to her bus after school when Roman tugged the strap of her book bag and told her he was driving her home. At his car Peter waited with Shelley; he was wearing an inherited plaid driver's cap and juggling three small rocks, she in breathless captivation. Thus far Letha's general impression of Peter was one of distaste. Not that they had had any real interaction, but he struck her as one of those boys with overly supportive mothers and proportionate grossly inflated sense of their own hotness. Which isn't to say she was not dismayed by his social ostracism in a generic state-of-the-world sort of way, but this did not detract from the pervert stare he gave any passing skirt with the apparent conviction when caught at it that his gross gawking was a kind of flattery. And this showboating performance right now, something inherently sad and stupid about exhibiting a pointless skill that required an investment of hours totally out of balance with its value, like the skater boys she always mentally crossed a finger would crash. The fact is, other people being jerks to you doesn't make you not inherently kind of a jerk. Then, the climax: Peter bending to one knee and catching two of the rocks in his hat and impeccably timing an am-I-forgetting-something face a split second before the third landed on his skull. Shelley applauded vigorously. And with that it is not so much that Letha revised her opinion as that the bottom of her heart fell open and swung slowly back and forth on its hinge. If you have never been a young girl you may not know exactly what this feels like.

"Got any other ones?" said Roman.

"Not with ladies present," said Peter, arching an eyebrow at Shelley. She hid her face behind her hands with glee.

They loaded up and hit the road. Roman asked if Peter and Letha had been introduced.

Letha turned to the backseat. She was puzzled. Somehow, in her appraisal of his round brown face and feral stubble and deep almond eyes as being vain and vulgar, it had eluded her that it was quite possibly the most *interesting* face she had seen in her life, a riddle yearning to be solved—the vanity and vulgarity twin guardians of some unknowable mystery it goes without saying she would have to possess. She left her hand on the headrest fearing that if she lifted it to shake his she would reach and touch his face, the precise reason she couldn't stand museums. Who wants to sit around looking at things?

Peter wondered why Roman's cousin was looking at him like that, and why she wasn't shaking his hand. This family.

"How would you like to do us a favor?" said Roman.

"Roman Godfrey, don't tell me you had an ulterior motive," said Letha.

"You know that guy we almost creamed? The one who saw Brooke Bluebell?"

She was suspicious. "Yeah?" she said.

"Talk to your pops. See if you can find out more about him. Stuff that might not have made it to the papers."

There, the wrinkle. Her immediate assumption at the presence of the other boy was that Roman was hanging out with him to piss off his mother, but there being some other moronic and potentially calamitous object was no surprise.

"What are you two up to?" she said.

"That's on a need-to-know basis," said Roman.

"We're hunting the demon dog," said Peter.

Roman gave him a look in the mirror. Peter shrugged. The open statement of their retarded mission surely less incendiary than an apparent conspiracy.

"No you're not," said Letha, less of a contradiction than wishful thinking.

"We think there are mitigating circumstances," said Roman.

She gave him a *Do we?* look.

"The demon dog is really a person," said Roman.

"Have you been drinking?" said Letha.

"Letha, this guy is hurting people," said Roman.

Letha tallied on her fingers: "(A) it's not a 'guy,' it's an 'it'; (B) saying you had a single good reason to think it was a person, you cannot seriously believe you're better off than trained professionals to go running after him; and (C) A and B aside, what do you think a mental patient is going to be able to tell you?"

Roman was quiet.

"Is that a yes?" he said.

"(D)," she said, "saying it is a person, and saying you find him: What are you going to do?"

"What do you think, sweetheart?" said Roman. "Put him in the pound."

Letha turned back to the obvious brains (if that was the word for it) of this operation with the look of chastising mother all women are born with. "Can I ask you what possible good you think is going to come from this?"

He met her look with a face evincing that great rarity: not even the hint of need for self-justification.

"No," he said.

They stopped at a red light abreast a garbage truck and she studied him and wrestled with the conflicting impulses of the ever Herculean endeavor of saving Roman from himself, and in her new faith-filled condition saying yes to whatever this mysterious moron asked of her as her ears were filled with the implacable grind of the neighboring trash compactor.

○

Roman dropped off Peter after Letha and told him he'd be back to pick him up at midnight. He added that it would be for the best if Peter didn't drop by his place anymore—getting himself mixed up in a series of grisly killings was exactly the kind of thing his mother would view like showing up to a dinner party without a bottle of wine: in poor taste. Peter was not heartbroken. He was not convinced as had been the majority of his ancestors that the Evil Eye could kill but neither would he bet the family farm.

Inside the kitchen, Lynda looked out to see an ill-made giant in a mule cart bouncing and creaking up the hill. She squinted, her cigarette precarious over an unbaked casserole.

"Well I'll be goddamned," she said.

○

The twins came to stay over with Christina. They brought her homework and a box of cookies they could vomit later and a get-well mixer album. Alyssa told her she had a killer reputation and Christina said that was nice. Alexa asked her if she was on awesome tranquilizers and Christina said she was. Alyssa asked if she was okay to talk about it.

"There's not much to talk about," said Christina. "I found half a person."

The twins were quiet.

"Also, I made out with her," said Christina.

The twins were quiet.

"I thought it was fake, you know?" said Christina. "Like someone's idea of a joke. So I kissed her. I thought it would be really funny."

The twins looked at each other. And then at the same moment they burst into a fit of hysterical giggles.

"Lez!" shrieked Alyssa.

Christina expressed no shared amusement. It was not that she was upset but that the sound of their laughter was the first time she felt like a living person since discovering the werewolf's discarded one, and she was too occupied trying to get purchase on that, to be here with that just a little while longer.

Alexa's tone grew cautious once more and she asked Christina if she had seen the papers.

Christina toyed with the drawstring of her pajama pants. "Yeah. Mom tried to hide it from me, but I heard something on the radio and looked it up online."

"Do you . . . still think it's that guy?" said Alyssa.

"It is," said Christina.

Alexa worried the CD open shut open shut. She abruptly stood and said, "I'm going to play this. Oh, my God, it's so awesome. All necrophiliacs should be so lucky."

She put the CD in. Alyssa sat on the bed a couple of feet from Christina and said to come here and Christina laid her head in the other girl's lap and closed her eyes as the first track played and Alyssa stroked her hair. The first track was what had been the defining song of two summers ago that over the course of those months the three of them had sung along together so many times at sleepovers and the pool and the mall and the backseat of the poor sheriff's car that when fall came they ceremoniously melted the album in the microwave with the shared revulsion of a thing once so consumingly loved. Christina lay there with those fingers running through her hair and mouthed along with the words. A response more involuntary than breathing because you can choose not to breathe when you are awake.

Then Alyssa's hand stopped without warning and Christina opened her eyes to see the girl peering down at her with a screwed-up face.

"What's that?" said Alyssa.

Christina was at a loss.

"What's what?" said Alexa. She crouched down and brought her face in near Christina's.

Alyssa sifted through Christina's bangs and pinched an isolated strand, pulling it out for examination, and Christina's eyes flitted from one girl to the other hovering over her in close scrutiny. The twins looked at each other frowning and Christina's face was hot and her breathing shallow and she wondered what could be so troubling about the object of study when with an efficient flick of the wrist Alyssa plucked the strand and held it dangling for its former owner to see: this single hair had gone white, as white as the moon.

○

At 12:40 a.m. Peter and Roman passed a pair of shovels and a canvas bag through the wrought-iron bars of the fence around Sacred Heart Cemetery and scaled it. They made their way through the rows to a fresh grave itself buried under the histrionics of grief that they brushed aside. The night was clear and cold and they began to dig. Metal carving earth, grunts and steaming breath. The damp smell of carrion earth, death and the weft of life.

"Did you know that people used to think the dead came back as bloodthirsty revenants because the bloating of internal organs made them belch up fluid from inside the lungs?" said Roman.

"Terrific," said Peter.

"The only reason we started burying the dead in the first place was to keep predators from getting a taste for human flesh," said Roman.

"Is there like a summer camp for serial killers?" said Peter.

Roman shut up. They dug.

"How many funerals have you been to?" said Roman after he had been shut up for as long as he could.

Peter grunted, hard to count. "Rumanceks are reliably kicking it as a result of positive lifestyle choices," he said.

"What are funerals like for you people?" said Roman.

Peter was thoughtful. "Committed," he said. "You're not allowed to wash or eat. Mirrors are covered and all the dead guy's stuff is burned."

"Why?"

"Because a Rumancek should not be remembered in this world for his things."

"Shee-it," said Roman.

"Shee-it," said Peter.

They dug.

"How did Nicolae die?" said Roman.

"Colon cancer," said Peter. He was reflective. "I was thirteen and had only just started to turn that year." He shook his head affectionately. "Man, was Nic something. Watching him, you couldn't swear on the Bible his feet were touching the ground."

Peter leaned his shovel against the headstone, took out his wallet, and produced from it a wrinkled photograph that he showed Roman. It was a picture of a slim white wolf racing through pine trees and you could not have sworn on the Bible its legs were touching the ground. Lynda had taken it when they knew he didn't have much time left. In Peter's own maturation he never failed to marvel in retrospect at the white wolf's patience. How little he minded the hindrance of a dumb pup. The fastest thing on four legs and he was simply in no hurry. It was still well outside Peter's grasp: the ageless wisdom that permits you to wait for others to catch up. What a drag.

Roman handed him back the photo and they dug.

But it had been different the last time, Nicolae's last turn. That night the white wolf had vanished, leaving Peter with no chance of catching up or scent to follow. Peter hunted for him all night but with no hope of success: Nicolae had affairs to settle on which Peter had no business intruding. Peter howled his loneliness to the night's listening ear and wound up just going home and scratching at the back door and curling at the foot of his mother's bed. After the sunrise Peter went to Nicolae's room to find the old man snoring like nothing was different. They didn't discuss it; in this matter Peter would have to catch up in his own time. The old man died before the new moon.

"They let me do it," said Peter. "At Nic's funeral."

"Do what?" said Roman.

"Cut off his head. Things happen to our kind after we die if you don't cut off the head."

They dug.

"So . . . what kind of things?" said Roman.

"Bad things," said Peter.

There was the dull voiceless drone of a helicopter behind the hills. They dug.

In time, despite the coolness of the air, their faces began to shine with the sweat of their labor, and Roman wiped his brow and looked into the night where a ring of cloud was passing in the breeze. He put his foot on the pile of dirt and crossed his arms on the shovel, resting.

"I've been to two funerals," said Roman. "One was my dad,

in '99. It's all pieces. I remember hearing the shot and going downstairs. The way Mom was sitting on the couch, the look on her face like she forgot why she'd walked into the room, you know. He was on the floor. It smelled like her favorite perfume, he'd soaked himself in it. I remember thinking how much trouble he'd be in for wasting it."

He drifted off, other fragments coming to him. His uncle coming by later that night. He was the one she called, and that was when Roman knew about them. He was too young to know what he knew, but nevertheless. His mother sitting with him every morning and reading out loud what the newspapers were saying. If he was going to hear it he was going to hear it from her mouth. Dr. Pryce dandling Shelley at the service—looking at her like their father never had. Like something of his.

"People like to say it was Mom, but no way," said Roman. "She would never have done it on that rug."

"Who was the other funeral?" said Peter.

"Shelley's," he said.

○

It was near dawn with threads of mist playing cat's cradle between the graves when they hit it. Roman climbed up to the ground and pulled on his palms to stretch his cramping forearms and the night air felt good on the callused pads of his hands. Peter braced his legs against the side of the hole, wedged his shovel under the lid, and pried. Lisa Willoughby was in a satin blouse safety-pinned at the bottom and completely surrounded with stuffed toys; each had the painstaking imperfection of having been made by hand. The bottom half of the casket was weighed down by sandbags where it was not weighed down by Lisa Willoughby. Peter lowered into a hunker unfastening the safety pin at the hem of the blouse and asked Roman to hand down the bag but got no response.

Roman was fixated on something staring up from near the

head: a plush cardinal, the bead of the moon on the curve of its black eye. Roman stared into its black eye lost suddenly to another childhood memory, one of his earliest. A third funeral that had previously escaped him. He had been in bed and jarred awake one morning after a late winter's snow by a sharp bang against the window. He got up and opened it and poked his head outside. There was a cardinal down on the ground. It was late February and it lay there in the snow, wings spread. He went downstairs and hunched over it, mesmerized by the brazen redness but unspeakable delicacy of the thing. Its black eye quivered and he expected it to roll down like a teardrop. He watched, not noticing the cold, for he didn't know how long. Until the quiver stopped. He felt a hand at the back of his neck and looked up at his mother.

"Where did it go?" he said.

She pointed into the sky, and he tried to follow her finger but had to look away in the bright.

"Earth to fucknuts," said Peter.

"Sorry," said Roman and handed him the bag.

○

When the sheriff picked up Alexa and Alyssa three hours later, both said "Shotgun," but as their father called it Alyssa had been a hair quicker and he cocked a finger at her. Alexa climbed grudgingly into the back and their father said to just hold on now while we get ourselves combobulated and handed Alyssa a brimming cup of Dunkin' Donuts coffee. He backed out of the driveway and asked how Chrissy was holding up.

"We told you not to call her Chrissy anymore, it's infantilizing," said Alexa.

"She still says the demon dog is Peter Rumancek," said Alyssa. They went over a pothole and a spurt of coffee came through the slit of the lid and onto the webbing of her hand. "Ugh, coffee burp," she said.

"She says it's going to happen again the next full moon," said Alexa.

He reached for the cup and gingerly took a sip. His saliva spanned a membrane over the slit and then popped.

"Does she," he said.

Inch by Inch

That afternoon Peter had company for lunch. This was unusual. For a while he'd sat at the table with the kids who wore dog collars and misquoted the Existentialists, but then they started sitting somewhere else, even the girl called Scabies Peter was pretty sure had left him anonymous voice messages of just moaning a couple of times. He didn't follow; more to say for eating alone than running around after a girl called Scabies. But today a brown bag was set down across from him and he looked up from his motorcycles and tits magazine to find Letha Godfrey joining him. She opened a container of fruit salad with exaggerated casualness and said, "There's a rumor going around you're a werewolf?"

Peter sipped his orange soda. He'd caught that one.

"Well, are you?" she said.

He looked at her. *What do you think?*

"You know, you really scare people," she said.

He shrugged. He was darker and poorer and had conspicuous style. People didn't need their little girls to be found in pieces to fucking hate that.

"What are you doing with my cousin?" she said.

"What needs to be done," he said.

"You know we're in the cafeteria and not a Clint Eastwood movie?" she said.

"When you go to the bank do you ask for twenties or wheelbarrows?" he said.

"Lazy!" she said. "Money doesn't make you dumb."

Peter did not disagree—it just made you used to people caring what you think.

"Do you want my help or not?" she said.

"If things keep going down this road, someone very important to me is probably going to get hurt," he said.

"Who?" she said.

"Me," he said.

She was annoyed to find she couldn't dispute the logic; she had already decided she was in, as if exclusion was even an option, but had been looking forward to making him work harder for it.

"Well, I'm glad you're friends, anyway," she said. "Roman doesn't have enough friends. I mean, there's those people." She nodded her head toward Roman's lunch table. "But all they care about is the name. Nobody really knows him. Least of all, Roman."

She leaned in with a confidential aspect and looked at him intently, and Peter saw now with clarity. Her soul's light, the wide-eyed mysticism that set her apart from the rest of these dipshits. Right. The thing Roman didn't know it but he was really in this for, Order of the Dragon my ass. Good to know, unless it wasn't.

"Promise me something," she said. "Promise you won't let things go too far. Promise you'll keep him from doing anything stupid."

Peter made a solemn face and smiled inside: he enjoyed the ceremony and impressiveness of making promises completely irrespective of his intention of keeping them.

"I promise I won't let that happen," he said.

They were quiet within the cafeteria babble. She shifted one leg over the other under the table intentionally grazing his shin, for which she falsely apologized but he paid no heed at all, filling her with the surpassing desire to give it a sharp kick. Then she realized it was the table leg she had artlessly footsied and projected on her face the exact opposite of how much dignity she felt.

"Can I ask you something?" said Peter.

She consented.

"What can you tell me about Roman's mom?"

"Aunt Olivia? Why?"

"Curious."

She bet he was. "What do you want to know?"

"What do you know about her?"

She thought, and shrugged. The truth was, nothing. No one did. In the '80s JR had seen there was no way to compete realistically with the Chinese and decided to move from industry into biotech. He went abroad to inspect some facilities and came back engaged to the most beautiful and despised woman in the town's history.

"Where did they meet?" said Peter.

"England, I think."

"Is that where she's from?"

She was not sure.

"What about her people?"

She shrugged.

"Do you think there's any chance your dad knows more of the story?"

"Maybe. He was her shrink."

Peter's expression did not change but there was no hiding the crafty crackle this inspired.

"I don't suppose you might be able to fish around and see if you can fill in some of the holes," he said.

"Mixed metaphor!" she said.

He gave her a look that somehow made her feel dumb even though he was the one who went around mixing metaphors. This boy!

"Well, I don't suppose life was getting interesting enough already," she said.

"Life is always interesting," he said.

"Did you steal that from a movie poster?" she said.

He opened a box of Cracker Jacks.

"Ooh, let me find the prize," she said.

He held the box out, widening the opening between his grip, and she rooted with closed eyes, producing a plastic packet.

Peter looked at the prize and was quiet.

She opened her eyes. "Huh, weird," she said.

She was holding a translucent pink plastic ring, a little nub in the middle like the drawing of a planet in orbit. A snake—a snake eating its own tail.

Peter held out his hand, and she gave him the ring. He opened it. "Wear it. It's good luck," he said.

Across the room, Roman watched Letha hold out her hand and Peter slip something around her finger.

○

That afternoon Dr. Chasseur waited in the atrium of the God-frey Institute for Biomedical Technologies for an interview with its director. At the reception desk was a small man in a pink country-western-style shirt with rhinestone pistols at the shoulders skimming through an entertainment gossip magazine. Engraved in the marble flooring of the entrance was a horizontal line followed by an omega followed by another horizontal line:

$$\underline{\quad} \; \Omega \; \underline{\quad}$$

She asked if this motif had any meaning. The receptionist shrugged. He licked a finger and turned a page.

Then there came from behind her the sound of footsteps approaching from the bank of elevators and she turned to see a man who appeared no older than forty, though he was over a decade past. His hair was black but tinted gray to suggest his real age and his face was a firm polyethnic blend. An uncommonly dense musculature was visible under his suit. He held out his hand. His hands were small in comparison with his build, and of almost feminine delicacy, curiously smooth even of the calluses along the pad of the palm common to bodybuilders.

"Dr. Johann Pryce," he said, and there was a certain spurious slickness to his carriage and his smile that brought to mind the rainbow patina of oil on a puddle.

"Dr. Clementine Chasseur," she said.

The receptionist, sipping a Diet Coke, abruptly coughed it back into the bottle. They looked over. He gesticulated at his tabloid.

"He's marrying that whore!"

Pryce asked Chasseur if she objected to holding this interview over lunch.

Chasseur said that would be fine and Pryce escorted her outside and around the building. In the front lawn there was a cloistered quadrangle surrounding a carefully tended rock garden in the spiral pattern of a nautilus shell. She followed him to a white van in the parking lot, with the same omega motif repeated on the door.

"A hieroglyph, of a fashion," Pryce answered, preempting by a fraction of a second her actually asking the question. "Adapted from the code of the samurai: no matter the length of the journey, it must be taken inch by inch, like the measuring worm."

She looked again and saw it was in fact a literal visualization of that process:

$$\_\_\_ \ \Omega \ \_\_\_$$

He took out a set of keys and punched the button to unlock the van. "Truth be told, a lunch break will be the closest thing I get to a vacation this week," he said.

She looked up at the White Tower. "Doesn't it make you a little crazy?"

"Does the name Noah Dresner mean anything to you?"

It did not.

"He was the architect of the institute, which was to be the summation of his life's work. Dresner was something of the Ahab of sacred geometry: the Fibonacci sequence, geomagnetic alignments, all that hokum-pokum. His intention was to culminate his legacy with the proverbial axis mundi: the connecting point between earth and sky. Upon the completion of this opus he took the elevator to the summit but collapsed and died of a brain hemorrhage by the fifth floor."

Chasseur suggested this did not exactly answer her question.

Pryce tapped the side of the van with his knuckle. Inch by inch.

They relocated to an upscale Asian fusion restaurant near the mall.

"People inform me the sushi chef here is quite good," said Pryce upon seating. "I wouldn't know. If you told me tartar sauce on Styrofoam was a delicacy, I'd probably believe you. It's all glucose to me. I'm not Asian, incidentally."

"You're German and Brazilian," said Chasseur. "You came to term at twenty-six weeks of age but after fairly spectacularly staging something of a prison break from your own incubator were diagnosed with the condition of myotonic hypertrophy. Superstrength, to us mortals. And you're allergic to peanuts."

"You read the Sunday *Times*," said Pryce, in reference to a *New York Times Magazine* profile titled "Man and Superman" of which he had been the subject the previous winter, the sort of puff piece focusing on the more sensational aspects of his biography that he submitted to from time to time in order to hide in plain sight, diverting attention from the nascent stages of a project of unusual sensitivity.

"I have a hideously abusive relationship with the crossword," she said. "But I keep on going back."

His mouth smiled before his eyes did.

"Are you going to be recording this conversation?" he said.

"I hadn't intended to, Dr. Pryce."

"Johann. But I am, just so you know. Which is to say, I have been this whole time. Just so you know. You understand."

She did not object. "So what exactly is it you do, Johann?" she said.

"Pretending you don't know."

"We're strangers on a train."

He smiled at the unusual prospect of play in the middle of a working day.

"I'm the director of the Godfrey Institute for Biomedical Technologies."

"Whoa, Nellie, that sounds fancy. What do you do there?"

"The gamut. We design diagnostic equipment, prostheses, artificial organs, etc., and stand at the vanguard in pharmaceuticals, genetic manipulation, and nanotechnology today. We're about to roll out a series of biosynthetic masks for burn victims that will convey human empathy via facial expression mirroring."

"Does that explain your receptionist?" she said.

He was confused at first, then realized it was another attempt at humor, and again attempted to appear like he went in for that sort of thing. "No, we can't take credit for Cesar. Actually, if you'd like to know a trade secret, all nonspecialist personnel are hired largely on the basis of an obvious disinclination toward natural curiosity."

"You don't want anyone asking questions."

"We certainly don't."

"What kind of genetics experiments are you doing?"

"Principally gene therapy," he said. "JR Godfrey foresaw, correctly, that while the malleability of material properties was what defined the crucial advances of the nineteenth century, it is the malleability of life itself that will define the twenty-first. And so his mandate was that the name come to mean for healing backs what it once did for breaking them, which happily aligned with my own inclinations. I can't really discuss much of it, but then you would probably only be so interested in the treatment of vein graft stenosis in adult dogs anyway."

"You do animal testing?"

"I respect you're asking out of diligence, but do I really need to answer that?"

"How exactly did you get this job?"

"Because there is no one in my field working at a remotely comparable level."

"But your own area of specialization is one of contention," she said. "Exobiology, a highly speculative field dealing with possible nonterrestrial systems of life. In fact, I had some difficulty following the premise behind your first published and highly controversial paper. I found no shortage of . . . interpretations, but if you wouldn't mind walking me through it."

Pryce nodded. "You mean the one that has become popularly called 'Better Reincarnation Through Chemistry.' Certainly. In theory, if one took an existing but inanimate carbon-based structure—"

"A corpse," she said.

"—that was still in a relatively labile situation—"

"A baby's corpse," she said.

"—one might weave into the existing structure the element phosphorus, which is capable of forming chain molecules of sufficient length and complexity to support life, new life. But phosphorus alone is dangerously unstable. However—in theory—a stable bond can be achieved in combination with nitrogen. Though we're not quite out of the woods: molecular nitrogen is practically inert and very difficult to convert into energy—a necessity to an organism constituted of the stuff. But a rather dynamic solution could be found, of all places, in the bean world. Legumes host within their roots bacteria that fix soil nitrogen in exchange for resources from the host. So a subject as described might survive by hosting these bacteria in, say, for the sake of argument, the feet, requiring simply a ready supply of dirt. In theory."

"A theory that discredited you in the eyes of many of your

peers before your career even started. You were, if I might speak candidly, a provocative choice for one of the most competitive posts to open in your field."

"An infuriating one!" said Pryce. "Oh, the shoes that were eaten that day. But just as Westinghouse patronized the future in alternating current, JR was a man more concerned with what lay past the horizon than with clinging with both hands to the sagging teat of orthodoxy. He was not, to use the vernacular, a complete fuckwit. Which cannot be said of many of my contemporaries."

She noted he did not echo her use of the word *peer*.

"Do you mind," said Chasseur, "if I ask you a personal question?"

"Insofar as we've been discussing my work, you have been all along."

She nodded as one who could relate. "What attracted you to such a controversial discipline in the first place?"

His expression drifted and subtly dulled as though animating energies were absorbed for internal distribution, and studying this void it occurred to her she was seeing him for the first time fully inhabit his natural character. And as someone uniquely adept at not showcasing her emotions she realized that this subject accomplished the reverse trick in animating his face at all.

"Shortly into my eighth year I read for the first time the most important book ever written, *On the Origin of Species by Means of Natural Selection*," said Pryce.

Chasseur nodded that that was indeed a dandy.

"I was enthralled," said Pryce, "and yet troubled at the same time in a way I couldn't identify, until I sat down and made a simple calculation." He gestured at her as a for instance. "There is an exponential increase in system complexity through the upward progress of levels of organization. So I calculated the statistical probability of a system as stupefyingly complex as human consciousness arising from random mutation in the geologic age of the Earth. And I concluded that it is not. Probable. Or, for that matter, possible. By random mutation. Draw your own conclusions."

By now she had quite an inventory.

"Now do you mind if I ask a question of my own?" said Dr. Pryce.

She made a hand gesture: *Go ahead*.

"You completed a doctorate in predator ethology at the University of Texas in 2004," he said.

She did not reply. This was not a question, and he would not have chosen his words casually.

"How is this of any possible interest to the U.S. Fish and Wildlife Service?" he said.

She looked down. There was a glass top over the table that reflected the skylight above in such a way that it contained her doppelgänger peering back at her from within a lighted shaft. She looked back at Pryce with amiable surrender.

"You got me," she said. "It's not, I suppose. They just give me a lot of rope to do my job, and I have my own method. It's a little elliptical."

"If I'm not mistaken, to complement your training in sociobiology you have some experience with the Reid technique of interrogation and have been asking tangential questions to establish a rapport with the suspect as well as elicit behavior symptoms of truth and deception preparatory to a more direct confrontation."

"Johann, is there any chance one of your test animals could have gotten loose?"

"No."

"What about a test subject?"

"You mean a person?"

"Yes."

"None whatsoever."

She regarded him. And if moments before, the vacuum of basic human vitality in his face had been a momentary lapse, it was now strategically deployed: he had become such a blank that he could have been napping right there with his eyes open, or breathing dead. She had never before looked into another living person's eyes and not found incontrovertible evidence of the human soul. She had never seen anything more terrifying.

She snapped her fingers. "Rats. And here I thought I'd cracked it. You wouldn't have any of your own ideas on our demon dog, would you?"

His point made—you will get nothing from me that I don't give you—Pryce suffered imitation of life to reinvest his features.

"I understand the animal has left no tracks," said Pryce.

She nodded.

"I understand canid scat was discovered in the area containing large amounts of human hair, but from an adolescent male, of which none have gone missing. Further, I understand analysis of this scat revealed abnormally low levels of adrenal glucocorticoid, indicating that the animal not only had not recently engaged in an act of aggression, but also is by nature non-aggressive."

She did not bother to inquire how he came into possession of this information.

"Your conclusion, Johann?" she said.

"I conclude I'm glad it's your job to make sense of it and not mine," he said. "However, considering the parallels between both killings, I would calculate the probability that these were not premeditated acts of a pathological sexual predator at within an order of magnitude of one in ten million."

"But a person wouldn't possibly have the ability to do what was done to those bodies. Not bare-handed."

Dr. Pryce nodded. He reached into his breast pocket and produced a digital voice recorder. He held it in his soft, feminine hand and, giving her a collegial smile, made a fist that he tightened and tightened until its shell ruptured and its gadget innards spilled onto the table, which he tidily swept into a napkin and set aside.

"If a problem can't be solved within the frame it was conceived, the solution lies in reframing the problem," he said.

Hello, Handsome

Immediately after dropping Shelley off, Roman went round to unhitch the cart. Olivia emerged on the porch and watched him. She could see that someone was sitting in the car, but she was not wearing her sunglasses and the sun's glare reflected from the window hit her eyes and she shielded them with her hand. Roman whistled an old Rodgers and Hart standard.

"Where are you going?" said Olivia, massaging her eyelids and causing a neon flare of blood vessels.

"Nowhere," said Roman.

"Will we be returning again at five a.m.?"

"We'll see." He lowered the cart and resumed whistling.

She blinked through a haze of phantom color as her son pulled from the drive but through her own galled determination made out the passenger, slouched and superstitiously averting his face from her direct gaze: Peter Rumancek. Olivia lightly traced her finger along the rail and pressed down on a knot in the wood.

She turned and was startled to find Shelley standing in the foyer studying her. Looming with nervous sensitivity to climatic shifts in her mother's mood. Olivia made an effort to slough off some of the tension the girl tended to absorb.

"And *what*," she said, "have we been told about how bloody *disconcerting* we are when we sneak up on people?"

She made her hands into pincers and pinchedpinchedpinched at Shelley's sides and the house shook with thunderous laughter.

○

On the parkway, Roman said, "So was that a nice little lunch date?"

"She pities me," Peter said. He didn't have to put his finger to the wind to know that extreme caution was required here.

"She's all heart," said Roman.

They entered a tunnel.

"Can I ask you something?" said Roman.

"Go ahead."

"What do you do when you get horny? While you're turned?"

Peter looked up at the lines of parallel lights extending into the white vanishing point at the tunnel's far end. He didn't answer.

They drove to the Pittsburgh neighborhood of Shadyside, making a detour at a health food store and then arriving at a crumbling yellow brick apartment building. Peter rang a unit on the second floor and they were buzzed in and Roman followed Peter upstairs. An elderly Italian woman passed by them and, making an educated guess of their destination, cast her eyes to the carpet and fished a crucifix from her breast, muttering "*Strega*."

Peter stopped at the predicted door and knocked and they were greeted by a young woman in her late twenties. She was brown like all Rumanceks and had on a boy child's G.I. Joe shirt stretched over an infelicitously modest chest, in a family of epic-bosomed women, and a small pair of cotton shorts. Her lean arms and legs and exposed abdomen were tight with springy muscle indicative of a stars-defying attitude toward exercise encountered in certain young women from closely knit ethnic enclaves who have witnessed too many members of their sex undergo the near universal ballooning of hips by thirty. She pulled Peter into a hug and kissed his cheek and gave his ponytail an annoyed jerk and harangued him didn't he have a girlfriend to make him cut his hair.

Peter introduced her to Roman as his cousin Destiny Rumancek. Roman held out his hand, which instead of shaking she held firmly palm upward and inspected with knit eyebrows and grunted speculatively and released.

"Come in," she said. "I'm finishing up with someone, but it won't be a sec."

They followed her into the apartment, which in contrast with the inauspicious conditions of the rest of the building was painted in welcoming primary colors with laminate flooring and appointed with attractive and ergonomic Scandinavian furniture and the sort of tranquillity fountain you see in an airplane catalog and wonder who besides massage parlors would buy such things. Destiny went into the bedroom, where Roman caught a brief glimpse of an overweight black man lying on the bed with his pants bunched around his knees, and over his genitals there was a washcloth damp with a substance that filled even the outer room with a bitter and pungent aroma. Destiny shut the door. Peter sat down and turned on the television, skimming for a sports station. Roman cocked an ear to the closed door.

"Let's see how we're doing over here," said Destiny.

There was a pause and then a gasp and whimper. Roman looked at Peter, but he was disinterestedly watching a recap of the Steelers-Colts debacle.

"Now I need you to listen to my voice and keep breathing deep deep into your diaphragm," she said.

The whimper modulated into long, trembling breaths.

"Look how good we're doing!" she said. "Now I need you to imagine your solar plexus as a golf ball of pale, dim light. Feel the flow of the energy and love flowing in and nourishing it, and as it brightens I want you to draw energy down from your own

Manipura, your city of jewels that also nourishes and loves, and would you look at that little ball—it's so bright and happy to be here it can give you a suntan!"

The breathing increased in volume and tempo before cresting and falling into an infantesque burble.

"Yay!" said Destiny, clapping her hands.

Soon after, both emerged. The man had tears streaming down his cheeks. He did not acknowledge Peter and Roman, or did not even see them.

"Now," said Destiny, "I want you to find time every day to be mindful of the love and nourishment flowing from your Manipura, and lay off the simple sugars. Only whole grains and starches. And if she still has the same complaint—well, there are plenty of fish in the sea."

He thanked her, settled up, and left. Peter looked inquiringly at Destiny.

"I crushed up some Viagra in his tea," she said. "But really he just needed to feel a pair of hands down there that don't care if he unloaded the dishwasher."

He nodded. It was understood among possessors of inherent magic that it is irrevocably corrupted when expended on the poor souls who try to buy it; as with love, its success on the open market was predicated on the consumer's need to believe in its authenticity.

"And I made that up about the sugar," she said confidentially. "I just thought his diet could stand to improve. Now, you gentlemen have something for me?"

First Peter handed her the bag from the health food store containing a box of her preferred brand of organic dark chocolate. The Rumanceks preferred trade to charity out of principle, and chocolate was Destiny's Achilles' heel.

"What a sweetie!" she said.

Second, Peter placed a mason jar filled with Lisa Willoughby's entrails on a counter. Destiny crouched with her hands on her knees and eyeballed the jar.

"Do I want to know?" she said.

"No," said Peter.

She rose.

"Look at me and tell me why this is better than running," she said.

Peter exhaled. "By now it's the difference between being fucked in the face and the ass," he said.

Uncertain, she nodded, then picked up the jar and unscrewed the top. Roman and Peter covered their noses. She went to the window where a fern was sitting on the sill, dug her fingertips into the fern's soil, and after a little rooting plucked out a pale worm as thin as but twice the length of a string bean.

"Hello, handsome," she said. She crossed back and dropped the worm into the jar, screwing the lid back on.

"How long?" said Peter.

"Overnight for good measure," she said, and she walked into the kitchen to wash her hands. Roman keenly watched the exit of her little shorts.

"I think my Manipura needs some nourishment," said Roman.

Peter punched him in the chest.

○

Dr. Pryce stood looking out his office window. The light was dimming over the neighboring hilltops and the ghost of his own reflection made a palimpsest over it.

"He found himself back within the precinct of the perennial riddle of the American experiment colon," he said, as was his habit in private moments of feigning dictation of the biography he hadn't the slightest intention of ever authorizing. "That its only native-grown philosophies of consequence were comma of course comma pragmatism and transcendentalism comma and the higher one esteemed the latter the more it indentured him to the former full stop. This dilemma embodied fully by the day's earlier encounter comma of which he had not stopped thinking full stop. It was not that the woman posed a meaningful threat em dash it was if anything poignant how ignorant she was of the true stakes at play em dash but a pebble remained in the shoe nevertheless ellipses an all-too-human ambivalence over what she would find waiting for her once her inquiries inevitably took her to the door of Godfrey House full stop."

He noticed the reflected flash of his computer screen and turned to his desk, regarding the message. He drummed his fingers on the desk blotter.

"Naturally it was absurd that both disruptions in a single day could be coincidence comma," he said, "but it was only to be expected since the beginning of this phase of the project that the dike would rupture in unforeseeable ways comma and to that end rest assured there was a finger at the ready full stop."

He pressed the intercom and told his assistant to inform Dr. Godfrey he'd be here all night.

Forty-five minutes later he admitted his second caller.

"Norman, it's been too long," he said. "Congratulations. As it were."

Dr. Godfrey ignored the hand offered him. "What's Ouroboros?" he said.

"Can I get you something to drink?" said Pryce. "Brandy? Diet Dr Pepper?"

"Johann," said Godfrey.

Pryce regarded his nominal employer. The man had never looked worse in their two decades of acquaintance. There had always been a baldly adversarial quality in Pryce's relationship with JR's pricklier sibling, who had objected to his appointment from the first on moral grounds (his position being that the office should go to a candidate *possessing* morality), and after the Shelley incident considered him no less than a war criminal of science whose Hague someday somehow awaited. However, the antagonist who stood before him was less the lion of proud imperial hypocrisy than a version thereof that had been put through a paper shredder and Scotch-taped back together. It saddened Pryce to see him this way. This was why he hated the political exigencies of his position; left alone in his tower he didn't have to expend these mental resources on something as capricious and fallible as empathy.

"Ouroboros," said Pryce, "is a project we're working on, and not a terribly significant one. Pit vipers possess heat-sensitive organs called thermoreceptors that more or less enable them to see in the dark, which we are studying with an eye as it were toward treating blindness. Christ, Norman, look at you. I'm getting you a brandy."

"Why," said Dr. Godfrey, "would a homeless man in my care be raving about pit vipers?"

Pryce produced a bottle of brandy from the cabinet and decanted a glass. Godfrey did not decline.

"This wouldn't happen to be a Francis Pullman, would it?" said Pryce.

Godfrey said nothing.

"Mr. Pullman volunteered to participate in an experiment with us."

"Volunteered."

"Yes. We covertly recruit volunteers for certain studies. It's not illegal, it's simply unadvertised. You are, of course, entitled to verify this in our records, as a member of the board. This particular study involved a soporific we're developing, with all the efficacy of a barbiturate but none of the side effects. We have yet, however, to perfect it, and in certain cases it has acted as a mild hallucinogenic. What soon became apparent in Mr. Pullman, however, was that despite his relatively clean psychological history, he suffers from an undiagnosed case of PTSD. But then, we're not psychiatrists. At any rate, in Pullman's case the drug was . . . contraindicated, so we cut him from the study.

More than adequately compensated, I might add. But we may be confident that went straight into his veins."

Godfrey nodded and looked at Pryce with blunt prosecution. "Not good enough. Why are both he and my niece referring to a paranormal entity called the Dragon?"

"If you'd like," said Pryce, "I can show you."

Rational Agents

Pryce and Godfrey stood before a long serpent after the Chinese fashion. Its scales were flaming red and orange and it had white eyebrows and a long mustache. On its torso was a Steelers jersey and it grasped in its talons chopsticks that in turn held the tip of its own tail. Its jaws were wide for the first bite and one eye was closed in a wink. The mural covered the double doors of the Herpetology Lab, with a quotation under it:

> I cannot tell how it mounts on the winds through the clouds and flies through heaven. Today I have seen the Dragon.—Confucius

"The Sleep Lab is that way," said Pryce, gesturing down the hall. "I also sometimes take Shelley there to monitor her REM activity."

He turned back to the dragon and smiled as though in paternal affection at a child's drawing. "I encourage little whimsies like this. It promotes group cohesion. And in the face of all we're doing, reminds us we're still human. Shall we?"

He stepped forward and the doors slid open. He gestured Godfrey inside. It was not immediately distinguished from any other laboratory in the Tower, except for a dozen dozen or so cages of transparent plastic containing what at first glance might seem to be dark, coiled tubing. But then: the eyes. Pryce approached a lab tech sitting at a monitor and thumped his shoulder.

"What's the word?" said Pryce.

"Some interesting discrepancies between *Trimeresurus trigonocephalus* and *Gloydius shedaoensis*. Oh, wait, no. There's the decimal."

Godfrey was grudgingly impressed. He was aware that he was standing on a stage of plausible deniability, but to what end God only knew, and if he pursued it, it would only call into question his own objectivity with the balance of control between himself and Olivia precarious as it was. He could only stay the course he had had faith since day one would result one day in Pryce's destruction: give him enough rope.

Godfrey looked into one of the cages and met the sensual gaze of a languid diamondback and to his surprise found himself nineteen years younger and in the basement of a rural Kentucky Pentecostal church one August morning. Nominally he had been researching the phenomenon of snake handling, but really he and Olivia had been looking for a plausible reason to get away for a night and had not even made it to the service itself but to a dark storage room in the basement where Olivia sat on a metal locker and he slid his hand up her skirt and the sweat rolled down them in sheets when there was a sudden *thump* as though the metal on which she was seated had been struck by a fist. They stopped, unsure what to think—Could a person be *in there*? Another *thump* followed, and then another. And it came to them both at the same moment. It was a snake. It "saw" their heat and was instinctively striking for it, their sheer physical need exciting the umbrage of primordial beasts.

"Norman?" said Dr. Pryce.

Godfrey had seen enough.

They returned to Pryce's office, where he refreshed his visitor's glass. Godfrey held it between his thumb and index finger and brooded.

"These would hardly be isolated examples of minds within

these walls taking certain flights of fancy," said Pryce. "It's not dissimilar to a cathedral in its tendency to collaborate somewhat spiritedly with the imaginations of our guests. But really, Norman, you look like misery in Dockers. How are you sleeping?"

"If you have some pills you want to give me, I'll pass."

Pryce smiled. "You just look like you need someone to talk to."

"We're not friends, Johann."

"Well heavens, who's contesting that? But it doesn't mean I can't see when a person is under too much stress. If you were working for me, I'd make you take a vacation."

"But you work for me," said Godfrey, more resigned than reprising.

"Speaking of," said Pryce. "You can expect to be contacted by an organization called Lod LLC with a bid to buy you out."

Godfrey was not surprised; it was not the first time Pryce had conspired with enigmatic third parties for his emancipation.

"And how many layers of this onion would my lawyer have to peel to find out whose interest Lod LLC actually represents?" he said.

"Too many to be worth the time of a person who would just as soon disavow the whole institute. Simplify things for everyone. You can buy yourself the highest horse in the land and self-flagellate to your heart's content just in case anyone hasn't gotten the memo on your feelings about having been born into the House of Godfrey."

"I have yet to resolve to my professional satisfaction whether you're evil or just autistic," said Dr. Godfrey. "But for your proposal to make any sense there would have to be a sum of money in the world more valuable to me than sending you to prison, a moment I have been awaiting with profound anticipation from the day you first got your hooks into my niece."

Pryce leaned back in his chair and steepled his fingers. "Would you have rather she died?" he said.

"She did die. I would rather you had been honest with my brother about the procedure."

"I don't believe there was a great deal of ambiguity. He knew the ramifications."

"He was grief-stricken. You knew he wasn't emotionally competent to make that kind of choice and you exploited it."

"I knew waiting wasn't a luxury available to us. And would you care to tell our girl you see her conception as the result of emotional incompetence?"

"Well, it's the only goddamn thing about her that's normal!" said Godfrey.

They looked at each other and smiled with the ease of old enemies. Godfrey slugged his drink and replenished it himself, now reminiscent.

"The first time we met," he said, "I pulled JR aside and said, 'You can't be serious about hiring that sociopath.' And he told me that sociopath was going to do for medicine what Bessemer did for steel. He said you were a genius. I said, So was Mengele." He ran his finger down the petal of a potted orchid.

"I have a teenage daughter I'm taking to the OB-GYN tomorrow," he said. "If I get solid evidence you had any involvement in that, I will have you killed. That is not an exaggeration."

He drained his glass, placed it on the cabinet, and left.

Pryce laced his hands behind his head, bemused.

"Of course comma," said Pryce, "if he had learned one lesson in his years within the gulag of academia comma it was that anyone who made decisions based on the premise that other human beings were rational agents acting in accord with what was of greatest benefit to themselves and their environment was a peerless cunt full stop."

○

Olivia found herself, as was from time to time her wont, with a case of the nibbles. She and Shelley were watching an old movie when she found she was sucking on the collar of her own shirt, an undignified habit from her early youth that reemerged during periods of pronounced nerves. She released the fabric and the hickey of her own saliva was damp on her skin. That. Goddamn. Child. She felt a tingle and saw that the hair on her arms was standing on end. As happened sometimes when she got caught up in a strong emotion around her daughter. Olivia kneaded Shelley's thigh with exasperated tenderness; in her years of experience in the theater and the particular specimen of adolescent female it attracts she had never encountered this degree of goddamn sensitivity.

"Oh, Shelley Belly," said Olivia.

A car parked outside then and Olivia felt a frisson pass through the hair on her arm as though from a soft breath; a concurrent increase in the girl's unease with her mother's ire. The front door opened and Roman passed through the foyer. Olivia muted the television.

"Roman Godfrey," she said.

He appeared and stood with his hands in his blazer pockets and waited with an affected and overcooked boredness and Shelley tensed, spine rigid and arms unnaturally straight with hands braced on her thighs, and Olivia was suddenly almost too fatigued by it all to get on with it. Like a night when the energy is bloody unsalvageable but the show must et cetera. Domesticity. Times when one wonders if *Medea* is a tragedy or goddamn wish fulfillment.

"Is there anything you're of a mind to share?" said Olivia.

"Not especially," said Roman.

"The news tonight said that Lisa Willoughby's grave was terribly violated," said Olivia. "They're offering ten thousand dollars for information on the culprits. Would you care to be more *specific* about your social agenda?"

He said nothing.

"You're lucky I don't phone the police right now," she said.

"Go nuts," he said. "Just gimme a minute to powder my nose if I'm gonna be on the front page tomorrow."

Shelley's breath became hoarse and shallow.

"Sarcasm, the enemy of wit," Olivia said witheringly.

"Pithy," said Roman.

Her face clouded darkly and she spoke with dread calm. "You think you can hide behind your name like every other time, but I have made my position clear on your association with that Gypsy trash. And whatever *preposterous* goddamn game you think you're playing to get a rise out of me, you have a rather great deal more to lose than that thick, spoiled head is allowing for."

Roman did not immediately respond, and wanting least in the world to bring attention to herself Shelley held her breath and there was only the high-frequency pitch of the muted television.

"Jesus, you need to get laid," said Roman.

Shelley gasped and raced from the room. Olivia looked at Roman. He was too pleased with himself to be finished, so she waited.

"Is Norm busy?" he said.

Now there was the rush! She rose and stood before him, regarding the child with a thrill of gall. And then she slapped his face with such force it knocked him back over the end table, and he made no attempt to protect himself as she knelt over him and slapped both sides of his face until his cheeks were an angry rose red. Then, suddenly short of breath, she backed off and turned away, leaving him on his back. There was a flicker in the window, the reflected screen of the television. The film's spurned heroine on a chaise smoking with languid animus. Olivia stared captive as the image diffused into a liquid flux of the light and dark and she felt herself sinking, sinking somehow away and into it at the same time . . .

She felt a pair of strong hands steady her shoulders and Roman caught her just before she fell.

These Lowly Creatures

Dr. Godfrey sat in the OB-GYN waiting room, where a sitcom he vaguely remembered loathing played as an otherwise emaciated young woman in her third trimester shrilled over it into her cell phone the excruciating details of her proud triumph in one of those squalid sexual potboilers that so frequently end up arbitrated in front of the cameras of daytime television judges. Next to her was a morbidly obese friend or relative who nodded and *mm-hmm*'d through the story as if on a pew. On her other side was a lean man years her senior in a sheriff's deputy uniform with a nose that led not just his walk but his slouch. His arm was around the pregnant girl. Godfrey thumbed through the lone *Sports Illustrated* he assumed was here to reduce the chances of expectant fathers taking flight.

"And I says Mom, I says Mom, you just tell him that demon pig bitch and anything that smells like her is gone by this weekend or he's never touching *this* again."

"Mm-hmm . . . Mm-hmm . . ."

Despite his evident sexual proprietorship over the prize in question, Nose had little enough stake in the drama; rather, his focus was on Godfrey, to whom he had now sent enough dagger glances that it could not be coincidence, though whether it was because of some inadvertent offense or the alpha-male hostilities that Neiman Marcus cuff links and a well-shined shoe instinctively arouse in a certain species of blue-collar man could not be said.

Godfrey employed a mental exercise. He had read at a young age a guiding principle that had changed the course of his life: The first step to liberty is respecting the rights of others. This had made him something of an aberration in the Godfrey line, the idea that each and every soul with whom you share this planet, no matter how unlike, much less appalling to yourself, was worthy of empathy and respect in all circumstances. So the exercise was simply continuing to sit here with this magazine whose words were a blur of irritation and trying to find a modicum of generosity toward this particular segment of humanity instead of escaping to the car and having a slug from the flask that he rationalized he wasn't hiding because the glove compartment wasn't a hiding place, it was a perfectly innocent compartment. What distinguished this exercise from punishment was a question of degree rather than intent.

Suddenly there was a report like the firing of a gun and Godfrey's head snapped in alarm. But there was no threat, no threat to his daughter, and the sound's provenance became clear as the obese girl slid to the floor: an existing hairline fracture in the leg of her chair had snapped under her weight.

She lay dazed on her back like a tortoise carved out of butter as her friend cackled into the phone.

"Oh my holy shit!" said her friend. "Guess whose fat ass broke the chair!"

Godfrey put down the magazine and rose. He went to the fallen fat girl and held out his hand.

"Are you okay?" he said. "Are you okay, sweetheart?"

Afterward, passing over the Hot Metal Bridge, he asked Letha if she'd like to go to lunch at the club.

"Are you sure you have time?" she said.

He didn't. He nodded.

"She has irises," she said.

He didn't know what she meant. And then he did and found himself at a momentary loss as though any second now words would be invented.

"I wonder what color her eyes are," she said. "I need some fresh air, okay?"

He did not object to fresh air and she cracked her window and her bangs danced in the wind.

O

Just upriver Olivia leaned against the hood of her pickup, smoking a cigarette in the shadow of the Dragon. This local luminary was a sculpture of rebar and oxygen hosing of a serpent's head. It stood roughly thirty feet in height between the mill building and the hot stoves of Castle Godfrey. What castle complete? The sculpture's author was a mystery; the figure made its first appearance on the property in 1991 following the aborted attempt at removing the Bessemer converter for scrap that resulted in the death of one worker and a half dozen injuries. Fearing the hand of some millenarian cult, the sheriff's department destroyed the statue, only for another of identical placement and proportion to take its place soon after. This process was to repeat itself several times before it graduated into a received part of the landscape, like the pornographic graffiti or scrap pile of exploded electric appliances or pieces of furniture dropped by the more enterprising of bored local youths from the ore bridge.

Sun glinted off the water, causing Olivia to wince and the cigarette to fall from her lips. She crushed it with the toe of her shoe and walked to the entrance of the mill unevenly in heels and went inside. Several minutes passed. There was a breeze and the hawk glided into it, coming to a standstill, wings tilting to and fro like a child on a balance beam. Then the old doors slammed open with a rusty whine and Olivia came stumbling out and, bracing herself on a wall, heaved a dark and glutinous puddle on the ground. She retched herself into dry heaves and then eased herself to the ground and lay on her back. She fished her phone from her purse and dialed. It took a minute to connect with the person she was looking for.

"Sheriff Sworn, Olivia Godfrey . . . Yes, yes, and yours . . . Well, I was wondering if it wouldn't be too much trouble if you would request your men to keep an eye out for any unusual activity around the mill . . . Precisely . . . Quite, cheers."

She stretched her arm and dipped a finger to the puddle and brought the fingertip between her lips.

○

Peter was doing a card trick with the Major Arcana for Shelley in the school parking lot when Roman approached and said it would be better if he didn't come along for the follow-up. Peter gave him an inquisitive glance as he produced the Hanged Man for Shelley. She shook her head and he flicked it aside.

"*Der Führer*'s panties are in a bunch," said Roman. "I'll come by your place in the morning."

Peter flashed the Hierophant. She shook her head again and the card was discarded.

"What is she so afraid of?" said Peter.

"Her talons slipping out," said Roman.

Peter nodded. Then his nose wrinkled and he doubled over in an explosive sneeze and a card fluttered to Shelley's feet faceup. The Wheel of Fortune. Shelley grinned.

"Gee, I wish I was cool enough to know magic tricks," said Roman.

He drove Shelley home. An institute van was parked in the drive. When Shelley saw it she clapped her hands and leaped from the cart, which lurched and rocked from side to side. She landed with a *whoom* that sent a rippled wave through the grass and she bounded to the door, stopping herself short of inadvertently battering it from its hinges. Steadying herself, she attempted to properly turn the knob in a ladylike manner. She was spared the effort as her mother opened the door and stepped out.

"Darling," she said, "you have a visitor."

Dr. Pryce stepped into view. "Hello, Glowworm."

Shelley seized him by the chest and held him aloft, mustering her fullest restraint to prevent herself from spinning.

"Do settle down, dear," said Olivia.

Shelley set Dr. Pryce back to his feet. He smiled indulgently.

"I was wondering if my best girl would care to join me for a walk?"

She tipped up and down like a child on the edges of her cubes.

"Hello, Roman," said Dr. Pryce.

"Hey," said Roman, passing by. He and Pryce had never had anything but a superficially civil relationship. The doctor fell into the rare category of person that gave even Roman the creeps.

"Any designs on the evening?" said Olivia.

"*Nein*," said Roman with a crisp Nazi salute. He went inside.

Dr. Pryce threaded his hand through the crook of Shelley's arm and they strolled around the house to a trail through the tree line in the rear. She left quadrangular imprints in the ground and bare leaves clumped to her feet. There was gloaming light through the naked trees and he noticed the tip of an earthworm protruding from loose earth. He knelt and pinched it and stood once more, holding its dangling, dirt-speckled pink to the light.

"'It may be doubted,'" he said, "'whether there are any other animals which have played so important a part in the history of the world, as have these lowly creatures.'"

They admired it a moment and then he delicately replaced it. They went on.

"Would you like to know a secret, Glowworm?" said Pryce.

She looked down at him. Did he even need to ask?

"Through some quirk of design, I was born with a sense of

self," he said. "Can you imagine anything so horrific? It's like the terror of waking up and not knowing where you are and the terror of the most lucid nightmare all at once. And if that wasn't enough, I was born twelve weeks premature. It was no bracing swat on the behind and delivery into loving arms that welcomed me to this world, no—it was the loveless mercy of an artificial womb. My first weeks as a sentient being were spent in solitary confinement. But I've always taken issue with that phrase. If anything, it's lucky I have no tendency toward agoraphobia; the microcosm mirrors the macrocosm, from particles of atom to the far reaches of the universe encompassing thirty powers of ten in space, all *within the apparatus of the mind*: the firmament without and the firmament within merely opposing sides of the glass. And in that pacific solitude, in full awe and dread: I saw it. Destiny is no more than the fulfillment of purposive potentialities within us. The human cerebral cortex is a single sheet composed of more neurons than there are stars in the known universe folded like a paper crane to fit in a quart-sized cubbyhole; there is enough potential energy in a single person that if released would equal thirty hydrogen bombs. Destiny is nothing to sneeze at! And there I saw my own. So I willed the power to hatch myself from that incubator because my Work in life illumined before me as perfect and outstanding as a single star at night, and I had no time to lose."

There was a slim tree felled in their path about four feet from the ground. Shelley grasped it and lifted it over her head as they passed under it, letting it crash back behind her.

"I understand," he said, "you have a certain confidence with your uncle."

She tensed in expectation of chastisement. He put a pacifying hand on her arm.

"I'm not cross with you. I'm not Olivia. But there is something I have to do, something very important, and by necessity very secret. Have you ever shown your poetry to your mother?"

She looked at him in alarm.

"Exactly. There is nothing wrong with secrets. You know, the alchemists believed that a creative work has a sort of life all its own independent of the creator, straddling the worlds of psyche and matter, of both and neither. A subtle body, they called it. Can you imagine anything so beautiful and precious? All creative expression a reverse eucharist: providing a spirit body! Can you think of what you wouldn't do to protect such a spectacle of fragility? There is no shame in hiding some things. Now, you've done nothing wrong, but, Glowworm, I do have to ask you, as a personal favor, to repeat nothing I tell you. To anyone. Ouroboros is that important and that vulnerable. Just . . . trust me that it's for the best."

Shelley met his eyes and nodded gravely.

"I am in my best girl's debt," said Pryce, "and even more deeply if she gives me a smile."

She grinned.

"I suppose we should turn back. You never know what you'll run into in the woods these days. And I don't suppose you'd have room for a slice of pumpkin pie?"

She nodded vigorously. They turned back on the path and a low-lying branch caught in her hair.

"Oh dear," he said and stood on a large rock, gently disentangling it. He brushed away dry leaf particles.

"I'm so proud of you, you know," he said. "It's not for nothing. Your time in this incubator."

Her cheeks flashed dimly like lightning behind cloud.

O

Destiny stood at the sink and unscrewed the lid and reached in and pulled out the worm, which she rinsed under the faucet. It had gone from white to a pale blue-red, and while skinny before it now bulged lasciviously.

"Down the hatch," she said and tipped her head back and swallowed it whole. She sat down and nodded to Peter. On the kitchen table were two leather belts. Peter looped one belt around her abdomen and arms and fastened it tightly. She crossed her ankles and he bound them to the chair with the second belt.

"Are your feet ticklish?" he said.

"It would be your last act on this Earth," she said. "Don't go far. This can get a little bumpy."

Peter stood behind her, bracing her shoulders. Suddenly she sucked in her breath as though at sharp abdominal pain.

"Be quick," she winced. "It passes fast."

Just then her head whipped forward and both belts strained taut, catching Peter by surprise and causing him to lose his grip; he only just managed to catch the back of the chair before it tipped forward. Her breathing now hoarse and erratic, she snapped back upright and her hair lashed Peter's face; her spine arched rigid and her extremities strained as she panted through her nose and began to wrench violently from side to side; the chair lurched and rocked in Peter's grip. Then she fell limp and the breath rolled down her nose. Her hair draped forward so all he could see were her lips, a loose strand of spittle issuing.

After a moment Peter said, "Can you talk?"

"Yes." Her voice was brittle and diaphanous, like the wings of a dead insect.

"What can you tell me?"

"I hated butterscotch. I was good at trig and liked to sew. All my life I was more afraid than anything of swimming where you couldn't see the bottom but one day I just wasn't anymore. I was planning on giving Scott Buford a blow job on his birthday but would have chickened out. My parents always loved me more than my sister. I hope they get that sorted out."

"What can you tell me about your death?" Peter said more specifically.

"I came to Hemlock Grove because of the invitation. It was dark, and I didn't see anyone else, but I thought that was part of it. So I parked a little way off and doubled back, like it said. And there he was. I couldn't tell what it was at first, waiting there in the mist. I'd never seen anything like it. But I wasn't afraid, not yet. I was in a dream. And then he came to me, but slowly. Like a friend. I could see now it was a dog, but not like any other dog. He was so big. So big and so black. He came to me and I reached out and held out my hand for him because I've always had a way with dogs. This close I could see how tall he was, his head was as high as mine. And so skinny it hurt my heart. Skinny but still strong. Some animals you can just feel it in the air around them, how strong they are. But I wasn't afraid. I have a way with dogs. I reached out to pet his cheek, and that's when I saw those eyes. Horrible yellow eyes."

"What was the invitation?" said Peter. "Where were you?"

Destiny convulsed. She looked up at Peter through eyes that looked far past him.

"The way he looked at me with those eyes," she said. "That helpless way a dog looks at you when it can't tell you what it needs."

Just then Destiny belched once and then twice and her head dropped and the worm slid out of her mouth and slopped to the floor. She looked at Peter.

"Let me up," she said.

O

After cleaning up, Destiny put a hold-on hand to Peter's arm at the door.

"Another thing," she said. "How much do you know about this place, Hemlock Grove?"

"It's a place," he said, trying to look terribly blasé.

"You can play Mr. Big Stuff with me but I've seen you cry your eyes out when Nicolae said the utilities guy was Leatherface," she said.

"What should I know?" he said.

"You need to be very careful around Roman Godfrey and his mother," she said.

"The little prince has no teeth," said Peter. "And the queen is an actress. Underneath the mask she's just bored."

"He has no teeth yet. But I could see with my Third Eye a trouble with his Anahata chakra, and just like I knew there would be, there's a dangerous conversion of his fate line and his heart line. He is going to face the hardest choice he will ever have to make, and however he falls will have very very large consequences for anyone around him.

"And you should watch your step around an actress whether or not she's *upir*. Because you never know how many masks that crazy bitch is wearing."

Peter nodded. She tightened her grip.

"Make no mistake about their kind," she said. "I was in love with an *upir* once. Someday when I'm drunk enough I'll tell you about it. But please take my word for it: Never forget what he is. Especially if he has."

"Okay," said Peter, impatient. There being no naturally occurring balm for exactly your own doubts quite like the implication that you don't have them under control.

He paused.

"What do you think of angels?" he said.

"Angels are messengers that help us understand God," she said. She looked at him. "Why are you asking me about angels?"

"There's this girl at school," he said.

"What is it with you and crazy girls?" she said.

He didn't have an answer. He wished he did.

No Upward Limit

That evening Roman stood nude facing the bathroom mirror with the blade of a box cutter pressed just to the side of his pubis, and he made a small incision. He was in the habit of on occasion cutting open—nothing excessive—his chest or his abdomen; not to release any inner pain or cause a fuss, but simply because he liked to, liked the feeling of hot blood trickling down his belly or his legs or his cock, liked the complementarity of it, that life was in essence liquid, not solid. He watched in the mirror the rivulet curve with his hip down his inner thigh and the hairs of his legs stood, the warmth of it versus the cold of the tile under his feet. He tightened his core and clenched his buttocks to increase the flow.

"Bloody invigorating!" he said.

Then his phone rang; the ring was the song "Common People."

"Shit," he said, reaching for a hand towel.

Downstairs, Roman told his mother he was going to pop off to Letha's. She searched his face, and finding a trace of that subtle glow his cousin tended to awaken in him that he was not sufficiently artful in mendacity to fake, said, "Fine."

He continued past but she stopped him. "Just a moment, darling, you've got an eyelash."

She put a hand to his face and looked into his eyes.

"Where's Peter?" said Letha.

"Otherwise engaged," said Roman.

He lay on her bed and she sat Indian-style on the floor.

"So you have dirt for me," he said.

"In spades," she said. "I was actually surprised I could get Dad to go into it, but he's just carrying so much these days he seemed relieved to have an excuse to talk about it. He can't get away from it, you know. It's on all sides. But he'll get through it. He'll get through it when he holds my baby."

Roman did not respond.

"So it turns out before Pullman saw the attack he was a test subject in a sleep study at the White Tower," she said. "He thinks it was connected with an experiment called Project Ouroboros where he was killed and brought back to life."

"Huh," said Roman, thinking of Pryce's unexpected call. "What's your dad think?"

"He doesn't know what to think. Considering there were no tracks, if what this guy thought he saw was actually a hallucination it . . . makes a lot more sense that you guys are right." She looked down and picked at fringe on the carpet. "That it's a person."

Roman nodded. Then he stopped abruptly and looked at her with a blank expression.

"What?" she said.

"The institute is one of the most advanced medical centers in the world," said Roman. "The only thing that matters is where the baby will be safest."

A moment passed and Roman continued to nod, but now with some confusion. She was confused too. They looked at each other. It passed. Letha turned her head to the side, cracking her neck, and reached back to squeeze a knot in her trapezius.

"Want a back rub?" said Roman.

She scoffed, as a selfish person offering an unselfish gesture can expect.

"Come on," he said. "You can't tell me those tits aren't murdering your shoulders."

"Shut up!" She folded her arms around her chest.

Roman patted the blanket. She bit her lip.

"Your token display of resistance fools no one," he said.

"Yeah yeah," she said and climbed next to him, lying prone. He straddled her and took a seat on the cushion of her posterior and tucked her hair to the side.

"You'll have to excuse me if my performance isn't one hundred percent," he said. "I'm not used to doing this through a shirt."

"You're so gross! If I wanted to hear about your whoredom I'd pay more attention in the girls' bathroom."

He dug his thumbs into her trapezius and made slow semicircles, radiating outward to her deltoids. She inhaled sharply and let it out in a long slow breath. He worked his knuckles into her scapulae.

"You *are* good at this," she said. "Gross!"

Her nose wrinkled from an itch and she rubbed it with the back of her hand. He took her wrist and regarded the ring on her finger.

"What's this?"

"A prize. Peter said it was good luck."

Roman said nothing. He worked his thumbs incrementally down her spine, then slid his fingers under her shirt and kneaded her waist and the dimples of flesh on either side of the small of her back.

"Right there. Ohmygod right there," she said.

There was a clipped knock and then Marie Godfrey entered before waiting for a response.

"Honey, that dancing show you like is on," she said.

"Thanks, Mom," said Letha.

Marie hovered at the door, in a conundrum over her disapproval and lack of theoretical ground to protest.

"Ooh, am I next?" she said with a laugh of unpleasant brittleness that her ears regretted registering as her own.

"Absolutely," said Roman, giving her a wink that made her wish she was carrying a hatpin.

"Oh, Mom," said Letha, "I think I'm going to see about switching treatment to the institute. I know Dad will have a conniption, but it's one of the most advanced medical centers in the world, and the only thing that matters is where the baby will be safest."

O

Dr. Godfrey sat with the phone to his ear, drumming his fingers on a jar on his desk containing two fist-sized skeins of intricately woven crimson fibers: the blood vessels of the brain cast in colored polymer—a gift from the Women's Psychiatric Society for his generosity to their cause. He inquired of his wife what precisely he was supposed to do about it.

She apologized. "I meant to call someone with some kind of control over what happens under his roof," she said.

Dial tone filled his ear. His hand fell away but he did not replace the phone in the cradle. He sat regarding the dead pinholes of the receiver.

O

"How very goddamn *mysterious*," said Olivia.

She closed Godfrey's office door behind her.

"The monsieur summoned?" she said.

He didn't get up from behind his desk. She sat on the couch, reclining.

"What is Johann up to?" he said.

"Why on earth should I know?" she said.

"Anytime I try to pick up his leash he goes hiding behind your skirts. Why is that?"

"Because as long as I'm apprised of quarterlies, I concern myself as little as possible with . . . whatever it is Johann does," she said.

"My daughter has decided she'd like to pursue treatment at the institute," he said.

"Sensible," she said.

"It won't happen while I'm alive."

"You're looking at me like I'm supposed to argue about something that's none of my business."

"What about the bid to buy me out? That's your business."

"If someone wants your share, it's news to me," she said indifferently.

"When you're lying about something I know you know, exactly what do you want me to believe?" he said.

She rose and went to his wall cabinet and took out a bottle of scotch.

"From what I've seen, people believe exactly what they want to, independent of your encouragement," she said. She poured a glass.

Godfrey looked at her. The first time she had been in his office since she was a patient. Eliciting the same response she always had then, never replicated by another: outrage over his own inability to control his feelings.

"How can you not care after what he did to Shelley?" said Godfrey, ears flushing with a rising anger happier than any drunk. "Do you have antifreeze in your veins?"

She didn't reply.

"What kind of mother are you?" he said, unfair, awful, and exalted.

She replaced the scotch on the shelf, putting the bottle on its side without screwing the cap back on and shutting the door. She returned to the couch as the liquid began flowing from the crack in the door down the paneling and puddled on the carpet.

Godfrey rose and went to the couch, standing over her.

"Stand up," he said.

"Thank *God*," she said. "I was worrying you only had me over because Marie doesn't listen anymore when you're feeling boorish."

He took the glass out of her hands and put it on the table, then reached his hand under her skirt and jerked on her panties, which slid down to her shoes. They faced each other. She breathed the smell of scotch into his face.

"Does that help you get it up these days?" she said.

He took her by the shoulders and turned her around and forced her down to her knees doubled over the couch. He knelt and hiked her skirt over her waist and slapped her with force on the buttocks. She breathed out sharply. He slapped her again, and again, and again, and she let out a cry and braced her hands on the cushions to push herself up. He reached with his left hand and gripped her by the neck and held her in place as he struck her with greater abandon, her shoulders racking with low sobs now and her bare flesh imprinted a luminous mottle of sunset red over a glimmering vulva like a heat mirage on the highway, the sight of which gripped his heart like such a vista of natural beauty one desires with every molecule but never can possess. He sank down, encircling her thighs with his arms and running his lips and his tongue over her rear and the small of her back. She pushed back against him and sank to the floor, reaching for his crotch and removing his belt and tossing it to the side. She unclasped his trousers and lay back and he parted her legs, entering her gently and kissing the wetness of tears on her face. She looked him impatiently in the face.

"Like you mean it," she said.

He thrust.

"Yes," she said.

He quickly built up a new head of steam. He felt like a rabid little rodent. He felt like a god of carnage. How he felt mattered much less than the fact of feeling so much of it.

Later he stood and took a box of tissues from his desk and handed it to her. She seized his hand.

"Come here," she said.

He allowed her to pull him down. He lay with his head to her breast and she ran her hand up and down his back. Their first time had been on this floor many years ago. If it had seemed like he couldn't have felt worse about it then it was because he had been too young a man to know yet that time is cyclical, that there is no upward limit to the number of times you can make the same mistake.

"My poor, poor Norman," she said.

He would have liked to lie here weeping for a while but was too depleted to cry. It felt like all the world's kindness was in the flat of her hand.

A Large Bad Thing

The next morning Roman and Peter went to 7 Royal Oaks Drive in Penrose. There was an SUV parked in the driveway with a bumper sticker for the losing Republican ticket of the latest gubernatorial race. On the porch hung a Thanksgiving flag of a cornucopia and lying over the mouth of one garbage can on the sidewalk was a mat with a paw print in place of the *o* in *Welcome*. A pale middle-aged man answered the door. He was wearing glasses with a fingerprint smudge on the edge of one lens and a Steelers T-shirt and sweatpants, his neck and chin pink and red stubbled with razor burn. He had not clipped his toenails recently.

"Can I help you?" he said.

"Mr. Willoughby?" said Roman.

"Yes?" He was medded out and apathetic about their identity or the purpose of their call.

"Is Mrs. Willoughby in?" said Roman.

"No, she isn't."

Roman looked him in the eye. "Why don't you go take a nap."

Mr. Willoughby went inside to a couch and lay with his back to the room like a cartoon drunk. Peter went to the stairs but Roman lingered over the man. He removed the man's glasses and breathed on the lens and wiped the smudge with his blazer. Peter looked at Roman and jerked his head in the direction of the stairs. Eyes on the ball. Roman set the glasses on the table and followed him to the second floor, where they began opening doors. Peter found the bathroom and Roman what appeared to be a teenage girl's room. Peter looked in and said, "This bed has been slept in."

The next room they tried was Lisa's. The bed was made and would not be unmade soon. On one wall was a corkboard with pictures of Lisa and her friends tacked to it as well as a hodge-podge of images of popular musicians and exotic travel destinations and a magazine fitness regimen. On her desk was an artist's dummy in a miniature ballroom gown doing a pirouette on top of a sewing machine. Roman went through her dresser, and Peter her desk. Peter flipped through all her letters and school notebooks and college brochures. He found a doodle she'd apparently done during social studies of a Pilgrim woman being chased delightedly by a Native American with a massive erection tenting his loincloth, and a single sheet of computer paper with a heading on the top: HOW TO CHANGE. The rest of the page was blank. He replaced her things in the order he found them.

"Anything?" he asked Roman.

Roman held up a pair of white panties with cotton on the back like a bunny tail. "Hippity hop," he said.

Peter dug through her closet, Roman pulled a box of child-hood photos and mementos from under her bed.

"What if it's in her car?" said Roman, neatly stacking elementary school class photos and construction paper valentines. "What if it was in her purse?"

"I'll never understand what a person can do with so many darned shoes," said Peter, who himself wore only the things as often as custom or climate made necessary.

Roman added a program for an old *Swan Lake* recital to the pile. He held up a picture of eleven- or twelve-year-old Lisa in the costume of a Depression-era hobo with a five o'clock shadow done in charcoal. "Riding the rails," he said.

"What are you looking for?" said a girl in the doorway.

Roman and Peter turned. She was about fifteen, with the unappealing variation on her sister's beauty, and overweight. Roman glanced at Peter, who held up his hand. He would field this one.

"We're looking for a piece of mail that would have come for your sister," said Peter. "We think someone might have killed her."

"Someone like you?" she said.

"Touché," said Roman.

"Roman," said Peter. "Shut the fuck up."

"Were you the ones who dug her up?" said the girl.

They were quiet.

"I don't care," said the girl. "Like that's so much worse than what already happens when you die. There are things living inside you right now that will eat you from the inside out. It's called symbiosis. Mom used to call me 'the sentimental one.' She's out taking Gary to be put down now. She can't handle a dog being around, and Dad can't handle the dog Lisa loved so much having new owners. I always thought he was an annoying little fucker, but it still seems like a bit much for a Boston terrier."

The girl looked at them with eyes as opaque as candle wax.

"I have it," she said. "What you're looking for. I'll get it." She disappeared.

Roman looked at Peter. "Sorry," he said.

Peter said nothing.

The girl returned moments later with a blank black envelope.

"I wanted to borrow a pair of socks and I found this," she said. "I wanted to come along, but she wouldn't take me. I . . . had an, I don't know, a flash. Maybe at the time it wasn't really a flash of anything, it just feels like it looking back. But you know how it is when you're mad at someone when they're leaving and part of you thinks, What if something happens and I never see her again and what I say now is the last thing I ever say? And I looked at her and she was always so fucking pretty and I said I hope she ends up left in a Dumpster."

She handed the envelope to Peter.

"I showed it to my parents, but they just got pissed," she said. "They think it was just an animal. They think it was just me trying to get attention."

Peter opened the envelope and pulled out a card of black construction paper with lettering of glitter and glue and read it. He looked at Roman.

"You're Roman Godfrey, aren't you?" said the girl.

"How do you know who I am?" said Roman.

"You're a Godfrey," said the girl.

"What is that?" said Roman. "What does that say?"

"I thought you might be here for me too," said the girl.

Peter handed the card to him. Roman looked at it and was quiet.

"I guess you're not," said the girl, morose.

The card was an invitation to a party. The party was INVITATION ONLY and you were not to tell another LIVING SOUL. SHHHHHHH, it said. The party was being held at Castle Godfrey the night of the full moon.

"Do you have any idea who might have sent her that?" said Peter.

"No, I don't. She didn't have any friends from Hemlock Grove that I knew of. But someone did steal her wallet out of her purse at a Starbucks there a couple of weeks ago. I figured you guys might have it."

Roman didn't respond or seem to be paying that much attention anymore. He held the invitation with his name on it as he would a sacred text.

"Thank you," said Peter. "This is a lot of help."

"Why are you looking for him?" said the girl. "The one who did this?"

"Because he's going to be joining Gary," said Roman.

O

Olivia took Shelley on a trip to the library. They branched out to different sections, Shelley physics and Olivia periodicals. Shelley passed the children's section. A woman in a rocking chair was reading to a semicircle of children on the rug. "Not by the hairs of my chinny-chin-chin," she said. Then she stopped as Shelley passed and the children turned. Shelley was immobilized—all those little eyes Lilliputian stakes. A little girl slid out and touched one of Shelley's cubes with an expression of awe. The right side of Shelley's face curled into a smile. A dark stain formed in the lap of a quivering boy and he began to cry. The storyteller knelt forward and shushed the boy but his tears began to spread from child to child like match heads flaring too quickly for the storyteller to contain. Shelley moved on.

Olivia heard the dim chorus of terror and hummed quietly to herself, selecting a wooden-spooled *Wall Street Journal*. It is commonly expected that wealthy families go from shirtsleeves to shirtsleeves in three generations, and JR, being of the fourth and solely responsible for saving the Godfrey fortune from certain ruin, believed this could be forestalled largely by the concerned parties being able to make hide or hair of the financial page without the assistance of flunkies. Early in his education of his wife she had balked—the only figure she could be expected to be overly troubled with was her own—but surprisingly got the hang of it upon realizing its relationship to her own art: once decoded, the market, like the stage or the heart, was simply another arena in which desire went to war. An elderly man of the sort that can be found at libraries with a preference for print periodicals, sitting at a nearby table, said, "At the risk of sounding old-fashioned, I'm always damn impressed to see a lady with a nose for business."

She turned to him, and seeing that the nose in question was connected to Olivia Godfrey, the affability drained from his face and his mouth spread wide in a death grin.

"Why, thank you," she said, herself old-fashioned enough to receive a man's compliment in the spirit it was intended.

Olivia and Shelley convened at two armchairs upstairs overlooking the windows. The springs in Shelley's chair sagged nearly to the floor as she opened her book. Olivia craned her neck, reading aloud over her daughter's shoulder:

"'Of course, minute as its impact may be in our physical universe, the *fact* of quantum entanglement is this: If one logically inexplicable thing is known to exist, then this permits the existence of all logically inexplicable things. A thing may be of *deeper* impossibility than another, in the sense that you can be *more deeply* underwater—but whether you are five feet or five fathoms from the surface you are still all wet.'"

Shelley clapped the book shut and folded her arms in a pout. But then her eyes lit (not a turn of phrase) and she rose, waving vigorously. Olivia looked over. The object of her daughter's enthusiasm was a girl of approximately her own age accompanying an old woman with a stack of trashy detective thrillers, a small girl with a black raven's nest bramble of hair and one glaring lock of white bang that to Olivia's authoritative eye was not a dye job. The girl, if she was not mistaken, who had found Lisa Willoughby.

Christina responded to her classmate's cheer in seeing her out and in good spirits with a smile of her own, but it faltered under the refracting blackness of Olivia's sunglasses. She hurried on with her grandmother.

Disappointed, Shelley sat, and in so doing the afternoon light glinting off cars in the parking lot caught Olivia's eye. Olivia tried to look away but could not. Suddenly and irreversibly at its mercy. The light transfixing her, the shadow closing in.

The shadow just waiting for her to get distracted by the light shimmering gold like a field of—

Shelley looked up as her mother braced one hand on the arm of the chair and drew the fingertips of the other softly down her own her face and her eyelids fluttered and she said, "The sunflowers . . ."

And with that crashed to the floor.

○

"It's just an empty, out-of-the-way place," said Peter as he exited the car. "It doesn't mean anything for all we know."

Roman looked off to a patch of bare rockface in the hillside where a tree grew outward in the shape of a J.

"Do you know what that's called?" said Roman. "When the root system is right there in the rock. Do they have a name for that?"

"I don't know," said Peter. "A lot of things have names."

They agreed to convene later in the evening and Peter went inside where Lynda was watching TV and putting together a jigsaw puzzle of a commonly reproduced Monet.

Lynda told Peter Lisa had stopped by.

"'Lisa'?" said Peter.

○

From the archives of Norman Godfrey:

NG: I spoke with Dr. Pryce.
FP: . . .
NG: Do you know who Dr. Pryce is, Francis?
FP: Yeah. I know him.
NG: He says you participated in a medical experiment at the Godfrey Institute. Is that true?

FP: So what?

NG: Is there a reason you didn't mention that before?

FP: I did tell you. They killed us.

NG: According to Dr. Pryce, you took a highly experimental barbiturate.

FP: I'm not a fucking liar.

NG: No one's saying that. I just wanted to get a better sense of what you're going through.

FP: They fucking gave us something, all right. They killed us and brought us back.

NG: Francis, can you possibly help me understand the . . . mechanics of that?

FP: Today I have seen the Dragon . . .

NG: Can you elaborate on the things you see?

FP: Things . . . come in my head.

NG: What kinds of things?

FP: Baby in a blood pouch. River glowing red. Dog hatching from a big black egg. Needle the size of a sword. Demon with a crown of light.

NG: This needle—was it some kind of drug?

FP: This is not about goddamn drugs! This is some evil, unnatural shit that has no business happening. You think this is just some junkie bullshit, talk to one of the other guys, see how they're sleeping. I even got a name for you, saw it on the chart by mine. Varga, H. You talk to H. fucking Varga before you start looking at me like I'm making this shit up.

NG: Francis, please calm down. I'm not jumping to any conclusions.

FP: Yeah. Godfrey's your fucking name. I bet it'd be real nice for you to come to the fucking *conclusion* this was all just some old nigger junkie bullshit.

NG: Francis, please, I'm here to help you. I'm a doctor, I just want to help . . . someone.

FP: . . .

NG: . . .

FP: Then make it stop.

(*Nurse Kotar enters.*)

NK: Doctor, I'm sorry to interrupt, but you have an urgent phone call.

Wouldn't You Love to Think So

Olivia was sitting under a tree, wearing her sunglasses, with her legs crossed at the ankles, plucking petals from a dandelion. Shelley diligently standing over her—shade. Olivia looked up and tugged at Shelley's hand.

"Look at the sour apple pretending he's not happy to see us," she said.

"What happened?" said Dr. Godfrey.

"Took a bit of a spill. I'm feeling rather light-headed."

"Why didn't you call an ambulance?"

She waved her hand at the idea of such a fuss. "And who would get Shelley home?" she said.

"Why didn't you call your son?"

"I tried. No luck."

"I think you should go to the hospital."

She wrinkled her nose as though he had proposed she wear rhinestones before sunset—the idea of attending to something so precious as your *health* in the horror show of a hospital. "I'll be as healthy as a horse after a nap," she said.

Godfrey rubbed his chin, appraising. She plucked the last petal and discarded the stem, regarding him over the top of her Jackie Os.

He turned to Shelley. "Care to give me a hand with the patient, nurse?"

Shelley grinned.

Godfrey drove them home in Olivia's truck. Olivia inquired into Letha's health.

"What if we don't talk about our kids," said Godfrey.

"Well, that sounds goddamn *divine*," she said.

She slid off her shoes and put her feet on the dash.

"Objections if I smoke?" she said.

"Yes."

She depressed the dashboard lighter.

At Godfrey House, once Olivia had been safely installed in bed, Shelley hovered in the doorway but was dismissed for Mummy to restore her energy.

Shelley looked reluctantly from Olivia to Dr. Godfrey, longing for some way for this adventure to continue.

"Mummy's very tired, darling."

Shelley turned dejectedly and went upstairs.

Godfrey stood at the foot of the bed, arms akimbo.

"Sleep," he said. "Eat something. If this happens again, I strongly urge you to consult a physician."

"Come here," said Olivia.

"There's no reason for me to go over there."

"Norman, please, you can give me a kiss good-bye like a grown person."

Godfrey hooked his thumbs in his belt loops and gave her his long-perfected shenanigans look.

"Olivia—was this staged?"

She laughed. "Wouldn't you *love* to think so? No, actually, I would leverage neither my goddamn health nor my daughter's safekeeping as a snare for *your* attention. I simply needed a hand and it was lovely of you to extend one."

"Have you been taking the pills?"

"You've made your position on that subject clear enough."

"That's not the same thing as yes."

"Yes," she said. "Believe it or not, I don't hold your medical opinion lightly. Even if you've got the bedside manner of a

mongoloid. Now stop being boorish and give me a kiss good-
bye."

Godfrey looked at his watch without consulting the time.
Then he went to the bedroom door and closed it.

○

"Your office, this bed. We are making the rounds, aren't we. Shall
we sneak off to the mill some night?"

Godfrey shifted away from her and sat on the edge of the bed
and looked at his rumpled pants on the floor like shed snake-
skin.

"This isn't then," he said.

"God knows. Then that goddamn moose head JR was so
pleased with himself over would still be over the mantel."

He said nothing. She hooked like a question mark toward
him and laid her head in his lap. She could smell herself on him.
She smiled but he looked ahead.

"Norman, look at me."

He looked ahead.

"Norman, look at me."

He looked down and met her eyes.

"The institute is one of the most advanced medical centers
in the world," she said. "The only thing that matters is the safety
of the baby."

Out the window, a doe had appeared from the tree line, stopping at a salt lick on a stump. It was as boringly mystical as all
deer. He was not sure if he had been watching it for a few moments or a day.

She drew his hand backwards and guided it between her legs.

"You still make me as wet, you always have," she said.

He stood, feeling a swell of pity. He didn't know if it was for
her for that to prove anything, or for himself because it did.

○

Roman walked back up Indian Creek toward his car. He threw Lisa Willoughby's bunny tail panties into the water and wiped his hands on his pants. There was a discarded beer can in his path and he kicked it, banking off a rock and into the mouth of a drainage pipe.

"Goal!" he said.

He removed his phone from his pocket and turned it back on. There were eleven missed calls.

"Shit," he said and jogged for his car.

When he arrived home, Dr. Godfrey was sitting at the dining room table with a glass in his hand.

"Your mom's upstairs sleeping," he said. "She's fine." Then, in response to a question that wasn't asked, "I'm just waiting for a cab."

"I can take you home," said Roman.

Godfrey waved away the suggestion. "Thanks, he's on his way."

"It's no problem. I'm right here."

"I'll be fine."

Roman shrugged and continued to pass through, the foregoing exchange the most words that had passed between them in months. Godfrey sipped and held the drink on his tongue and swallowed.

"After this drink," he said.

As the Jaguar crept out of the drive, neither noticed the crackling umbrage of the silhouette observing from the attic window.

"How is she doing?" said Godfrey on the road. "Your mother. Overall."

"Psychotic," said Roman. "So, more or less status quo."

Godfrey chuckled and looked out the window. They were passing a strip mall in front of which was a bus stop where a young, overweight black boy in a Ninja Turtles T-shirt riding up the folds of his belly sat with a push-up ice cream that he was not eating, just staring blankly as he pushed the ice cream from the tube and pulled it back in and pushed it back out as though it had been a task assigned him in the underworld.

Roman looked at him. "How are you?" he said.

Godfrey was surprised by the question. But why should he be? The boy shared his blood and his name; why should it be surprising that the offspring of two of the closest people in their own ways in Godfrey's life was also a human? He was not sure how to respond and realized he cherished the confusion: in this moment he was neither father nor doctor nor in any meaningful way uncle and in fact had no clearly defined role or expectation whatever.

"Do you know who knocked up my daughter?" he said.

"No," said Roman. "If I did, he'd be at the bottom of the river right now."

It astounded Godfrey that he had missed what a charming young man his nephew had become.

Roman, wanting as only the mother-raised can to get the most of the older man's approval, tried to think of something useful to add.

"If I knew more than you did, I'd tell you," Roman said. "If that's what you're asking. But all I can say is that she seems . . . happy. I don't know if that's a red flag or not."

They passed an open manhole cover with a rope feeding into it that a line of men in hard hats were hauling up from the inner dark.

"Neither do I," said Godfrey.

○

Letha informed Peter he was just in time to escort her to get frozen yogurt, so they went to the Twist and she brought him up-to-date on the other half of the reconnaissance she had done with her father.

"So Aunt Olivia isn't one of his favorite subjects, but I did learn a little. Still not sure where she's from; I guess JR just fell for her when he saw her onstage. Which, I mean, of course he did. (Man, I don't know how many goats you have to slaughter for your butt to look like that at her age . . .) But when she was Dad's patient I got the sense she had some pretty serious problems, before Roman was born. But it was JR who totally lost his grip in the end. Apparently he made some pretty wild accusations about her."

Peter picked up a straw and flattened it.

"Like what?" he said casually.

"He wouldn't tell me anything specific, but it must have been some serious crazy person stuff; Dad was still pretty obviously upset by it. And it turns out there was a suicide letter that came in the mail . . . the day after. He never showed it to anyone. I was going to ask him what it said, but I could see in his face it was time to change the subject."

He folded one end of the straw and fitted it into the other, forming a quadrangle.

"What exactly is it you're looking for?" she said.

He smoothed out the edges and made of the straw a window through which he looked out at her.

"What are you going to do if you find it?" she said.

He took a bite of pie and chewed thoughtfully, trying to give the appearance that he had an answer of too great consequence and sensitivity to share rather than the truth that he had none.

Suddenly she leaned forward. "Do you know them?"

He followed her sight line. The twin tarantulas in little-girl suits that hung around Christina were at another table across the food court with several other freshmen, staring.

"Oh, they just think I'm a werewolf," said Peter.

Letha glared at their table. "Who wants to be seconds!" she said.

The twins turned away and there was hushed twittering.

"People suck," said Letha.

"People are just people," said Peter, enjoying the feeling of being simultaneously wronged and magnanimous.

"Little whores," said Letha.

Peter smiled; he got a special charge out of flares of female rivalry.

Letha wanted to wipe that jerk smile off his face with a sandblaster; she wanted to paper her walls with it so she could feel it with her eyes closed.

The Most Fun a Girl Can Have Without Taking Her Clothes Off

It was uncanny. Not only was the spot they had dyed yesterday as white as it had been previously but also the number of infected strands had doubled.

Alexa frowned. "That's really annoying," she said.

"I mean, it's not your fault," said Alyssa, eyeing Christina accusingly.

They were helping Christina prepare for her date, because it had been decided between them—Christina had not been consulted—that there was nothing to help her get over the trauma of discovering half a dead girl than the trauma of a first date with a whole live boy.

"We'll just have to make do," said Alexa wearily. "Have you thought about an outfit?"

Christina showed them what she had planned to wear and received a simultaneous and emphatic no.

"The jeans aren't too . . . frightening," said Alexa consolingly.

"But the shirt is way more sort of church picnic than wild sex goddess," said Alyssa.

"I don't know if wild sex goddess is my sort of look," said Christina.

But they ignored her; she had only really asked in the first place for sociological purposes—they had brought what she was to wear.

"I like these jeans," said Christina.

"Totally. For something to look cute painting in," said Alyssa.

Alexa laid the shirt they had furnished on the bed. The shirt was the color of pink frosting and had a pattern on it to imitate sprinkles.

"I . . . I can't wear that," said Christina.

"Christina, don't be difficult," said Alexa.

"I can't wear that," said Christina.

"Christina, we're only . . . *bitch!*"

Alyssa had sharply pinched the skin above Alexa's elbow between her fingernails and indicated Christina with her eyes. The pallor in her face.

"Okay," said Alexa. "It's okay, sweetie."

They selected a cream sweater that after some discussion they decided was acceptable as long as she was sort of bitchy the first half hour, and proceeded with their combined efforts to squeeze Christina into the jeans they had furnished. Then they turned to the situation of the hair. The process was foreign and mysterious to Christina. She had not been conferred with a practical sense of how one went about this strange and all inverted business of being a girl, where seemingly natural stuff like going on about all the great things you just learned about Siberian tigers on National Geographic was suddenly weird, but totally weird stuff in and of itself like drawing around your eyeball with a pencil became normal, and it impressed to no end that it was a product of meticulous effort that made the twins seem so perfectly and effortlessly feminine. But it worked—they were always so, so pretty.

At seven Tyler came and took her to the roller rink. Initially Alyssa vetoed this plan as silly and juvenile, but Alexa thought about it and pointed out that it opened the door for hand-holding that didn't necessarily reveal intent and planted suggestive make-out music while on the surface deceptively silly and juvenile. Christina did not interject that she liked roller-skating.

On skates Tyler was endearingly klutzy, which calmed Christina's racing heart. He said he hadn't put these things on in years, and when they stepped on the rink he humped back and forth to maintain his balance, throwing his arms up in mock triumph when he fell.

"Here," said Christina, holding out her hand.

"You sure?" said Tyler. "If I go down, you go down."

She noted his palm was as clammy as hers. Well!

Tyler and Christina had first had a moment during drama class when they wound up partners for the mirror game. Tyler was a gangling boy, all knees and elbows, making him the star physical comedian of the HGHS stage. When Christina missed a couple of days of school he dropped off the DVDs of the first season of *Glee*. There was nothing imposing about him other than the fact of his sex; when they had changed into skates she noticed his pinkie toe poking through a hole in his sock, the adorable way he'd tried to hide it.

They were passed by a very skinny very pregnant lady in denim short shorts and a lime green tube top who was skating like greased lightning.

"I'm glad you're feeling like better and everything," said Tyler.

"Oh, I'm fine," said Christina, affecting breezy nonchalance.

"You look fine," said Tyler, and Christina blushed.

The pregnant lady did a pirouette and Christina saw that she had a long and ratty goatee, and Christina realized it wasn't a lady at all but a man dressed like a girl carrying his beer weight in his gut.

"Hello, nurse!" said Tyler, and Christina giggled, per the twins' instruction to laugh at *everything* he said. She had her own doubts about that one—it seemed like it would make a person feel like some kind of circus clown—but the twins seemed, as usual, correct: she noticed that the more she tittered, the more generally pleased he seemed.

After a couple of minutes the rink darkened and a disco ball spun slowly. It was the couples skate. A Madonna song played. Other skaters joined hands.

"Now I'm not the only one who looks special ed," said Tyler.

When you call my name it's like a little prayer

His grip tightened. A simple adjustment, or was that a squeeze?

I'm down on my knees, I wanna take you there

The movement of his feet became less jerky and halting, falling into rhythm with hers. They made a full, smooth pass.

"You're *getting* it," said Christina, imitating the kind of coo she would envision the twins approving of.

"Whoops," said Tyler. His left foot slipped out and he fell, legs splayed, Christina coming down right on top of him. It was the first time she had felt the body of a boy beneath her, the solid and the warmth of it. She would have to remember to make a note of the sensation later, how these poor innocents have no idea that they are prey to the budding writer's catalog of impressions! Then she realized she probably should get off him; he appeared to be in serious pain. But he laughed through his grimace and some wise guy yelled to get a room and Tyler said, "Warned you."

When they were done skating, he asked what she wanted to do and she shrugged. Her curfew wasn't for another hour.

"We could just, like, figure it out in the car," said Tyler, reaching for his shoe.

Oh, will we now, Christina thought, and she reached and pinched the protruding toe and wiggled it.

"This little piggy went to market," she said.

They drove to the 443 Sunoco, which was on a bluff overlooking the river.

"Do you want anything?" said Tyler, which impressed her as chivalrous.

She said, A cherry Coke if you please, and he went inside. But he did not lock the door behind him and she worried for a half second it would be rude if she did, but the car was parked in the penumbra of the nearest streetlamp and one glance at the darkness beyond the hood and she reached over and slapped the button. Just a precaution; there was nothing to be afraid of here.

"Remembering that you don't have to be afraid is a Positive Coping Strategy," she said.

Her hands were restless waiting, so she flipped down the visor and regarded herself in the mirror. The physical activity had disheveled her hair somewhat, but rather than fix it she decided she kind of liked it—the effect combined with the white striation was in its own way kind of hot. Fierce, even—like you didn't know what you bargained for letting *this* out of its cage! Or was it? Really, it was just as possible she looked retarded. Suddenly, as happened with some regularity, she hated the twins. What were they thinking, letting her in this situation by herself? How she wished they were here right now.

Someone worked the door handle and she gasped in surprise, but of course it was Tyler who entered and handed her a cherry Coke.

"Scared you," he said.

They sat looking out over the guardrail. The dark treetops on the ridges of the hills over the opposite bank like the bristling of massive beasts and the shimmering river a long lady in a black and sequined dress.

"It's really pretty here," said Christina, grasping the bottle with both hands between her thighs to hide her nervous fidgeting.

"I used to know the graveyard dude," said Tyler, nodding to the store. "He hooked me up. Now it's some fat dyke. She probably just got dumped by her Facebook girlfriend or something."

Christina nodded. Her job now to wait and embarrass herself as minimally as possible. But wait for what? Her stomach was all tied up. She knew the sort of things boys were supposed to expect going into these things, but being in the thing itself she had no idea what he expected. She had told herself, before, she was more ready than anyone would have expected of her, but now that there was this big, warm thing taking up all that space so close to her, she was so scared. Could it possibly be as enjoyable as this tension was unbearable?

They both sat staring out the windshield. About a half mile down the river stood the remains of Castle Godfrey, its chutes and furnaces in the dark giving it the appearance of some nightmare burlesque of an amusement park.

"I was inside there once," Christina said, pointing to the mill. Making conversation because just sitting there not saying anything felt like that millisecond right after hearing tires screech and not knowing whether the crash would follow, that millisecond stretching on and on.

"Yeah?" he said.

"My friends and I were walking on the tracks this one day and we were just messing around."

"What's it like?" he said.

She rubbed the sweat of the bottle with her thumb. "It's . . . so big. And so empty. Except for this giant whatchamacallit— this cauldron thing they used to make steel in, like a giant black egg with a hole at the top, that's still there, on its side. It's supposed to be cursed or whatever. So I went to check it out, you know, peek inside. Put my head in."

"Put your head in!" he said.

"Oh, you know," she said airily. "Just gathering material."

"You're a really good writer!" said Tyler, impressed.

She neglected to mention that she couldn't sleep with the bedside light off for weeks afterward, that she had never hated or misunderstood the cruelty of the twins more for daring her to do it, for knowing she would because they wanted her to.

Tyler nodded. He was reminded of his brief experience dating Letha and how he could never know conclusively that the bouquet of severed doll heads attached to plastic flower stems the opening night of the previous spring's production had been related or not.

"Those Godfreys," he said. "You're lucky the elephant girl didn't jump out and eat you."

"Shelley's okay," said Christina, chastising. She was surprised and pleased at her own conviction coming to the other girl's defense.

"I didn't mean anything," said Tyler.

"It's okay," said Christina. "I just don't know if we . . . get her."

They were quiet. Then without warning he reached and touched her white bang. She flinched. He withdrew his hand.

"I'm sorry," he said. "I . . . thought it was cool."

"It's okay," she said. "It's okay, sorry. You . . . I think you should."

She touched her hair nervously. He touched his own in the same place. She realized he was playing the mirror game. She giggled, and so did he in imitation. Feeling much more lighthearted, she did a jazz handsy sort of thing and so did he. He puckered his lips. Oh did he! She puckered her own. He leaned in and so did she. She tasted sweet boy breath and felt inexpert boy lips. The soft insistence of his lips. Wet, moving lips.

He made a noise between an exhalation and a moan and he did not notice as all the fingers on both her hands extended fully and she placed her rigid hands to either side of his face and shoved him off, then fumbled for the door and fell to the pavement, screaming and screaming and screaming.

The Crucible

"I can feel it when you're doing that," said Marie. "I can feel it when you're just lying there, worrying. It keeps me awake. Will you please go downstairs?"

Godfrey rose, leaden, and obeyed. In the kitchen he poured a scotch and poured an equivalent amount of water back into the bottle. He suspected she was monitoring. He looked at his reflection in the window, catching himself in the act, and made a ray gun out of his hand.

"Zap," he said.

Disintegration: literally, the loss of integrity. But if the mind can be described as one's subjective experience of the brain, then what is the self but vagrant fluorescings of neural constellations, individual states of consciousness determined by mercurial configurations of amplitude and alliance? And yet: he was not convinced, never able to shake the conviction there was so much more to lose . . .

He drank. Was his wife really snooping? Marie ran the Godfrey Foundation, the family's charitable arm, and it had to be admired how good she had gotten at not bringing her work home. Although, to be fair, if she *was* snooping it was not entirely unjustified given how much he was drinking, albeit as an unusually educated self-prescription: in his medical opinion, if one must choose between the physiological deterioration caused by oppressive, neuron-murdering stress versus intoxication, who does one think one is possibly kidding?

His eyes fell to his phone but he looked away. No. Not that.

Bludgeoning himself with liquor was one thing, but fucking Olivia twice in one day for the first time in thirteen years in a feckless rage of potency would be a violence to his own soul. It was dangerous even to be thinking about her again. Fucking in the old places, thinking about her like he used to. Missing her exactly like he used to.

He poured more liquor into his glass and more water into the liquor. The front door opened, startling him so he nearly dropped the bottle. But this was absurd. As though thinking about Olivia was an act in which he might be caught. This was totally absurd.

"Letha?" he said.

She appeared in the kitchen, to his delight. But now shouldn't he have some reason for summoning her beyond simple conjuration? Name, face. Or, as progenitor, did he? On balance he could be asking for a lot more in return for the fact of her existence. Like oh for instance getting an abortion. Kill it, kill it while there's still time. But Godfrey was contorting himself through the motions of trying to see the potential for good to come from her decision; stranger things, in his professional experience, had happened. But down back the hill it rolled; he hated it, he hated the thing inside her and it pumped his stomach with battery acid every time he thought about it, which is to say, all the time. All the time it felt like this. He had the familiar impulse to pour a fresh drink with a full one in his hand.

"I'm told you had a gentleman caller this afternoon," he said. (In fact he'd been told she'd gone *gallivanting* off with some ponytailed *hoodlum*.)

"Oh," she said, "Peter."

"Peter who?" he said.

"Rumancek. He's a new kid."

"The werewolf," he said.

"He's otherwise very nice," said Letha. "I'm told you were Aunt Olivia's white knight today," she said, changing the subject.

He nearly spilled his drink. But she didn't know. Somehow, still, no one knew. A feat of willful ignorance, as impressive as the pyramids.

Except Roman. Almost certainly an unspoken knowing earlier today in the boy's eyes. Godfrey House was made of secrets, and he knew as well as anyone what the slightest creativity and stealth could uncover. But there was no way to ascertain without asking, an investigation he had no interest in pursuing. And assuming the boy did know, he was discreet about it. Criminal, his lack of generosity to his brother's son. But didn't it worry the bones to hear Letha speak Olivia's name. When Marie did, it was invested with reassuring malignity; the way Letha spoke, it could have been anyone's kindly old aunt.

"She fainted," he said.

"Who faints?" said Letha.

She kissed him good night and he found himself left to the sudden onset of a complete and primordial sense of aloneness for which the only thing was the trivial distraction of modern technology. He went to the computer and surfed to distraction. Holes in the Steelers offense, reviews of books the likelihood of his ever getting around to reading decreasing each year, a vulgarity he'd meant to look up on Urban Dictionary. Then, for curiosity's sake, he performed a search on Lod. Not that he expected it to generate any hit, but just supposing it did. And as it happened there were quite a few entries, although none of them from the corporate sphere. Lod, a city on the Sharon Plain of Israel: birthplace of the most venerated saint in Orthodox Christianity, Saint George. He looked at this useless incongruity on the screen and drank, the warm numbing finally offering the promise of sleep.

But there was something else he'd been meaning to look up, something to do with a case. But which? Which else? He searched for "H Varga" to see if perchance it would yield some sort of contact information. It did not, but there was a small news item from a few weeks ago. So there would be no confirming Pull-man's story with Hollis Varga: his body had been dredged near Penrose with iron weights in his pockets and a one-line note in a ziplock bag:

Today I have seen the Dragon

Godfrey shut down the computer and swiveled the chair and regarded Letha's framed childhood silhouette on an end table across the room. *So where are we?* He knew enough about their shared blood that she was going to be having the child, and enough about Johann's slime trail that it would be impossible to follow without slipping. But the one, it had to be admitted, had nothing to do with the other, and in a time when the imperative of fathers was thrown into tragic and urgent relief his own cold crusade did not have the luxury of priority. Letha was having the child. The institute was one of the most advanced medical centers in the world. And the only thing that mattered was the safety of his baby girl.

○

Roman pulled into the empty gravel lot abutting the rail yard and Peter told him to kill the headlights. Roman said there was no point because no one gave two shits what happened out here, but Peter said to humor him. Roman killed the lights and pulled forward and parked by the electrical substation. Peter exited but Roman did not.

"What?" said Peter.

Roman regarded the clock in a cold sweat: 1:11. There was no way to convey how fatal an augur it would be to embark on this task when the time was a succession of primes that added to the worst of primes, so he didn't bother. He waited until it turned 1:12—a cumulative 4.

He exhaled in relief and got out. They both carried flashlights, and Roman a bolt cutter. They passed the Dragon. Roman waved his arms irreverently and said, "Ooga booga!"

"Please don't," said Peter.

"Why?" said Roman.

"Humor me," said Peter.

They walked to the main entrance of Castle Godfrey. Roman hefted the chain, noting that there was no rust on it; it had been recently replaced. He notched a link and sheared it and pushed the doors open. The whine of the hinges echoed within the mill building. They stepped inside. It was cold and smelled like metal and mud. The floor was covered with slag and graphite and broken glass and their feet crunched on it.

"You know how when you close your ears sometimes the sound of your heart is like a little man walking through snow?" said Roman.

"Yeah, that's weird," said Peter.

They turned on flashlights. There was a crane system overhead and at one end an immense, shadowy mass like a dead whale, or sleeping. On the wall was a Steelers logo next to the words SAFETY'S NO. 1! in gold.

"Any idea what we may be looking for?" said Roman.

"Driver's license," said Peter. "Social Security card. Dream journal."

"Kiss my big black ass," said Roman.

They split off, taking different halves of the mill. Peter turned his flashlight to the mass, revealing it to be a Bessemer converter. It was larger than his trailer and lay on its side, a fissure in the cement snaking away from the mouth from a past seismic impact. Peter crouched behind a row of pallets and pointed his light. Empty. Roman climbed the stairs to the crane pulpit but found nothing, and combed the locker room to the same end. Peter went into the office. He pointed his beam into a corner and a sleeping bag came into view. He went to it and knelt and ran his finger along a caking of dust on the nylon. He noticed a spoon, the convexity blackened, and nearby on the floor a patch cleared of the old blueprints and beaver mags. His beam lighted a large burnt-looking stain on the floor that was shaped symmetrically into a pair of wings. Blood, a snow angel of blood. Peter turned to call for Roman, then didn't. It was clear this had been here since long before the *vargulf*, and not knowing what to make of it himself, he decided Roman's energies were better kept undistracted.

His beam lighted a pair of boots, at least as old as the sleeping bag, and by them another pair of wings. A quick sweep revealed perhaps a half dozen more on the walls and ceiling and Peter's bones went cold. It was time to go, he suddenly knew. To get out, and especially get Roman out. The energy here had no good in it, there was no good in exposing Roman to it, he felt in his balls. But in turning toward the office door his light illumined the hollow of one of the boots and with it came a flash of inspiration that he did not like, he didn't like anything about it. Not least of all that it meant not leaving yet.

Reluctant every step, Peter walked out of the office and across the floor and stood before the Bessemer converter. He gagged at the stench issuing like pestilential breath and he muffled his nose and shone his flashlight into the mouth. He held it there and unsettled dust danced in its shining and he said nothing.

"What?" said Roman. He came beside Peter. The stench hit him and he averted his face as though struck, but not before getting a look at what was inside.

"Oh, man," said Roman quietly.

The lining of the interior was encrusted with sticky brown black and at the base was what appeared at first to be a comically large meat-stripped wishbone. The wishbone wore candy-striped go-go boots. The outstanding half of Lisa Willoughby.

"Should we . . . tell someone?" said Roman.

"Tell them what." said Peter. He lowered his flashlight.

Roman was quiet and his eyes lingered on the blackness of the Bessemer. The panties he stole had smelled fresh and sweet, like fabric softener.

"I'd like to go," said Roman.

They walked out in silence and when they emerged into the air Roman fished for a smoke. Then the shadows of the black willows rose and fell like the spokes of a turning wheel as a light streamed through and Peter and Roman looked at each other, realizing at the same time. Another car.

"Inside," said Peter, already slipping back within the shadows of the mill.

"He'll see the car," said Roman, squinting to get a better look at who was approaching.

"That doesn't mean blow him a fucking kiss," hissed Peter's disembodied voice.

Roman withdrew and they both watched the car pull into the lot and come abreast of Roman's. A sheriff's department cruiser. Two figures emerged: Neck and Nose. They inspected the Jaguar.

"Young Master Godfrey's, if memory serves," said Neck.

Nose pointed a flashlight to the mill and Peter and Roman hugged the wall.

"You may as well get your tight ass out here, because I'm going to be real pissed if I have to go in there," he said.

Peter looked at Roman. "Get rid of them."

"With pleasure," said Roman, and there was something in the way he said it that filled Peter with misgiving, but there was nothing to be done as Roman stepped out.

"Well, olly olly oxen free," said Neck.

"You know Chuck E. Cheese is that way, kid," said Nose.

"Can I help you gentlemen with anything?" said Roman with a gentility that did not help Peter's unease.

"Maybe you can start with what the hell you think you're doing out here," said Neck.

"Well gee, I was sitting quietly by myself playing solitaire," said Roman. "I hope I wasn't disturbing anyone."

Peter's balls aged in dog years.

Nose closed in aggressively on Roman. "You think we won't run you in, you goddamn little punk?" he said.

Roman turned back in what Peter at first feared was for the purpose of some kind of stage wink or equally bonehead gesture but instead he swept his arm at the side of the building—to what end Peter did not know but he could not imagine what was preventing him from employing the one thing he was reliably good for.

"The eyes," Peter whispered desperately. "Do the crazy roofie eyes."

In fact, what Roman was indicating was the faded six-foot white lettering on the side of the building: GODFREY STEEL COMPANY. And he had seen his name put to too much ill use this day to resort to parlor tricks; real things were at stake here and had to be put to right.

"Okay, I'll level with you," said Roman.

"We're all ears," said Neck.

"I was actually jacking off to French postcards of your mother and would prefer a little privacy, if you wouldn't mind directly fucking off and staying away from my property or I'm reporting both you illiterate assholes for harassment," said Roman.

Neck and Nose exchanged looks.

"Best news I got all week," said Nose.

He seized Roman by the arm, roughly wrenched it behind him, causing him to emit a sharp cry of pain, and slammed him face-forward into the side of the building.

"At the request of Olivia Godfrey, I'm placing you under arrest," he said.

Once the taillights of the cruiser had vanished and Peter was in darkness he began to breathe normally again. He took a final look at the converter and walked out of the mill. The keys were still in the Jaguar. Wheeling it around, the headlights hit a white patch that caught Peter's eye. A scrap of paper. He left the car idling and got out and knelt to the ground. It was a page ripped from a book, weighted by scattered pebbles. He brushed it clean and held it to the light of the moon.

She clipped a precious golden lock
She dropped a tear more rare than pearl

Those Who Are Able We Invite You to Rise

On the way home Roman sat in the passenger side of the pickup with his head leaning against the window. He tapped his knuckles against the door paneling in time with the passing of lampposts and telephone poles. Olivia's eyes were fixed ahead and there was a standoff as each waited on the other. Roman reached to turn on the radio. Olivia hit the brakes, coming to a sudden stop in the middle of the road.

"Jesus," said Roman.

She took his chin in her hand and roughly turned his face to hers.

"Jesus," said Roman again.

"I will cut you off without a cent," she said. "You think I won't?"

He looked at her without saying anything.

"You think I won't?"

Her fingers made white bruises in his jaw. The breath from his nose rolled over her knuckles. He cast his eyes down.

"I'm sorry, Mom," he said. "I'm really sorry."

She released him and rested her hand on the gearshift. Her hand was shaking.

"I just—" she said, "all I want is—"

She didn't finish the sentence as her eyes drifted to a malfunctioning lamppost, the light waning to a glow of filament and then sputtering out and then flaring once more, and the shaking of her hand passed through her body in a shudder. Her eyelids fluttered.

"Mom, are you okay?" said Roman.

She inhaled sharply and her eyes refocused.

"Mom . . . I see them too," said Roman.

Olivia started the engine again and put her hand on Roman's knee.

"All I want in this world is what's best for my baby."

O

From the archives of Norman Godfrey:

From: morningstar314@yahoo.com
To: ngodfrey@hacres.net
Subject: none

To begin, a blunt admission, because there is hardly any point proceeding without it. Upon reflection, that you and Mother should have a—what dismay in giving irrevocable shape to the words—sexual affair is, on its face, unsurprising. Terribly banal, even. Is there a commoner platitude: these things happen. As though commonness in any way trivializes it. Birth is common, the hour before sunrise.

Betrayal. What could be commoner?

But an accounting of your heart is neither my place nor purpose, I simply feel I must be honest with you because if I was not it would mean irreparably to lose you. So please forgive my honesty in order that I may forgive you. I cannot lose you, Uncle.

Especially now, my purpose in writing not my own unhappy discovery but another of larger consequence.

To begin, Roman was arrested last night. He was caught on the mill property (in the company, one might surmise, of Peter Rumancek, but as to the purpose of their errand your guess is as good as mine), where he earned, in Roman's inimitable fashion, the disfavor of a pair of policemen who brought him in for "malicious mischief." Suffice to say the incident did not lighten Mother's disposition. For my part, I was actually greatly relieved: I had cloistered myself in my room all evening and thought some ongoing row might further divert attention from me. But today relations reached a striking armistice. Roman's manner was polite, even solicitous, in an unspoken (not to mention out-of-character) gesture of contrition, and Mother's rancor (also uncharacteristically) showed no residual traces. By lunch they were conversing idly about Monaco or Provence for Christmas, the whole time my own head was lowered as I counted the seconds before I could excuse myself without attracting notice.

But just when it became possible to inconspicuously leave the table, I felt it, the first tickle. A single mote of dust: fate's siege engine. And then I sneezed—hopelessly disrupting my most deliberately fashioned hair.

Roman gave his blessing, before seeing. And then he stared, alongside Mother.

And here we must back up to yesterday afternoon when, once alone, I made an illicit expedition to the mall, where my wonderfully wicked Jenny was only too delighted a coconspirator in a petulant revenge against Mother for, well, being Mother. And yes, if I was so anxious after consideration of the consequences I could have more easily removed and discarded all evidence of its doing, but one needs no advanced expertise in unraveling psychic mysteries to see that the dread of discovery did not overwhelm the desire—no, necessity—for it.

And this something more than childish spite—when Jenny first brandished the mirror and I experienced the simple feminine thrill of wearing something made to make a woman feel like a woman . . .

I am ugly, Uncle. There is no other way to put it. But that does not mean I am without pride, without joy, without the same entitlement to feel deserving of love from those not obligated by blood to give it. I may *be* ugly, but I can hardly imagine a reason to act like it.

Mother, of course, has always had a different opinion, insisting I keep my dress and hair as plain as possible (this in a family where more is spent per annum between her and my brother on plumage than a low-income family's total expenditure). But not as some arbitrary tyranny, no: out of concern that any attention I call to myself—even the audacity of wearing the costume of a normal person—would only expose me to unneeded ridicule and heartache. It is only my happiness she has in mind in extinguishing the notion of dressing the part of anything but a pitiful grotesque. Without question the kinder of cruelties.

So you might picture her face. Not half a day after retrieving her son from the sheriff's office, this new sedition. The shock and blow to her sovereignty.

"What," she said, once words returned, "have you done to yourself?"

Lacking a credible response, I vainly and foolishly bowed my head and covered my ears with my hands. She strode over and pried them off, taking one lobe between her fingers with furious delicacy.

"You perfectly idiotic creature," she said. "You great, lumbering *dolt*." She turned to Roman and demanded if he had had any hand in this.

He appeared conflicted, as though tempted to share and thereby ameliorate guilt but ultimately knowing his own standing too unsteady. He denied it, and of course I was partially disappointed he did not come to my rescue, but glad also: I had made a decision and it was my own.

"I—" said Mother, her attention back on me, "I am simply perplexed. You want to make a mockery of yourself? You would *connive* to demean yourself? At least I thought you had a [EXPLETIVE DELETED] *brain*. At least I thought you had that."

In the past there have naturally been times when I have caused Mother's frustration to flare, but never, quite unlike Roman, with deliberate forethought. And Mother, for whatever shortcomings she may possess, has made an effort of patience and consideration with me that is a great strain on her nerves. It must be said this is not easy on her.

She has never yelled at me.

I sobbed, helpless. She continued.

"Do you know what true *deformity* is, Shelley? The most intolerable and repellent of them all? Stupidity. Do you think for a moment I thought you were too young to understand what your father used to call you?"

The "abortion." She used to tell him not to call me that.

"This travesty ends now," she said. "Remove the [EXPLETIVE DELETED] things."

I fumbled for my ears, but my fingers, not the nimblest in the best of circumstances, had no hope the way they were shaking. She watched, her impatience excoriating as my clumsy efforts became all the more pitiable. Mercifully her vexation overtook her and she seized my wrists to do it herself.

And that's when it happened: the entire edifice of our home dissolved in one word:

"Stop."

Stated, not vehement, but with what I believe could fairly be described as heartbreak, Roman told her to stop.

"Stay out of this," said Mother dismissively.

But Roman repeated himself. Looking at neither her nor me, his face lacking in affect like some ventriloquist's tool.

"Let go of her," he said.

"Excuse me," said Mother, less dismissively, "was that a *command*?"

He folded his hands on the table and now he met her face. "Leave her alone," he said.

Mother laughed like a nail. "Amazing," she said to some imagined and equally unbelieving audience and reached once more with that terrible delicacy for my ear. "Hold *still*."

Roman put his hands flat on the table, pushed himself back, and came around to us. He clamped his fingers around

Mother's forearm. My head was a helium balloon that had slipped its knot and my breath came in shallow gasps.

"Let. Go," said Mother.

"Leave her alone," said Roman.

She struck him with the back of her free hand. He closed his other fist around that arm. She tried to wrench free, but he held. My head fell and I began rhythmically to lift it an inch, two, and let it drop on the table. Dishware rattled.

"So help me," said Mother, "you will end up in the gutter, you [EXPLETIVE DELETED] little rodent."

A spherule of blood beaded at the corner of his mouth from where he had been struck.

"I've seen the will," said Roman.

Mother was quiet. My percussions sent a glass over the end of the table and it shattered.

Roman released her but she did not move. I held my head suspended, confused by the significance of this admission.

"Last year," said Roman, "when you didn't like the settlement Annette got you for the Black Derby incident." (Referring, in case you have forgotten—or, for that matter, were not in her company—to legal complications arising from Mother, dissatisfied with the service at a cocktail bar, entering into a dispute with the bartender requiring stitches for the latter.) "Do you remember what you called her? Not everyone likes being talked to that way. She called me into her office and showed me the will just to spite you, you psychopathic [EXPLETIVE DELETED]. I *know*."

Mother sank into his empty chair and he said the words that unglued what mutual understanding had ever existed among us.

"It's all mine," he said. "I'm sole beneficiary. And on my eighteenth birthday I gain control of the entire trust. Everything is mine. It's my house and my money and it always was."

He picked up a napkin—*his* napkin—and dabbed the blood from his lip. She looked past him. A fragment, a small diamond rainbow, flickered on the table—*his* table—refracted from the chandelier. This is what held her attention.

He backed away from her and lit a cigarette. Cigarette smoking was never tolerated in the dining room. Mother looked at that diamond and Roman smoked his cigarette. I wanted instinctively to reach for her, but in that moment it was understood by each that Roman alone had freedom of movement. He dropped his cigarette on the floor and stubbed it out. He was as afraid as the rest of us of where we went from here.

Outside, a cloud must have passed over the sun and the diamond vanished. Mother's head snapped as though she'd been nodding off. We remained there in a silence that had begun some time before the beginning of the world, and though Mother adjourned wordlessly to her (or, Roman's) room where she remains, and I am in my (Roman's) attic, and Roman off to devices of his own in his fiefdom, in that binding silence we remain, just as I remain

Yours,
        S.G.

Roman stood in the doorway. She sat on the top mattress hunched and facing the window. Her back was as broad as a child with fully outstretched arms, and a glow under her shirt evanesced with her breathing. She did not turn to him. The mattress curled around her in a smile.

"That's not what I wanted," said Roman. "I didn't want to do that."

She didn't respond.

"I would never do anything that would hurt us," he said. "You know that, don't you?"

She turned now and looked at him. It was the first time she had called him a liar.

"I'll go," he said.

She grunted no. He went to the bed. She lay back and he lay behind her, working his arm under her head. She knew his arm would be crushed numb in moments but he could live with it. He saw she had removed the earrings. He shut off the bedside lamp and the star and moon stickers glowed.

Later, when her breathing had become a regular saw, Roman extricated his arm and rose. He went to the door, shaking the needles from his arm. The easel caught his eye. She'd been working on this one awhile, it seemed nearly finished. A single vertical white bar against a dark muddle of night, and directly beneath it some subterranean chamber within which was a ring with a sort of node at the top.

A snake—a snake eating its own tail.

Roman took his hand from the door and went back to the bed and climbed on with his arms outstretched and laying his cheek flat against the echo chamber of her heart.

A Measure of Disorder

The phone rang, ending a brief and halting sleep. Dr. Godfrey picked up.

"Okay," he said finally. "Okay, calm down. I'll be right there."

In the dark he found a pair of jeans and a sweater.

"Was that Olivia?" said Marie.

"No," he said absently. At some distance he was aware how treacherous and truthful it was that in a semilucid state this was the first thing to occur to his wife. But he could worry about that later; it would have to take its place in the queue. He looked out the window. There was a misting of dew that made the night outside look like wine through a glass and he had the strange and pleasing thought: No time like the present for a swim. It occurred to him he may actually have said this out loud, but he wasn't sure and Marie gave no indication. He laced his shoes.

Down the hall, Letha was in the bathroom. She heard her father's descending footsteps and quiet exit, and waited another few moments for any sign her mother was going to stir. Then she crept down to the study and knelt at his file cabinet.

○

The police were already at the Neuropathology Lab, waiting for Godfrey's arrival. Nurse Kotar came to him. Her eyes were red and her hair looked like she had just been given a serious going-over in the bedroom, an appearance so unlikely it could only spell disaster. He put his hands on her elbows and told her to go home and take a few days off.

She nodded docilely, then abruptly clung to him tightly and shook like a child.

"Go home," said Godfrey again, his gentleness of tone hiding his resentment that to some this remained a solace.

Sheriff Sworn waited for her to leave, then approached Godfrey with a smile meant as a frown.

"Some funny math here," he said. "You have a highly disturbed individual and a straightforward—or at least these days close enough—suicide, whole thing caught on camera. But. The security situation here, it's no joke, right?"

It was a rhetorical question, but Godfrey nevertheless confirmed no joke.

"Thing is," said Sworn, "you watch the tape, this wasn't a break-in, but there was no assisted entry either." He paused in considered disapproval of a world that had once held up its end of what he'd considered an understanding. "The door, it just opens up for him. As if . . . well . . . as if to say, Come on in, pilgrim."

Dr. Godfrey looked to the floor of the far end of the Brain Barn. Francis Pullman lay on the floor. There was the plunger of a syringe in his hand. There was the splintered needle of the syringe in his temple. What was that Dorothy Parker line? *I'd rather have a bottle in front of me than a frontal lobotomy.* Godfrey stifled the only sane response to this tableau, the latest somewhat dramatic addition lying at the wall of three thousand orderly Tupperware-housed specimens. The only response a certifiably sane person could have in this asylum. But it would not be appropriate for a man of your position to laugh.

○

At first light the master bedroom door opened and Olivia emerged. She wore a white satin robe and passed down the hall and stopped at the door with the Dragon on it and entered. The room was dark; morning light visible around the edges of the curtains. He was still sleeping. She came forward and stood over him. His bare chest and neck were long and lean and white. She placed the backs of her fingers to his neck and felt the living miracle of the young heart in his chest, the conduit between it and her own. His eyes opened. She caressed his face and his scalp.

"We'll need to bleach you soon," she said. "Your roots are showing."

○

On his way to homeroom Peter stopped at his locker and found sticking through the slats a folded page of notebook paper. He looked at it and he knew in his Swadisthana that it had been delivered by the same hand that had sent Lisa Willoughby the invitation. He took the page and unfolded it. There was no writing on it, only a picture. A crude drawing of the severed head of a brown wolf. The head lay in a pool of dried blood that in color and texture was clearly real blood, and the head itself seemed at first appearance to be brown shoe polish but no. He realized, after a moment, that's not what it was. Peter grimly folded the picture and placed it in his backpack. He looked at a poster on the wall of a hand with an extended index finger with the caption WHEN YOU POINT ONE FINGER, YOU POINT THREE BACK AT YOURSELF.

"Shit," he said.

He turned to head down the hall but saw Roman approaching.

"Shit," he said again.

But this had all the trimmings of one those days. They

stepped out an eastern exit next to the loading zone and over-looking a steep embankment over a housing development. They kept the door open a wedge with a half brick to keep it from locking behind them and Roman lit two cigarettes and handed one to Peter and said he had a lead.

Peter looked out. It was the sort of day that had the birds all in a dither. They gathered by the dozens on high wires like dark clothespins against slate sky only for some mysterious bird-brain impetus to send all of them into drunken wild flight, God shaking pepper into a whirlwind, and then just as suddenly to alight once more on the same wire, but facing now in the op-posite direction. Whatever it is that gets into birds on days like today.

"I think something is going on at the White Tower," said Roman.

Peter smoked and watched the birds.

"I don't know if it's connected or not, but I can get us in," said Roman.

Crosshatching the sky were gauzy tendrils of black. Rain later.

Roman saw it in his face. "What?" said Roman.

"No," said Peter.

"What do you mean, no?" said Roman.

"It's over," said Peter.

"What are you talking about?"

"This is over. We're done."

Roman looked at him and saw he was serious. Suddenly he wanted to rip that faggot fucking ponytail out of his head. He wanted to find whatever words it would take to make him change his mind.

"Why?" said Roman.

Peter did not answer. He hated that he was having this con-versation; this sort of thing was no less suffocating to him than when he was younger and an older cousin would trap him in a blanket and sit on him and it felt like the worst of all possible deaths. Getting mixed up in other people's feelings, only himself to blame. Also he blamed Roman.

"What, you mean the cops?" said Roman. His tone reflected the boringness and triviality of the incident. "You said get rid of them and I did. Oh, and that was very considerate, dropping my car off with an empty tank, incidentally."

He waited to see if interjecting levity made the situation any different but it didn't.

"Okay," said Roman. "Okay, it was stupid. It was really stupid and I'm an asshole and what is there to say other than that I was being an asshole, but come on. Think about what you're doing. You can't walk away over a stupid thing like that. You can't walk away from . . . this."

He pronounced *this* in the phonetically correct fashion, but somehow it still rhymed with *us*.

Peter thought about how he might explain things to Roman in a way that wouldn't upset him further. Explain that they were not alike, that however different from the rest of the world Roman felt, he was still rich and so tolerably different. He did not know what things were like for Peter, he did not fear the cage. The cage was the worst of all possible deaths. But there was no way to make that real for someone like Roman in the same way you could hardly say to a tiger in the jungle, Do you know how free you really are? Because how can he know any other way to be? There was no way to make this a picture in Roman's brain, so he bounced his heel off the railing for a while and wondered if he could get away with not saying any more than he'd already said.

"Will you fucking say something," said Roman.

"You should go," said Peter. "There's no good for you here. You should get away from this death and this town and your name. Make it all clean. And I don't know. Figure it out from there."

Roman regarded his hand. His hand was shaking and wasn't much use for holding a cigarette, so he flicked it. "I bet you'd like that," he said. "I bet you'd find that very convenient, you Gypsy piece of shit. You know if you fuck my cousin, I'll kill you."

Peter looked at him.

"You're not better than me," said Roman, bitter.

Peter kept looking at him.

Roman turned his head. "That's a faggot fucking ponytail," he said.

Peter got up and went inside. Roman looked up at the glowering sky. "Fuck," he said. There was a constriction in his throat.

Then there was a movement in the corner of his vision. Peter coming back out, not leaving it like this. Like before, Peter getting the hard-on thing out of his system but coming back to him. Roman looked pridefully ahead but knew he would let him. That was just his way, Peter was all right for a hard-on. Roman would let him come back again. But the door did not open and Peter did not come, and the movement he had seen was suddenly in the opposite side of his mind's eye, and it was like dark fingers of black shadow performing sleight of hand to get his attention. Roman's eyes fluttered. He bent and picked up the brick and the door closed after it and he hurled it over the hill. There was a metallic crunch and a car alarm went off and Roman sat against the locked door and after a moment held up his still-trembling hand palms outward and scurried his fingers in the air, watching the dance of spidery veins.

○

When school let out Letha appeared by Peter's side as he approached his bus and he did not question as she boarded alongside him. He walked to his customary seat in the back and gestured for her to sit and she did. She reached into her purse and pulled out an old, wrinkled envelope, which she handed to Peter. It was to her father, no return address. He raised his eyebrows and she nodded, pleased with herself.

"Did you read it?" said Peter.

She was offended. "I would never read someone else's mail," she said. "Unless it was about me."

He put the letter in the front pocket of his backpack, joining the fragment of *Goblin Market* and the shitty picture. He did not know if this would all ultimately come together as something meaningful or if it was like the opposite of those paintings made of dots, the illusion of order a consequence of proximity; if you stood at the other end of the universe seeking resolution you would just end up feeling like an idiot for trying.

When they passed Kilderry Park Letha looked out the window and said, "He's dead."

"Who?" said Peter.

"Francis Pullman. The one who saw. He stabbed himself in the brain last night."

"Oh," said Peter.

Letha moved her hand as if to take Peter's but changed the motion into picking at the duct tape patching a rip in the faux leather of their seat. The bus came to a stop at the mouth of Kimmel Lane and she got off with him and started down the hill. Still, neither commented that this was outside the normal run of events.

"Roman seemed weird today," she said.

"He's pissed at me," said Peter.

"Why?"

"Because there's a big Roman-shaped blind spot in the way Roman sees things."

"What happened Saturday night?" said Letha. "Were you there when he was arrested?"

"Your mom using the sheriff's department to give you a time-out isn't the same thing as being arrested," he said.

"What are the things you're leaving out?" she said.

Peter said nothing.

"You don't need to leave stuff out just because I'm a girl," she said.

Peter looked at her to see if she really believed that. He said nothing.

"I should sock you," said Letha.

As they approached the trailer, the rain that had been threatening all day began lightly to fall. They jogged inside. The car was gone and they had the place to themselves. They sat on the couch and listened to the rain.

"Do you believe in angels?" she said.

Peter saw no way out of this conversation and regretted for the second time today that it was only one night of the month that he got to drop his human mouth on the ground.

She clasped her hands on her stomach. "It scares my parents, because they don't believe me. But I guess I wouldn't either in their shoes. I know it sounds a little crazy."

"It actually sounds a lot crazy," said Peter.

"Do you believe me?"

"I don't know."

"Are you just saying you don't know because you think I'm crazy?"

"Well, I think you probably are crazy, but I still don't know."

She looked at him but he looked away. He felt her still looking at him and wished she would stop, but still tried to make his profile handsomely contemplative. The cat leaped onto the coffee table and sat on the jigsaw puzzle Lynda was still working on and began to groom, not actually disrupting any pieces but proving that it could.

Every cat is a woman, thought Peter.

"Well!" said Letha.

"Well what?" said Peter. He knew but had learned that if there was one advantage to the male sex it was that your obtuseness would never be underestimated; if you pretend you don't know what the problem is, half the time it just goes away.

"Are you going to try to fuck me?" she said.

Peter sucked in breath. "Well, here we are," he said.

"What kind of thing is that to say!" she said.

Peter grimaced.

"What is it?" she said.

His grimace tightened and he licked the back of his teeth.

"Roman," he said.

"What does Roman have to do with the price of rice in China!"

"You know," he said.

She was quiet.

"Do you like me?" she said.

Peter shrugged. He didn't *not* like her. Per se.

"Are you sure it's not—" She moved her hands over her bump.

"No," he said. "That's kind of hot."

"Pervert!" she said, beaming.

"Look," he said. "If the dynamite's on the tracks, you think twice about stepping on that train."

"Smooth talker!"

They were both quiet.

"You're really saying no?" she said.

○

Roman stood in his room regarding the coupling link mounted on the wall. While it looked like worthless junk, this was the first item produced by Jacob Godfrey for the Pennsylvania Railroad and its value was beyond measure: an empire had been built on it. Roman picked it up and held it in front of his heart and pulled with both hands as hard as he could, but to no avail even a century after its production: it was Godfrey steel. He put it back on its mount and went to his dresser, where there was a glass of vodka and ice and a small mound of cocaine on a pewter tray. He took out his mint container, where he stored a blade for a box cutter and segments of straw, and divided the cocaine into several lines and snorted them. He took a heavy sip of vodka. He looked at himself in the mirror.

"Godfrey steel," he said.

He held the blade of the box cutter to the corner of his eye and made a quick vertical slash down his cheek. He closed his eyes and felt the pleasing warmth as blood issued onto his face. He opened his eyes and put a finger to the cut and traced it under both eyes and over his lips in a parody of his mother applying makeup. He batted his eyes for the mirror and puckered his lips.

"Shut up and kiss me," he said.

The doorbell rang. Startled, Roman hurried to the bathroom and washed his face and applied a Band-Aid to the cut. He grabbed his drink and went to the foyer. The caller was a petite black woman wearing a dark trench coat and holding a badge.

"Are you Roman Godfrey?" she said.

"Yeah," he said.

"You're bleeding," she said.

"Close shave," he said.

"Let me see," she said.

"It's fine," he said.

"Hold still," she said.

She lifted the bandage, gauging immediately that the cut was superficial and self-inflicted. Further that the boy was high and recently had had his heart broken and that this made him defenseless and dangerous, so conveniently incautious for her purposes. She told him to keep it clean, but he'd live. She introduced herself but it was obviously not news to him.

"You know who I am," she said.

"You're the dogcatcher," he said.

"Might I ask how you know that?"

"Small pond," he said.

"Is your mother home right now?" she said.

"No."

"Do you expect her?"

He shrugged.

"Is your sister in?" she said.

"My sister doesn't go out."

"Do you think I might talk to her?"

"She doesn't talk."

"That's fine, I'd just like to say hello. If that's okay."

"Why do you want to meet Shelley?"

"Maybe I should come back when your mother is around."

This bluff trumped the boy's suspicion: he could not in good conscience make a choice that responsible.

Roman led her upstairs and she stopped short in the second-floor hallway.

"Is this your door?" she said.

"Yeah."

"What's this?" She pointed to the cross and serpent.

"It's from a video game. Why do you ask?"

"Just thought it looked familiar."

They continued to the attic. The door was closed and string music played softly from within. He knocked and said, "Shelley, we have a visitor who'd like to meet you."

Chasseur noted the softening of his manner. He held some things sacred. There was a pause and then a loud scraping noise followed by several slow creaking steps. The knob turned and the door nosed open and Roman pushed it and entered. Chasseur followed. The music was coming from a computer; on the monitor was the dense text of an academic article on biomimetics. Roman stood off to the side, his sibling awkwardly before her.

Dr. Chasseur was legendary for keeping certain physiological responses in check—her fame within her unit in the Corps dramatically increased one poker night when she won the pot with a royal straight flush with no hint of a tell, and a first husband who would never hear a woman say "I love you" again without flinching. But it took the full exercise of her talents not to gasp out loud seeing the elephant in the room, hands like gloves with hands inside them nervously fussing the folds of her dress, that brute face and eyes so bright and clear and sad.

"This is Dr. Chasseur," said Roman. "She's here to take a bite out of the *vargulf*."

She turned from the girl to the boy. "Excuse me?"

And she saw now his positioning was not accidental: he had strategically placed himself to cover an easel, but the outline was unmistakable. Ouroboros.

She looked back to Shelley with a smile and said, "I don't mean to be rude, dear, but I think I need to have a word with your brother."

A sound like a thousand lightly tapping fingers filled the attic: the rain had begun.

Roman and Chasseur went down to the living room and sat and she made her eyes into scalpels and cut him into very small pieces.

"Yes?" he said with badly feigned innocence.

She continued to look at him and he drank, uncomfortable.

"Roman, I'm going to ask you a few questions," she said. "But before I do, there's something I want you to do for me. I want you to think about what kind of person you want to be. I'm here because people are getting hurt, and the more honest you are with me the more it will help me do something about it. I want you to take a second and think about that, okay?"

Roman looked down at the glass in his hands. He set it on the coffee table and nodded.

"What is your association with Peter Rumancek?"

"We . . . hang out."

"Is there anything else you want to tell me about your relationship?"

Roman was quiet.

"Does Peter believe he is a werewolf?"

"No," said Roman. "People just say that about him."

"Do you have any idea why they would say those things?"

"They're afraid of him. You should hear the things they say about us. I guess you have."

"Do they have a reason to be afraid?"

"No. Peter would never hurt anyone."

"Why did you go to the first murder site?"

The word hung in the air for a moment like a smoke ring before it dissipates. *Murder.*

"I followed Peter."

"What was Peter doing there?"

"Rubbernecking."

"Did you dig up Lisa Willoughby?"

"No."

She reached into her coat and produced her badge and set it facedown on the table.

"Did you dig up Lisa Willoughby?"

"I said we didn't," said Roman.

She looked at him.

"Yeah," he said. "We did."

"Why?"

"It was a ritual or something. Some Gypsy thing. I don't know."

"Roman, desecration of the dead does not fall under the rubric of 'some Gypsy thing.'"

"It wasn't desecration."

"What was it?"

"Peter . . . thought he could help her."

"She's dead."

"Peter marches to his own beat," said Roman.

"Upstairs you used the word *vargulf.* Why did you use this word?"

"Because I don't want you to bother my sister."

"Why do you think I would bother her?"

"I don't want you to think she's the *vargulf.*"

"When you use this word, what exactly do you think it means?"

He looked down and fussed at his already smooth lapels.

"It's a kind of sickness," he said. "It's like . . . hunger with no appetite."

She was bemused.

"Where did you learn this word?" she said.

"I don't know where I learned it."

"Where did you learn this word?" she said.

"Peter," he said.

"Can you tell me anything about an experiment being conducted at the Godfrey Institute for Biomedical Technologies called Ouroboros?" she said.

"I know that symbol means something. I mean, all symbols mean something, but that one means something—I don't know, something . . . happening."

He picked up his glass and drank and set it down. His fingertips missed it so he picked it up again. The ring of condensation from where it had first been placed joined the ring from where he lifted it and made a ∞.

"I see things sometimes," he said.

She nodded.

"Do you know what it means?" he said.

She regarded the boy: a narcissistic, insecure, oversensitive, and underparented adolescent heir to a Fortune 500 company with a substance abuse problem and homoerotic tendencies—it would have been more surprising if he *didn't* "see things sometimes."

"I can't know what it means to you," she said.

He hunched and ran his thumb up and down the sweat of his glass.

"I can help you," he said.

"Your cooperation is very helpful."

"I can do more. The White Tower. Ouroboros—I can find out what it is. My father built that place. My name is Godfrey."

"A name is only a name," she said.

He was doubtful of this premise.

"It's good that you want to help," she said. "It's very good of you. But you can't."

She observed him try inexpertly to conceal how deeply this

cut and had intimacy with this pain. No insult to the heart like being not needed yet.

"Why not?" he said.

She looked at his watery eyes with impatient compassion. She knew what he needed to hear, the first and fundamental tenet on which the rest of her training was founded, though it was unlikely the boy was any more ready to hear it than she herself at enlistment age, when the fight was more important than understanding why you fought. Teenagers. How thankful she was to be needed for something other than maternity.

"God doesn't want you to be happy, He wants you to be strong," she said.

Roman's native response was to send an acid-tipped barb straight in the exposed heart of this display of conviction but his tongue was silenced by the sudden uncertainty whether this was the most shit-for-brains or most important thing he had ever heard.

She reached for her badge. Staying any longer would be redundant: there was nothing to take from here but pain.

"Roman, would you like to introduce our guest?"

They both looked up to find the boy's mother in the entryway, holding a grocery bag. Chasseur looked out the window and saw the black pickup. It had not been there moments ago but its silhouette in what was by now a shower gave it a quality like some monolith from a primeval age. The mother stood in a white velour track suit and sunglasses and both were dry.

"May I ask your business here?" she said politely.

"There are certain inconsistencies in this investigation," said Chasseur. "I'm just dotting t's."

"Say no more," said Olivia. "Of course we would be thrilled to offer whatever you would find of assistance. Not a pleasant business at all, anything we can do. May I offer you a tea or perhaps a brandy? Things are getting frightful outside."

Chasseur could imagine no climatic condition more forbidding than the smile on the lady of Godfrey House inviting her to stay. Chasseur made her excuses and gave Roman a parting look and that look was really a prayer.

Once they were alone Olivia took the glass from Roman and sipped. Her eyes flicked down to the beaded rings on the table, which she wiped with her sleeve.

"You know," she said, "there is no shortage of coasters in this house."

He mumbled an apology.

"What happened to your face?" she said.

"It's just a scrape," he said.

She smiled sadly.

"Silly monkey," she said.

His phone then rang and he stepped into the next room and answered.

"Marie is hysterical," said Dr. Godfrey. "But this place has been a zoo all day and I just can't get away yet. Do you have any idea where Letha might have gone?"

He stood by the hall window looking out at the rain and the trees.

"Yes," said Roman. "I have an idea."

○

"You smell nice," said Letha. "You smell sweet like a puppy."

She was sitting astride him on the couch and his shirt had made its way off but they were otherwise clothed. He ran his fingertips down the back of her arm.

She shivered and smiled and said, "Goose bumps." She walked her fingers down his chest hair to his navel and lay her hand flat. He was hairy and his belly gently convex like a glass filled just to the point of overflowing.

"Tell me a story about being a Gypsy," she said.

"Do you people realize I'm half Italian?" said Peter.

"Right, but who cares!" she said.

Peter thought about it.

"One time Nicolae caught a fairy," he said.

"What do you mean, a fairy?"

He was annoyed. "I mean a fairy, what the heck am I supposed to mean?" He went on. "I was at his house one night in the summer, I must have been eight or nine, and Nic said he wanted to show me something, and he turned out the lights and gave me this jar with a little light inside. I say, Nic, that's a lightning bug. He says, Look closer. So I held it up and it wasn't a lightning bug, it was a person, a girl, no taller than a thumbnail, with wings like a dragonfly. And she had this little light."

"What was she wearing?"

Peter arched an eyebrow.

"I say, Holy shit, Nic, where did you find her? and he says she was just flying around the porch light with the moths. First he tried to catch her with his hands, but she stung him."

"Fairies sting?"

"Are you kidding? Fairies are meaner than fucking hornets."

This news pleased her.

"What did you do with her?"

"Kept her. For a while."

"What did you feed her?"

"Flies."

She was indignant. "Pretty fairies do not eat flies!"

"Yes they sure do. Get 'em right in the air and tear 'em apart. It's better than watching a tarantula go after crickets."

She was thoughtful.

"What happened to her?"

"She died. They don't last so long in captivity. One day there was just this tiny old woman at the bottom of the jar. Her wings had fallen off. At first I thought she was just taking a nap so I shook it a little. Definitely dead."

"You didn't clap your hands?"

He gave her a look.

"Well it's a fairy!" she said. "They're magical."

Peter shrugged, philosophical. "Death is fucking magical," he said.

Letha was quiet. Then abruptly she pushed herself up so she was straddling him. "I'm sorry, these things are killing me."

She pulled her shirt over her head and reached behind her, biting her tongue in concentration, and unclasped her bra. Her breasts fell free, the undersides bitten by wire. She made a relieved noise. Peter ran his hands along the swell of her belly.

"Are you serious!" she said.

She moved his hands over her breasts, leaving her own atop his and slowly kneading. She exhaled with contentment. Peter watched this surprising gift of his hands on these swollen tits with ambivalence.

"You should know I'm not any good being a boyfriend," he said.

She looked at the ceiling in wonder. "Tell me how such a big hairy retard can smell so good?" she said.

"What I mean to say is that what you're talking about is a whole deal and everything," said Peter.

"Fucking?" she said.

For a young man who devoted a predictable amount of mental resources to who and in what manner he would like to fuck, he did not like this business of her using this word. It wasn't girly and made him ill at ease.

She sat on top of him and enjoyed his discomfort. She could pinpoint the exact moment that she decided Peter would have sex with her today and it had been this morning, when she had attempted and discarded in frustration numerous ensembles and realized it was completely for his benefit and if he was going to cause her all this hassle he had better hold up his end of the bargain.

But as to her virginity. In her view the reason most of the time a girl was a virgin amounted to she wanted to feel special and not like just any old whore. Letha had never considered this her own motivation. She thought it was the height of dumb that anyone could look at this nonchoice as some kind of accomplishment and if a girl wanted to have sex with a bunch of boys or a bunch of sex with one boy and that made her happy, what could be wrong with that? What could be wrong with wanting what makes you happy? So she had told herself that when she met the person she really really wanted to get to know without her clothes, all bets were off; she was just waiting for when it felt right.

Letha did not know if it felt right to have sex with Peter Rumancek; she could in fact find no shortage of reasons why it wouldn't. But something had happened. An angel with a halo of every color had brought her a miracle and after that happens you don't get to tell yourself lies anymore, the right has been revoked. And if Letha was honest with herself, there had been plenty of boys she wanted to get to know without her clothes— she wanted to feel their breath on her skin and to hold their penises in her hand and believably pull off lines like, Are you going to try to fuck me—but the thing that was really holding her back was the idea that this nonchoice was some kind of accomplishment, that she was special, not just some whore. And this was not acceptable anymore; lying about her deepest self was not an option in a world that had reached into her and left grace behind.

○

Roman watched.

Sheets of rain washed over the glass and Roman watched the two of them inside. They were on the couch. She was facing down and he was on top of her. Her arm was outstretched and his fingers laced through hers. Roman stood in the hemlocks with his hair matted to his forehead and arms dead at his sides and watched. Peter worked his hand under her and up her clit and her mouth made a moan and his hair brushed her face and her mouth closed. Sucking on it. Sucking his fucking rat faggot hair.

Rain hit a puddle by his feet like a thousand damned mouths wailing O.

Roman turned away and walked around front and got into his car. His wet clothes suctioned him to the leather and he tried counting the worms of rain racing down his windshield but they all ran together. It was nothing but a measure of disorder. That was all it was.

The shadows dancing in the corners of his eyes laced gently together now, forming a merciful black.

O

The walls went white as there was another *CRACK*, the kind like it's all coming apart, and Ashley Valentine yelped as the lights went out. Her heart calmed in the dark and she laughed. We can't know if we laugh at ourselves for being silly or to forget that we're not and that we are still here only by a sufferance that can be no more predicted than appeased. Like most things, probably a little of both. Ashley went to the window and looked out to see who else the outage hit. The whole block was dark and it took a moment to notice a strange shape in her yard. A person. A man. A strange man standing in her yard, unmoving. Her heart clutched and now she emitted no sound. Her parents were out and would not be home until much later. She fumbled for her phone, unable to take her eyes off the man in the rain and his weird stillness. She began to dial the police but it was then she noticed the car in the street, a Jaguar. She flipped her phone shut and went downstairs and opened the front door.

"Roman?" she said.

At first she thought he hadn't even noticed; he remained queerly still like a kind of retarded lawn gnome. But then he looked at her and said, "No light."

"Roman—are you all right?"

He turned his palms up and regarded the waterburst.

"It's just rain," he said.

"Roman, I think you better come in."

He did not disagree but did not move and she stretched her hand outside. There was a low roll of thunder. He took her hand and she led him upstairs to the bathroom and gave him her pink Victoria's Secret kimono.

"You have the legs for it," she said.

He handed her his wet clothes through the door and she put them in the dryer, then lit several votive candles in her room. When he entered she put a hand to her mouth to stifle laughter—that baby pink and his pale, skinny thighs.

"Here," she said. She sat him on her bed and pulled her comforter around his shoulders and sat on her rocking chair looking at him. Here he was, Roman Godfrey, cross-dressed and swaddled on her bed. Her heart was a flicked mold of gelatin.

Not that she had a thing for Roman. He was not just the worst kind of conceited jerk but a genuinely sick person, the kind who would come up to you at a dance and give you a corsage made of tampon wrappers—which he had in the ninth grade—and she had always prided herself on being immune to whatever inexplicable attraction he seemed to hold for other girls. But here he was. This poor soaking creature staring distractedly at a candle's flame—and even if you were absolutely immune to the charms—as if—of Roman Godfrey, how could your heart not go out to such a pitiful display? What a loser!

"What's wrong?" she said.

He lowered his head and did not meet her eyes. The candle flickered over the hard geometry of his face. She noticed the stain of red under the bandage on his cheek.

"Roman, what happened?"

He was staring blankly and his cheeks gleamed because he was crying.

"Okay," she said. "Okay, hey." She went and sat next to him and took his hand.

"Hey."

He did not raise his head.

"Why don't you tell me about it?" she said. "Maybe you should talk about it."

He shut his eyes and bunched his face into a hard ugly fist. He relaxed it.

"Roman," she said.

"I'm ugly," he said.

"What?" she said.

"I'm ugly. I'm an ugly person."

"Roman!" she said.

"I have an ugliness it's impossible to love," he said.

He withdrew his hand from hers and he put his face into his hands and he wept. The comforter fell away and his scapulae showed through the robe in sharp relief, racking up and down as though he was trying to fly.

○

Soon enough one thing led to another and Roman took one of Ashley's hands and guided it through the bars of the bed frame, followed by the other. He pulled the sash free from the kimono he was still wearing and tied it around her wrists in an elaborate and apparently practiced knot. She said he was crazy, did he know that? He kissed along the hem of her panties, and in her mind she said, *Finally* . . . She said he ought to be locked up.

He pulled her panties off. Her heart hammered and her wrists jerked, but wherever he had learned that knot, it wasn't for show—resistance only strengthened its hold. He knelt over her and the folds of the robe opened and his torso was like a tightly braided rope. He parted her legs and lowered his head.

The headboard rattled. After a few minutes he pulled away and she caught her breath.

"Your turn," she said.

He looked at her. There was something childish about the wetness on his face, and with his disheveled blond hair it gave him the momentary appearance of a Renaissance cherub.

"Your turn," she said again.

He stood and stripped off his Jockey shorts. Her tongue thrilled at his hardness.

"Untie me," she said.

Roman ignored her and took her ankles and flipped them purposefully, but because of her hands she could not turn all the way and ended up with her legs scissored unintuitively, and suddenly things were different. Ashley had heard girls tell stories of getting into situations and changing their minds as though this made them victims of what happened next, like that was how it worked, that you got so far and it switched off just like that and they were not themselves to blame for being little sluts and cock teases in the first place. But now she understood: it was not like that. Changing your mind was not the thing that happened at all, what changed was your body telling you what was right and what was wrong and before now she had never known the way things can just like that go all wrong. She worked at the knot but it held her tight.

"Roman," she said.

A quality of thereness was missing from his face, his green eyes were windows to nothing. He was mercurial.

"Roman, please untie me," she said. "I don't like this, Roman."

He braced her hip with a firm grip and slipped himself into her. She was very wet from her own arousal and his saliva and there was something uniquely horrible about the ease of this violation.

"Roman. Roman, hold on." Maintaining the remote hope he was just getting carried away as boys would from time to time. But that was not what she saw in his eyes: something had gone away to she didn't know where.

He thrust his hips hard and fast. She tried to twist her legs to force him out but he clamped a hand hard on her thigh.

"Roman, *stop!*"

The scariest part was, he could have at least looked like he wanted to do what he was doing.

Part of her broke off and felt unconnected with this hateful thing that was happening to her body but the headboard kept time with the violence, reminding her. She felt too terrified for speech but heard herself regardless, she heard herself crying and resisting and sounding exactly like the sort of hysterical female who would get herself hit or cut or whatever it would turn out a person capable of this was capable of. Be quiet, she communicated to her body. Whatever he needs for that, do not give it to him.

But her body did not cooperate. She heard it continue to fight him and beg him and reject that allowing this to happen until it was done was the best thing. It refused to accept this use of the flesh. And she resigned herself to the fact: her stupid body wasn't wrong.

Roman stopped then. He leaned forward and brought his face close to hers. Whatever he was capable of, now it was coming. He looked into her eyes. His eyes were windows to nothing. And then there were no windows, there was only the nothing.

"Want it," he said.

And then she found herself back in herself, in this room, in this bed, being fucked by Roman. His body clashed with hers like a wreck replaying on a loop: thin, hard veins ridged his neck and arms, the kimono fluttered wraith and ethereal behind him— and she wanted it more than having it could satisfy.

He looked into her eyes and told her to tell him he was ugly and she did. He made her repeat it again and again. It hurt him just the same every time. He looked into her eyes.

"Come," he said.

She shrieked as this command swept through her most inviolate regions of self.

Roman collected his clothes from the dryer and returned to her room and worked the knot of the sash and untied her. He pulled her panties up her legs and then a pair of pajama pants. He lifted her arms and pulled a T-shirt over her head. He pulled her comforter to her chin and took her hand and held it. He looked into her eyes.

"I was never here," he said. "Dream about something nice."

You Are Not on Solid Ground

The air was damp and smelled like mud and the bright sun baked bloated worms into the walk, causing Roman to deliberately place his steps on his approach to the White Tower. He stopped and produced a small vial of coke from his blazer pocket, feeling on balance pretty good about the limitless opportunities of this new morning. On balance all this goddamn pussyfooting was against his genetic disposition, and if there was any lesson to be taken from his lineage it was that history's great murderer of clarity was always other people. Jacob Godfrey once said that the one thing that others could be reliably depended to provide was gastrointestinal distress, and this had never been so poignant to Roman before now. But it was a Godfrey who had built this town, so it was only fitting that it would be a Godfrey to save it from itself. He didn't need them. They could suck each other's dicks. He didn't need anyone. He did a bump into each nostril and wiped his nose. The sun glinted off the side of the Tower and he found himself fixating on it, the light pulling itself to the center of his mind's eye as shadow found the fringes . . .

He shook his head. Not now.

"Goddamn pussyfooting," he said. He resumed his steps.

"They can suck each other's dicks," he said.

He entered the building and the sterile air enveloped him

and he strode with decision to Reception, where a slight man glanced up from the newspaper horoscopes.

"May I help you?" he said.

"I want to see Dr. Pryce," said Roman.

"Is Dr. Pryce expecting us?" said the receptionist.

"No. But he'll see me."

"And may I inquire our business?"

Roman put his hands on the desk and leaned forward. "What's your name?" he said.

The man made a God-give-me-strength face. "My name is—"

Roman cut him off. "I really don't give a shit. My name is Roman Godfrey. And I'm here to see Dr. Pryce."

The receptionist was quiet, then picked up the phone. So there you had it. How things got done around here.

Waiting, he paced the floor with restless coke legs. The overhead lights were jellyfish on the marble floor.

"Hey," said the receptionist, flagging his attention. "What's your sign?"

"Aries," said Roman.

The man looked at the newspaper. "'Senses will lie as dreams wake. You are not on solid ground. Don't look down.'"

"Is that a haiku?" said Roman.

The man started counting syllables on his fingers as Dr. Pryce emerged from the elevator and came forward. Any perturbation he may have felt at the interruption or what the boy might be doing here independent of his mother, at whose side he was as good as surgically attached at the public functions where their interaction was almost entirely localized, was not evident.

"The big man," said Pryce, shaking his hand. "Isn't this a nice surprise? What brings you our way?"

Roman returned his smile. "Project Ouroboros," he said.

Pryce pursed his lips, nonplussed. "Well, I can't imagine you'd find it very interesting," he said.

"Suppose I do," said Roman.

They looked at each other. Several lab techs entered and

passed through the mezzanine, glancing at this unusual impasse of lord and vassal. Finally Pryce shrugged and gestured for Roman to follow. He conducted Roman to the Herpetology Lab and repeated the same performance he had given Norman.

"Oh, wait, no," said the lab tech. "There's the decimal."

Pryce made a conciliatory face for Roman. "Not a thrill a minute, I suppose, but I hope it's what you need. If you want, we can drop by Prosthetics—there's a robot arm you can make play Nintendo with your own motor cortex."

Roman did not look at the lab tech. "Get out," he said.

The lab tech looked at Pryce.

"Did you just try to touch my dick?" Roman said to the lab tech.

The lab tech was alarmed.

"I'm calling the CFO right now and telling him you tried to touch my dick," said Roman.

Pryce gave the lab tech a nod and he exited.

Pryce was amiable. "Your dad was a real pistol too," he said.

"Show me what I came for," said Roman. "Project Ouroboros. The real one. It's underground and I'd like you to take me to it."

Pryce laughed. "If there's some secret underground experiment, I'd sure like to see it too."

"Do not fucking laugh at me," said Roman.

Pryce stopped laughing. He gestured for Roman to have a seat. Roman did not. They looked at each other.

"Relax," said Pryce.

"Who do you think you're talking to, Johann?" said Roman. He had never called Dr. Pryce by his first name before. He loved today. Yesterday and every day before he had allowed that greasy faggot to call the shots, but now look who was the warrior.

Pryce took a pen from his shirt pocket and twiddled it between his fingers.

"Of course," he said. "There is no presumption quite so infuriating as to be treated like the boy you were and not the man you've become. So. What can I do for you, young man?"

"I don't think I need to be clearer," said Roman.

"There is, however, a consequence to stepping into your father's shoes," said Pryce. "Or rather, a great number of them, compounding in interest until the day you die. It has been my experience—"

"Did I say, Talk to me like a little cunt?" said Roman. So down to business.

He looked Pryce in the eye. "Tell me—" said Roman.

Pryce clicked his pen three times in succession. *clickclickclick*. It cut Roman's focus off at the knees. Three. Atonal, asymmetrical, amoral. Bad luck's favorite number, its association with the divine the devil's hat trick. Roman sputtered, trying to expel this emissary of the dark place.

Pryce waited.

Roman shook it off and recovered, looking Pryce in the eye with renewed intensity.

"Tell me—"

clickclickclick

Roman sputtered again and then was still and ominously quiet.

Pryce watched him with concern now. "Do you need a glass of water?" he said.

Roman blinked rapidly and glared, willing his anger into a penetrating focus.

"Tell me—"

clickclickclick

"GODDAMMIT!" Roman roared and seized the pen from Pryce's hand and hurled it across the room. It bounced to no great effect off a cage, causing its inhabitant to languidly raise its head, find nothing going on of interest, and return to its meditation.

Roman fell into the chair previously offered him and wheeled it facing in the other direction from Pryce. His eyes had filled with useless water and the clicking echoed in his brain like the abyss in tap shoes.

Pryce stood over him and gently kneaded the boy's neck.

"Inch by inch," said Pryce.

Roman breathed and allowed the tension to release under the gentle hands behind him; he'd pissed away too much dignity to have any option left but submission.

"It has been my experience," said Pryce, as though he had never been interrupted, "that being a man consists in large part of accepting how little of it is getting what you want when you want it."

O

Outside, Roman headed back down the walk. His shoulders were clenched and his cheeks were as hot as though they'd been slapped, and so acute was his annoyance and embarrassment over this failure that he very nearly, without even thinking about it, stepped on a crack, catching his foot just at the last moment. He looked down appalled at this averted catastrophe.

"Fucking Peter!" he said. "Fucking goddamn Peter!"

On the next square of the walk an earthworm writhed speckled with little black ants, and Roman stomped on the entire squalid spectacle. He resumed his step.

clickclickclick

Roman whirled, eyes darting wildly, but no one was there.

"Breathe," Roman said. "Breathe."

He felt the ground under his feet. This was here. He took out his mint container and tapped out the rest of his coke on the back of his hand and sucked it with both nostrils, grinding his nose into it. This was really here. He wiped his nose with his sleeves and once more started walking.

clickclickclick

Roman froze. His blood went cold. Oh no. It had gotten in him. It had gotten in him and taken up a small chisel and *clickclickclick clickclickclick clickclickclick* it worked away at him. It worked away with purpose. It wanted something.

Roman whimpered. He covered his face with his hands. He

did not know if they were his own hands or the other hands. The dark ones. He did not know what was here and what was from the dark place they came from that he wanted so desperately to stay there.

"Please," said Roman.

clickclickclick clickclickclick clickclickclick clickclickclick clickclickclick clickclickclick clickclickclick clickclickclick clickclickclick clickclickclick clickclickclick clickclickclick clickclickclick clickclickclick clickclickclick CLICKCLICKCLICK

And then it was quiet again, and what boundary there was between Roman and the dark place fell away, and his eyes turned backwards and he saw the other side of it, he saw with clarity something he once knew, the most forbidden possible thing to know, the thing that Francis Pullman had seen when he looked into his eyes. The thing that had happened, and was still to come.

Roman screamed, and his knees buckled under him and he fell to the lawn screaming, and the ground around him buckled inward in a concavity of a perfect circumference that appeared around him, but he did not notice as the ground rippled and then fell away and he was swallowed by the pit.

○

Norman,

It's a funny thing how you can look at something a thousand times without really seeing it. This happened to me recently when I saw the word gentleman *in print and for whatever reason for the first time really saw it. Gentle* man. Oh, I thought, that's my brother. A gentleman is my brother, Norman.

But she won't let that stand. She will bring out all the worst in you and by the time you realize it it's too late, because she's already destroyed the best. I could see the look in your eye the last time we talked, but under the circumstances I hope you will understand how seriously I mean this.

Do not let her destroy you.

Also, just so it's in the record, I did attempt the other way first but it didn't fly. She won't let me kill her.

JR

Catabasis

From the archives of Dr. Norman Godfrey:

NG: How are you feeling this morning, Christina?
CW: It's very pretty here. I took a walk for the first time earlier. It was a very nice walk, although there were branches all over the place. That sure was a heck of a storm last night. My grandfather would call it a barn burner.
NG: Yes, it was. I hope it didn't upset you.
CW: Oh, I love storms. I can sit and watch a real barn burner of a storm all day. It's like the thrillers my grandmother reads, you know? There's no *literary* value, of course, but once the blood and guts start flying, oh boy! Nothing beats being safe and snug while things are just going to pieces, you know?
NG: You feel safe here?
CW: I mean, I'm not an expert on mental institutions, but this feels like a pretty tight ship. Kidding, I'm kidding. But yes. I do. It feels like nothing can get its hands on you in here.
NG: . . .
CW: I knew him, actually.
NG: Excuse me?
CW: You're thinking about him. That bum. Sorry, I shouldn't call him a bum. But he was your patient too, wasn't he?

NG: Yes, he was.

CW: My grandparents live by Kilderry Park, so I'd see him around a lot. I guess I shouldn't say I knew him. He had an entire life and parents and everything and I don't know anything about it. Except the obvious.

NG: The obvious?

CW: He watched him do it. He watched Peter Rumancek eat that girl.

NG: . . .

CW: Doctor, do you need a glass of water or something?

○

There was a silence of dread character when Dr. Godfrey returned from work. Marie was in the kitchen, scouring the counters, and there were eddies of tension around her neck and shoulders. There had been a time when he could have put his hands on her shoulders and it would have relieved that tension. There had been a time when kindness passed between them other than for an audience and their interactions had more underlying themes than blame. He stood in the doorway and she knew he was there and allowed a sense of foreboding to build, nothing good to come from a Godfrey woman doing her own cleaning, and he waited with habitual fatalism about what he regarded not just as the years' accumulation of domestic hostility and disappointment but also a cosmic punishment. Because she had never fallen out of love with him.

He looked at the face on the refrigerator door. The lumpy eyeless face, a goblin made of Silly Putty. And he had argued in favor of displaying Letha's ultrasound because . . . because he had lost the power to say no to her.

"She has nothing to say to me," said Marie finally. She did not turn to face him. "She looks at me like the goddamn grand inquisitor. Maybe you'll have better luck, Doctor."

In his near decade of medical training it had never occurred to him it would come to fruition with the honor of having this title spat at him like that.

He went to Letha's room. She was on her bed doing math homework and did not look up, denying him her attention with an air of beatific persecution. An unwelcome image came to mind of this "ponytailed hoodlum" bucking on top of her. This was the lot of man: you begin life as the young buck only to blink and find yourself the father of the young lady being bucked upon.

"I guess I'll run off and join the Calvinists," he said.

She ignored him. In the pains he had gone through in his own courtship days he could never imagine a denial more acute than his daughter's affection. But there were larger considerations. One of the biggest factors fracturing this household was Marie's perception of irrelevance; from her perspective it would seem more as factioning: her husband and daughter banding against her. Which they were; they were because he was doing everything to encourage it. So there was no choice. He would have to align himself with Marie, even at the risk of alienating his daughter, of his daughter looking at him as they did her, with such . . . disappointment. If he wanted to fix the one thing that was in his hands, he would be forced to take her mother's side. He closed the door.

"I'm not here to mom you," he said.

She looked at him and he felt the thing he knew was the last thing he should be allowing himself to feel: that he was winning. But right now his talents were needed elsewhere. He sat on her bed and fortified himself to disengage the father side of him and employ professional neutrality. Sword swallowers actually manage to rearrange internal organs. All manner of feats were possible.

"Was it your first time?" he said.

In a manner of speaking, he added silently.

"Yes," she said.

"It's not a bad thing," he said. "Don't ever let anyone put it in your head that it's a bad thing."

"Okay," said Letha.

"But . . . you have to understand our concerns. Look around you, sweetpea. The biggest thing was not knowing. You have to understand how we're going to take not knowing where you are."

"But that's not it," she said. "The biggest thing is Peter. And that's exactly why I didn't say where I was. Because I don't want to lie to you, but I knew you would react exactly the same either way. At least *she* would."

He concealed the satisfaction he took in the amendment.

"She's just as judgmental as anyone else," said Letha. "It's the same with Roman. It's confirmation bias. She's already made up her mind and will only see what makes her right."

"I'll have to look at my parenting rules of order, but I'm not sure you're allowed to be throwing around terms like *confirmation bias*," he said.

A plastic thread curled from her comforter and he pulled it straight and let it recoil.

"And," he said, "I have to ask you, how much do you know about this boy?"

He could see in her eyes a pulling away with the clarity of physical movement.

"Letha, I hear things," he said. "And this is a person I hear about more than some. Now, I'm tying pianos to my legs not to jump to conclusions, but this young man has quite a reputation."

She was quiet a moment and he wasn't sure if this was a losing battle. If there was any way to discuss it without making her hate him. If this was a defeat he could live with.

But then she looked at him and her eyes were glassy and she said, "Dad, I'm in love with him."

He said nothing. His eyes glassed too.

"People see what they see," she said. "They see someone like Peter and he's just a blank page that people can put on whatever they're afraid of. You know how people are."

He did. But he also knew this little girl who spoke with unearthly authority was very possibly insane.

He lay his hand flat on the bed. She put her hand in his. They were quiet.

The door opened and Marie came in. Invaded, was what it felt like. It felt like an invasion of privacy. He hoped Letha wouldn't move her hand and she didn't. So there.

"Olivia called," said Marie.

And so that was that. He knew what was coming, all these dumb-ass years coming, and in a single instant over, and what this instant revealed to him was that he was not simply prepared for it but elated. Elated because it was not in his cosmology to leave her.

He held his daughter's hand and waited for it to come.

"Roman is in a coma," said Marie.

○

Roman was in the attic at Godfrey House. Pryce had told Olivia that his EKG was stable but he strongly advised against bringing him home. This advice was overridden. Shelley had communicated that she wanted him to be up in the attic with her and received her mother's consent. Shelley carried his bed up herself. He lay there now in a gown from the institute. They stood over him, Godfrey and Olivia and the girls. There had been no pretense of Marie having any place here. Godfrey looked down at the boy, the boy lying there but with a kind of lack of thereness that looked exactly nothing like sleeping as the smell of his own childhood attic conjured reams of irrelevant memory, and needing some air he asked Olivia to come downstairs with him. The girls stayed. Letha looked up at Shelley. Shelley's eyes looked hard and cool to the touch like quartz. Letha wrapped her arms around Shelley's trunk. Her hands did not quite meet.

Godfrey and Olivia stood out on the back patio. The motion sensor light came on and threw their shadows lank over the lawn.

"You know he should be in a hospital," he said.

"He's staying here," she said.

Godfrey looked at the tall man he made on the grass. He had told her once, long ago, that he would without hesitation have her children taken from her if he ever thought there was a reason. But in this circumstance, where intervention was clearly justified, he suffered no illusion of his conscience holding any jurisdiction.

"How did it happen?" he said.

"A drug overdose. He was on narcotics and causing a scene at the institute."

"Why was he there?"

"I don't know."

He pressed a fingertip to the apex of the pyramid post cap of the railing.

"Olivia, tell me the truth," he said. "Do you know anything about Project Ouroboros?"

"I've told you I haven't got any better idea what goes on there than you do. Has it got something to do with Roman?"

"Why was he there?" Godfrey said again. "Something's going on here, you can't act like it's not."

She turned to him with a look totally incongruous of his experience of her. She looked at him with no agenda.

"Norman, the last thing I feel like right now is acting," she said.

She lit a cigarette. The motion light went out. The cherry of her cigarette glowed in the tears on her cheeks.

"Liv," he said. He had not referred to her by this glaring homophone of a diminutive in a very long time.

"Liv Liv Liv," he said.

○

That night after midnight Godfrey's phone rang. He said "Hello" and then "Oh for God's—" and then "No no, I'm on my way." He hung up and turned to Marie and began his cover but did not bother to finish; it was beyond redundant. Her impassivity over his leaving their bed inspired in him the morbid impulse to oversell his desire to return to it. He hovered over her, rubbing her arm, and said he would be back as soon as he could. She expressed no need for this to be any truer than it was.

Vindicated, he drove for the second time that day to Godfrey House and climbed into another bed and afterward engaged in an activity with Olivia they had not done in as many years as it had been since he called her by her pet name. They slept together. A phrase he had always failed to understand as a euphemism for fucking as though fucking were of intrinsically greater consequence.

Some hours later he woke suddenly, an animal confusion over being in the wrong bed. He was alone now in the bed, and having regained his orientation looked up to find her sitting at the bay window. She was nude and one knee was drawn up and the whisper of cigarette smoke was over her head. Lost in her own thoughts. Her own heartbreak for a world where these things happen to our children and there's nothing we can do about it.

O

Peter and Letha were eating lunch in the cafeteria and he felt it coming. He detected a kind of nervous energy in her, a distinctively female tension that when released would be no good for anyone. He felt it in his Swadisthana. A week had gone by. Roman was still under and Peter had made no headway in the investigation. He had done nothing at all; he knew the fight that was coming but did not know what new and inspired ways things could get fucked if he continued trying to get around it. For now the only thing was to take things as they came and avoid getting into any more grief-inducing scenarios. For now he was totally set on those. But the way Letha was worrying her yo-gurt it was clear that whatever was on her mind would soon be on his.

"Wow, do your earrings match your purse?" said Peter. As a rule he kept observations about fashion decisions women had made in reserve for diversionary purposes.

"I want you to come to dinner at my house," she said.

Peter was quiet.

"It would be kind of a big deal for them," she said. "It . . . would be kind of a big deal for me."

Peter told his mind's eye to picture the way the sun falls like honey on the grass in autumn and a low stream passing over round stones and the first angel's-hair sliver of the new moon. Make "this" a lot easier. So we're a "this" now. As if that wasn't the exact kind of talk that led to *boyfriend* and *commitment* and other words he was allergic to. Girls. The second you set up a perfectly reasonable boundary is the second they're shopping for bulldozers. Ever the foremost of ironies that men are considered the hunters of the species.

She looked at him, expecting. Expecting the ten million things that girls get it in their heads to expect. Obviously he was letting things come too far. Obviously she was hard of hearing in that way they get when you say "I need my space" and they hear wedding bells. He knew how to handle this. As Nicolae had said: nine out of ten times a woman is giving you an ache in the belly it can be easily solved by taking her home and giv-ing her the business. There it was. He would just take her home and give her the business like it was going out of style and there'd be nothing more to talk about. He smiled at her and nodded and she smiled back, thinking she was getting her way.

The subsequent evening Marie Godfrey could hardly con-tain her disbelief that she sat across the table from this greasy and quite plausibly lice-ridden thug like any school friend breaking bread with her family. Or at least the stand-in family whose resemblance to the one she had devoted her best years to diminished by the day. But it was still her table. Appropriate enough for the ritual sacrifice of what was left of sanctity. Classist! The nerve of such an implication when Marie Newport had grown up the daughter of an unskilled steelworker from a side of the tracks that neither her husband, daughter, nor any Godfrey had a conception of any more than the dark side of the moon. As though it made one some scaly old relic out of a Jane Austen novel for having some concern about one's only child ending up chopped up in a ditch. As though it made any difference how many charitable endeavors you were spearheading or that you would cut off your arm before voting Republican; that one look at the likes of a Peter Rumancek and you had a responsibility to your eyes irrespective of something so notional as class. Unless your name was Norman Godfrey. If this was your name your responsibility was to an argument against an ancestor who had been dead for nearly a hundred years.

But none of this was what caused the greatest strain on Marie's credulity. What astonished her most about this performance was her own collaboration with it. When Letha had first sprung this proposal, Marie's response was a hard and brittle laugh unpleasant to her own ears and an unequivocal "Absolutely not." But Letha had not bothered to argue her ruling or even look at her. She looked at her father in unmistakable collusion: he would handle it. Handling crazy people was his job. Marie wondered if there was a word for what she had become. It would be the opposite of an echo, a body severed from the voice. When all the voice wanted, if anyone could hear it, was to ask how they had let this happen.

After dinner she excused herself, claiming a sudden onset of fatigue, and Dr. Godfrey poured himself a drink and offered one to Peter. The kid earned it sitting under the klieg light of Marie's hospitality.

And now, upon meeting the accused in person, Dr. Godfrey

was more sympathetic to his daughter's point of view: Peter was a different breed. He was not our neighbor. He did not want the things we wanted. If you told him to straighten up and fly right he could only look at you in utter confusion: to his mind this was exactly what he was doing. Foremost he was guilty of civilization's unthinkable crime, as plain in his walk as a limp: he was not owned by anyone.

He did not want to be here right now, that was certain. But he was. He was here because Letha had asked him to be and this demonstrated a base level of integrity that in Godfrey's estimation earned the kid a fair shake. His darkest fear had been that Christina Wendall had concocted the werewolf story much as Letha had, as a psychological bulwark against the more disturbing reality, but his instincts drew him to another theory about that particular patient. Otherwise, it was in the water supply: people were afraid and someone had to account for it, and Peter was not One of Us. But here he was, making this effort (though would it have really killed him to wear a tie?), and besides, it could not be discounted that he had been kind to Shelley. Of all things, that could not be discounted.

Godfrey handed Peter the glass, which Peter held up to clink against his own.

"To . . . Roman," said Godfrey. He'd been searching for something leavening and innocuous but that's what came out.

"To Roman," said Peter, and in his eye was a sort of strange character Godfrey had caught at odd moments all through the meal, not so much a maturity as a nature consciousness as though he were at times a boy exactly of his years and others a soul out of time wearing a boy mask.

Godfrey noticed him squeeze Letha's leg, and that filled him with a gladness that surprised him considerably. But he was glad. That his strange daughter had found this strange suitor, that there was a person in her life to touch her like that. Here was a woman he had made.

Once the table was cleared he made a show of skepticism

when Letha said she would drive Peter home, but, as she pointed out, he'd been drinking, and neither broached the idea of rousing Marie. And by now he had privately abdicated any responsibility of being another obstacle between them. They would run into plenty without his contribution. He gave them the parting admonition "Behave," counting on that they would do the contrary. They would live.

A real live woman. What did you know about that?

○

From the archives of Dr. Norman Godfrey:

CW: It was that dream again, the one in the mill. But it was different this time, this time the moment comes, I don't know whether to hide or to turn and face it, but this time I can see someone outside, someone out the window. It's Francis Pullman. I can tell because . . . God, I hate saying this out loud, but because of that creepy dead eye. And that's the only thing that changes, he's just standing out there not saying anything, and I'm still stuck in the same place but with a dead man watching me.
NG: Do you have any idea what significance Pullman or Pullman's ghost would have here?
CW: I . . . This is going to sound a little crazy, Doctor.
NG: I think you're in the right place.
CW: The look on his face.
NG: What do you mean?
CW: He wasn't saying anything, but I knew he was telling me something by the look on his face.
NG: Is it something you're comfortable sharing here?
CW: He was telling me . . . You are going to lose your soul.
NG: . . .

Peter's Hierarchy of Shit He Can Live Without

It was the last day before the Snow Moon, and when the eighth-period bell rang it dismissed not only the student body for the day but also the last hot minute of denial on Peter's part of what he had been putting off for the last two weeks: now he would have to tell her. Women and talking, the way it just went together like drawn and quartered. He walked from study hall to his bus, wincing at the prospect, when Alex Finster and Tom Dublyk appeared at his flanks, with an additional one or two behind. This was not the reprieve Peter had in mind.

"Full moon tomorrow," said Alex.

Peter said nothing.

"You got spunk in your ears, Rumancek? I'm talking to you, you dirty Gypsy piece of shit."

Peter did not take his eyes from the exit sign down the hall over the wave of heads.

"Aw, he's probably just down his girlfriend's in a coma," said Tom.

The question, Peter knew, was simple: make it to the bus. They wanted him to give them a reason. If people were going to jump you, they just jumped you; these shitheads needed him to give them a reason. So it was the simple question of just keeping his mouth shut and getting on his bus.

Alex called him a deaf Gypsy faggot and as they passed

through the door the crush pressed their bodies together and Alex turned his head and breathed hot in Peter's ear.

"Probably needs to run home and suck Sleeping Beauty's dick," said Tom.

Just keep his mouth shut long enough to board bus 89. They wanted him to give them a reason but Peter had been on the wrong end of enough beatings to know that nothing was worth it. This was what made Peter not like Roman; Peter had control. When they can take that from you there is no floor under what else you can lose.

Tom drew two fingers under his own nostrils, inhaling deeply. "Is that pussy I smell?"

They were outside now and the buses were in an idling line no more than fifteen yards away. Fifteen yards, an achievable goal.

Alex put an arm around Peter's shoulders. "So where's the wolf half come from, anyway?" he said.

He thought this intrusive familiarity would goad Peter into reacting. Just enough smart to get on the bus.

"Your mom toss a steak between her legs and say, 'Come and get it, boys'?" said Alex.

Peter hit Alex in the balls.

Alex doubled over and tripped over his own feet and fell and Peter broke for it. The other boys were just behind him, but the moment's lapse in their reaction was all he needed to get to the bus, whatever was nearest, something at least he could hang on to and kick. He made passing eye contact through the bus window with those girls, the Sworn twins, staring at him with those spooky little eyes, but if staring was the worst of it there were things worse than eyes.

He leaped up the steps but then one of the twins' eyes widened (which?—lost to history) and she yelled, "Watch out!" but Peter knew: he had lost, and a hand seized him by the ponytail and wrenched him down off the bus and he was shoved to the pavement, finding himself in a ring of boys and looking up directly at

Duncan Fritz, 210 pounds of Duncan Fritz who had not been seeking this fight but now that a fight was in the air could not pass it up. This is what a fight cost you: the right to abstractions, like "fair." This is one of the things a fight cost you. Peter attempted to bring his hands up in protection, but before he could Duncan punched his face. It was like looking into a very bright spotlight, and a quick succession of half a dozen flashes of this spotlight followed before Peter was successful in getting his hands into place and curling his knees into his chest and wheezing blood into his palms and waiting for the kicking to begin.

But then sharp elbows broke through the ring surrounding him and another combatant entered the fray and he felt the weight of this new body come down on top of him and a pair of arms encircle his neck. It was not a lot of weight and the arms were shaking and skinny like a girl's. It was a girl. It was Letha. Letha had thrown herself on top of him.

Things were quiet again. Letha clung to him, shaking. There flowed from the center of her body a power so great even now Peter could feel it in his Swadisthana, and it caused her whole body to shake with her intention of not letting go of him.

"Aw fuck," someone said eventually. The party was over before it had begun: this stalemate alongside the immediate threat of some authority's arrival caused the mob to drift, deflated. As suddenly as the tribe lust for sacramental violence had arisen, the pregnant girl was a real wet blanket.

Letha helped Peter up. His hair was loose and in disarray and his face was red and bleeding from cuts over his eye and his mouth. And although he was standing now and okay what she saw in her mind's eye was that other boy standing over him and hammering his fist into him again and again. She had never herself seen such violence before but knew instinctively and unequivocally that the only real way to fight it was with its equal and opposite, and she kissed his face. She covered the face the other boy had beaten with fists with kisses that were the fluttering of moth wings. An eye for an eye.

Peter leaned his forehead against hers. He put his thumb to her mouth and wiped his blood from her lips. She was crying and mucus was leaking from her nose. He drew his index finger along her upper lip.

"Snot," he said.

He fished a spare hairband from his pocket and pulled his hair back in its ponytail. He took her hand.

"Let's go," he said.

"Hey!" barked a voice like clapper boards and Vice Principal Spears seized Peter's elbow. "Where do you think you're going?"

"He's coming with me."

The vice principal released Peter. His face paled twice in the twin reflections of Olivia Godfrey's sunglasses.

○

Peter and Letha went with Olivia. Shelley, for whom Olivia had come, sat in the bed of the pickup, and the three of them in the cab, Letha in the middle, tucking her legs to the side of the gearshift. Olivia had furnished Peter with her head scarf and he held it to his bloody mouth. The inside of his cheek wall was torn and he worried it with his tongue. Olivia, in response to a question that had not yet been voiced, said, "He's the same." She lightly rapped Letha's thigh, which at first seemed like a gesture of solace—but she needed room to shift.

She drove them to the Rumanceks' trailer. She told Letha, "I really should take you home, darling."

Letha said nothing. Olivia made a display of mulling her adult responsibilities and relented.

"Call your mother, at least. She is wound rather tightly these days."

At the sight of Peter's split lip and swollen eye, it took Lynda the better part of fifteen minutes to grieve and rage. She spat on her own breast, calling some of the more voluptuous curses on the poison wombs that conceived such monsters that could do that to a face so handsome. Then she calmed to practical maternal authority and cleaned him up and gave him a tea with two crushed aspirin and a joint and sent him to the bed with a Saran-wrapped frozen pork chop against the swelling. Olivia stayed to have a discussion with Lynda.

In the bedroom, Letha lay with him and draped an arm and a leg over his body. Still superstitiously keeping herself between this body and the world.

He prodded at the fissure in his mouth again.

Letha winced. "Stop that. I can see you doing that."

Peter looked at her. This funny little person who had put all the love inside her between him and a kicking that might have had who knew what end. One of Nicolae's main criteria in determining a woman's quality was whether or not she would help with moving the furniture. Not some womanly business like picking up the odd lamp or box of dishware, but really get in there with the men and put some teeth in it. What do you say to that, Nic?

But the fact remained that Peter still had to tell her what he'd been avoiding in the first place. He had to tell her what was going to happen tomorrow night and she was not going to like it. Especially now. She was not going to like hearing it any more than he was going to like saying it. But it did not change the fact that he had to tell her, and waiting would only make it worse. He shut his eyes and smelled her hair. In a minute.

There was a knock on the door. Lynda entered with Olivia. They had agreed it might not be safe for Peter to stay here. The full moon does bring it out in people, observed Olivia. Peter nodded, in no mood to challenge this unlikely turn of events. He rose and packed an overnight bag for Godfrey House.

○

Olivia set Peter up in a spare bedroom. In the corner there was an old mirror mounted on wooden trunnions and angled slightly up, and from where Peter stood it caught the reflection of the wall portrait of an old man with a hawk face and previously commented-on green eyes and the ghost of a smile like he'd just stuck the knife in without your even noticing.

Olivia put her hand on Letha's shoulder. "I took the liberty of calling your father."

She turned to Peter, looking at his mangled face. He could not read her expression behind the sunglasses. She put her fingers to his face but he didn't flinch. The soft knowing of her touch did not hurt him.

She left to give them a few minutes.

"Boys . . ." she said under her breath. "Boys . . ."

Peter looked into the mirror. His Swadisthana may have given him a heightened sensitivity to the frequency, but he had always been just as happy that this had never migrated up into the Third Eye. The Third Eye had struck him as depressingly literal. But tomorrow night would come the turn, the turn where he would have to do what had become inescapable since Roman got himself arrested. What the fact was, was inescapable since the night they found Brooke Bluebell. He would have to scent the *vargulf* and hunt him down and tear his throat out. It made him weak and he wanted just to lie down, but he was supported by the ongoing pain of the beating. Pain providing nothing if not a sense of priority. He did wish now for just enough of the Third Eye to provide him a view in the glass of how the world would look the morning after next, but all it contained was his own ugly beaten face. In the mirror, hands came around his midsection and clasped.

"Let's go see him," said Letha.

They went up to the attic. Shelley was downstairs; when not sleeping she held her brother's privacy as inviolate. He lay under the window. Pairs of owl eyes glimmering in the trees creating a flickering vigil. There was more natural black on Roman's scalp, and his cheeks were patchy with stubble. Letha knelt.

"I didn't even know he could grow facial hair," she said. She looked at his face. In the moonlight she could see the delicate veins in his eyes.

"If you were going to run away, would you tell me?" she said.

"I'm not going to run away," said Peter.

"I'll go with you if you run," she said.

He looked out at the round moon.

"I'm not fast enough to outrun this," he said.

She looked at the curl of Roman's ear, like a ?, and knew there was more to come and she would hate it just as much as she hated that her best friend was in a coma and seeing the beating of the first boy she had loved with all her body. She knew that whatever he was about to say was going to be like that, so she focused on the faintly luminous down of hair in Roman's ear and she waited for it.

"I need you to promise me something," said Peter. "Tomorrow night I need you to promise me you'll be home at sundown and no matter what that someone else is with you until the sun comes up. The whole night."

"What are you going to do?" she said pointlessly. She knew exactly what he was going to say and it wasn't going to improve anything hearing him say it, which made it no less necessary to hear.

"I'm going to kill it," he said.

She could just barely hear Roman's breath issuing from his nose.

"You know you're just a person, right?" she said. "That's what we all are. We're all just people."

"An hour before sundown," said Peter. "Under no circumstances leave the house. Under no circumstances let anyone in."

"And then what? The next time I see you you're in jail? At your funeral? Do I even see you again after that?"

Peter didn't have an answer and had taken too many hits to the head to make one up fast enough.

"I think you're full of shit," she said. "I think you're both fucking full of shit. You think I'm the one who needs protecting? Well, look at you. Look at both of you. What do you need to happen to understand that this isn't some kind of game? This is life."

Peter still did not answer; it was not because he didn't have one but because he was too tired to hear it himself. That what had happened the last two turns was going to happen again tomorrow night, and the whole town knew it. Unless he killed it. That this thing knew who he was and there was nothing he could do now to make himself not part of this. Unless he killed it. That he had a fear now even deeper than the cage and it was for what had happened to those other girls to happen to her, for her to be alive and watching while teeth and claws ripped open sacks of meat and jelly and shit and the life inside her. Unless he killed it. That life *is* a game, with the clearest stakes possible, and that losing it blows beyond all comprehension. He was not a killer, he did not want to kill anything, fuck all this killing.

He looked for something breakable but not valuable, punctuation, not passion. He selected a desk lamp and hurled it to the floor. Letha startled at the violence, which had been its intended effect, and he hated its efficacy.

"Either do exactly what I say or you will never see me again, you stupid little bitch," he said.

There was a wash of headlights outside; her father was here. Letha lifted Roman's hand and brushed the tears from her cheeks. She rose and smoothed out her shirt and looked at Peter. Her crying Godfrey eyes were red and green, like the worst Christmas in the world.

After she was gone, Peter sat on Roman's bed. He put a hand on Roman's shin and gave it a shake.

"Nobody here but us chickens," he said.

There was a creak and he looked up to find Shelley hovering in the doorway, reluctant to intrude. She looked at the broken lamp but would not have needed the evidence to know the air of people hurting. Peter said nothing. He bent forward and removed one of his sneakers, and then its mate. He tossed one sneaker and then the other into the air and she watched as he, with an elegiac grace, began to juggle in the dark room.

○

The following morning, Peter was prodded awake by his mother. His cheek was a welt of purple and there was a black crust on his lip that had leaked in the night and fixed to the pillow. He wanted to feel better now that he had gotten a night's sleep and his mother was here, but what he felt hadn't changed. Yesterday had still happened and so would tonight, and nothing in between changed that giant black hole of suck.

"How are you feeling?" she said.

"How do I look?" he said.

She spit on her shirtsleeve and dabbed at the side of his lip.

"Breakfast," she said.

Olivia had given Lynda the run of the kitchen and this was reflected in the volume of the offering. But it was times like these that require our greatest strength and it had just killed Lynda the night before that she couldn't feed her baby. Shelley attempted to eat with an exaggerated delicacy to compensate for the increased toll on her nerves, but every so often her salad tong clattered into the punch bowl of Cream of Wheat before her. When their eyes met Peter pulled one earlobe down and cocked the opposite eyebrow and this elicited a faint smile, but when he attempted to return it he only grimaced at the affront to his bruise. Olivia, meanwhile, hid behind smiling eyes and blithe gossip about the recent celebrity scandal as though just as pleased for this amusing disruption of routine. Peter did not know what to make of the *upir* woman's sudden hospitality, and didn't care. His mind was busy with the way Letha had flinched when he threw the lamp, and the lost look in Roman's eyes when Peter turned his back on him, and the moon that was now on the other side of the earth but couldn't have exerted greater pull over his thoughts.

After breakfast Olivia rose to take Shelley to school. Lynda took the other woman by the hand. "Your kitchen is really a dream," she said.

Olivia was demure. "One does one's best."

When Peter and Lynda were alone, Lynda rummaged for the liquor cabinet. She removed a bottle of whiskey and doctored their coffee.

"It's less than a day's drive to Toma and Crystal's farm," she said. "We can be there before you turn."

There was a hairline crack in his mug and he traced it with his fingernail.

"What if she's next?" he said.

They looked at each other and there was nothing more to say.

Peter sipped from the mug. When he swallowed, his throat was the eye of a needle. Lynda got up and came over to him and he wrapped his arms around her and buried his face into the folds of her belly and he wept and wept.

"Fuck all this killing," he said.

Someone came into the dining room and Lynda looked over. It was Roman. He did not display surprise at walking in on the Rumanceks in his dining room as much as the faint befuddlement of the overslept.

"What time is it?" he said.

PART III

THE FOREVER HOWL

The Fence

Peter and Roman sat on the hood of Roman's car and the sun was pink through the trees and the shadow of the electrical substation came at them like a slow attack of elbows.

"Will I be able to keep up?" said Roman.

"No," said Peter.

Roman threw his cigarette butt to their growing pile and lit another.

"I'm sorry I was a pain in your balls," he said.

"Don't worry about it," said Peter.

Roman looked at the crisscrossing tracks at the rail yard and straightened his arm, considering the intersection of veins at his elbow. Means of transporting iron.

"Do you love her?" said Roman.

Peter hunched forward, resting his forearms on his knees. "Yeah," he said. "Or whatever."

"Shee-it," said Roman.

"Shee-it," said Peter.

They were quiet. Peter reached into his pocket and pulled out the fragment of *Goblin Market* and handed it to Roman.

"What is this?" said Roman.

"I found it here last time," said Peter.

"What do you think it means?" said Roman.

Peter didn't answer. He was through trying to solve a wolf problem with people skills.

"Why are you giving me this?" said Roman.

Peter didn't say it. But if tonight went all to shit it would be on Roman to stay on the trail. God help us. He changed the subject.

"Do you remember anything from when you were out?" said Peter.

"No," said Roman. "Well, a feeling. I have a feeling. It's sort of like déjà vu but not. Like . . . something that's gonna happen but I forget what it is. I guess I'll know it when I see it."

He looked at the Dragon and knew now what if only he had known sooner. That it stood for something that was more powerful and more important than anything with the name Godfrey on it, and making fun of it had been a boner move.

They were quiet.

"Shee-it," said Peter.

"Shee-it," said Roman.

And then Peter felt it. Heard, that is. It starts when you hear it, in the rocks and trees and sky. Calling out your secret name. He slid off the roof of the car and undressed. He pulled his ponytail free and got on all fours. When the wise wolf stopped shaking and the red mist settled, it looked at Roman. It had the appearance of being stouter than at the previous moon; its winter coat was coming in.

"Peter?" said Roman.

The wolf looked at him but not in recognition, and then it looked away. It walked to the entrance of the mill with its head lowered and scratched at the door for entry. Roman went and pushed it open and stood back as the wolf trotted inside, nose to the ground. Roman waited outside; he accepted finally that the better part of valor was knowing when you were getting in the way. After a minute or two the wolf returned and nosed its way out and turned toward the rail yard.

"Is there a scent?" said Roman.

The wolf lifted its nose into the air.

"Do you have him?" said Roman.

The wolf shot through the rail yard for the trees. It was immediately apparent nothing on two legs could keep pace. Roman watched the wolf race over the muddy outskirts of the yard and leap over the fence. The hairs on Roman's arms prickled as he watched the wolf leap: clearing the razor wire with a brute and unsurpassable grace, its coat rippled like a breeze over a wheat field and if its paws never touched ground again Roman would have been just as happy, he would have been just as happy to watch his friend fly forever.

Then, faster than Roman could keep track, things went all to shit. A pained yelp issued from the wolf and it went all cockeyed in the air, body tumbling over legs and skidding into the brush. With whimpering pants it rose, stumbling, and attempted to push forward into the woods, but its shaking legs sent it into a drunken carom, walking into the trunk of a birch.

"Peter!" Roman cried, and he ran to the fence.

The wolf shook its head and attempted a few more steps before its legs gave out and it splayed to the ground.

"What is it!" said Roman, the panic in his chest so overpowering that it didn't occur to him he was talking to a dog.

A convulsion passed through the wolf and it was still. Roman cried out Peter's name again but the wolf just lay there. Its tongue lolled. The rise and fall of its ribs. A long, thin tube, Roman now saw, sticking from the ribs. That was the thing, whatever it was, the thing that was hurting his friend. Roman seized the fence and started to climb. There was razor wire along the top but he wasn't thinking that far ahead. He just saw his friend lying there helpless with a thing sticking out, and that was as far as he'd gotten.

"Get down."

There was a rustling in the brush and a person emerged from a few yards down, on the other side of the fence. It was Chasseur. She was camouflaged in dark khaki that was rank with deer piss to mask her own scent and she carried a rifle with a scope and there was a pack around her shoulders, and Roman realized what was sticking from the wolf: a dart.

"You don't understand," he said, still hanging on to the fence.

She stopped and shouldered the rifle and sited him.

"Get down," she said.

Roman dropped to his feet. "Listen to me," he said.

"Do not attempt eye contact," she said. "Stay ten paces back. Keep your hands visible. Do *not* attempt eye contact."

Roman averted his look. "It's not him."

Chasseur set her rifle and her pack on the ground by Peter. She did not show that she heard what he had said.

"I said it's not him!"

"How do you know that?" she said. Less to entertain the discussion than keep him amused while she did what she had to. She was willing to tranquilize him if pushed, but didn't want it to come to that. To the eye a shot is only geometry and yardage and wind, but to a still-beating heart pulling a trigger on another living body and watching it fall is to be avoided, it does not give you a good feeling. If you aren't a psychopath or a male.

"Because—" said Roman. How *did* he know that? "I was with him last time. The whole night."

"You're lying," she said. She undid the clasps of the pack.

"If you hurt him, you are dead," said Roman. "Do you hear me? *Dead*," he stressed pathetically.

"He's fine," said Chasseur. "And if you threaten me again I'll come over there and break your fucking teeth in."

She pulled a thin plastic loop from the bag and fitted it around Peter's hind legs and tightened it. Roman mashed his knuckles into his face, chastened and desperate.

"I'm sorry," he said. "But . . . I'm telling you, you don't know what you're doing right now."

She fastened another ZipCuff around his forelegs and pulled a conical steel and leather apparatus from the pack.

"It's not Peter," said Roman. "We were tracking him. That's why we came here. To get the scent."

She tucked Peter's tongue in his mouth and closed his jaws and fitted the apparatus around his snout. A muzzle.

"Just how much of what you think you know is what he told you?"

Roman looked up helpless at the spreading inkblot night. His foot sank into the ground with a mud belch. Abruptly he snapped his fingers and jabbed emphatically at the fresh paw prints.

"The *vargulf* doesn't leave tracks!" he said.

She did not deviate from fitting the straps of the muzzle.

"Didn't you hear me?" he said. "Peter leaves tracks, the killer doesn't."

"No tracks were found," she said.

Roman came forward to the fence and she put a warning hand on the rifle butt.

"It's going to be your fault," he said. "If there's another one tonight, it will be your fault."

She tightened the straps. "Roman," she said, "what can be done with fewer assumptions is done in vain with more. This is not your friend. This is not a person. I know it's hard for you to accept and I believe it's hard for him too. I believe that you wanted to find the monster, and so did he. Because he couldn't know that about himself. You can't know that about yourself and continue being a person."

Roman shook his head. "That's bullshit," he said. "That's just bullshit."

She gave Peter's restraints a once-over and stood. "This is an animal," she said. "That's what it is."

Roman looked pleadingly at her. She repeated her admonition about eye contact.

"If you're wrong, someone is going to die tonight," said Roman. "Can't you see I'm just trying to help? Why won't you let me help?"

"Because you don't believe in God," she said.

She pulled the dart from Peter. "Please go to your car and leave of your own volition. I'm going to be really pissed off if you make me shoot you."

For a moment Roman was still except for the play of shadow on the hollows of his clenching jaw. Then he turned his back to the fence and walked away.

"God doesn't want you to be happy, He wants you to be strong," she said.

She looked down at the truly marvelous specimen at her feet breathing the last of its free air. Questions of right and justness aside, the wolf would surely die in a cage. Its kind didn't know how to live in one. She knelt and placed her palms flat on its chest and belly and felt its breathing and permitted herself this one moment of pity before what had to be done was done. The death of freedom was always something to be mourned.

○

The van was parked along the train tracks a half mile away. Chasseur sat for a few moments on the back bumper and caught her breath, folding forward and pulling her lower back into a long stretch. It hurt more than it used to, humping a load that far. She didn't know whether it was her or this case, but it used to be that being in the field made her feel younger. She got up to close the rear doors but stopped, glancing a moment at the mud-caked paws. Doubt gnawed, but the method prevailed: replicable observation and measurement of material phenomena. The sanity of science of apostolic necessity in trafficking with mystery, God the most necessary hypothesis. She shut the wise wolf in.

"Take this sword: its brightness stands for faith, its point for hope, its guard for charity," she said.

She looked out at the river. On the other bank several streetlamps dotted their reflections on the water, making a series of stuttering exclamation points *!!!* She took out her phone. Holding her fingertips to the crucifix around her neck but not quite touching. She dialed.

"He's in bracelets," she said. "Make a bed."

She hung up and watched the light of her LCD screen slowly fade, then walked around to the driver's side of the van and came face-to-face with Olivia Godfrey.

"Hello again," said Olivia. She wore a satin evening gown as white as a grin and Chasseur could not account for how so glaringly absurd a thing could have gotten the drop on her, but it wasn't a priority.

Chasseur unholstered her .38 and aimed it at Olivia. Pulling a trigger on another body has its exceptions.

Olivia regarded her with a cocked head. "The cross you wear," she said, "it's not of your order."

"Mrs. Godfrey," said Chasseur, "I am going to give you one opportunity to slowly place your hands on the vehicle, and if you take one step toward me I will kill you."

Olivia's head cocked the other way. "Saint Jude. Oh, Little Mouse: What makes you feel so lost?"

She stepped forward. Her gown shimmered like the risen moon in the river.

○

And Peter woke.

He didn't know what had happened or where he was. He didn't know shit about shit. This is no way to go through life, he thought. He focused. He was nude and in a strange room—but he had been here before, the night before—he was in the guest bed at Godfrey House. And someone was standing over him. Roman. Roman was waiting for him to wake up. It was in his posture and his eyes. Roman had bad news.

Peter tried to sit up, but this was ambitious. There was a heavy groan and he realized it was coming from him. He tried to pinpoint the last thing he could remember but it was like looking at shapes underwater: nothing resolved into actual thingness and anything might eat you.

My heart really breaks for Peter here. He didn't deserve any of this, and it is with great melancholy that I picture him peeing on a tree, a lattice of diamonds imprinted on his bare back from the hammock, or pulling his hair fully around his face to become Cousin Itt, or chasing a squirrel—too slow!—up a gully. All in all, Peter's love of being Peter was so great that like an overfilled bucket of paint it slopped over even in the smallest moments of his day. No, Peter didn't deserve any of this. Though it could be said it was his fault.

"What happened?" Peter said. It was like sandbags were tied to his words.

"Alexa and Alyssa Sworn," said Roman. "The *vargulf* got the sheriff's daughters."

Peter looked at the ceiling. He had no idea what to do with this information; this was not a respectable way to go through life. Then he snapped upright and seized Roman's arm.

"*Lynda*," he said.

God Doesn't Want You to Be Happy, He Wants You to Be Strong

As Roman passed Kilderry Park he saw the black pillar of smoke issuing from down the hill and his stomach sank. He hurried, but when he reached the Rumanceks' plot there was nothing waiting but the scorched husk of the trailer. He got out and stood for a while as close to the black and buckled metal as the heat would allow. On the ground there was a carpeting of ash and debris and something fluttered into his jacket. He took it in his hands; it was the singed fragment of a Peanuts cartoon he recognized from the refrigerator. Roman released it and turned from the trailer. A broken compact mirror lay on the ground, open like a clam. It was cracked and reflected the wash of black smoke in the sky's white.

His phone rang. Peter. Destiny had had a dream in her Third Eye and retrieved Lynda in the night. They were in the city.

"How's it look?" said Peter.

"Like the last time Shelley made toast," said Roman. "Molotov cocktail, maybe. Or grenade."

Peter was quiet. Then he said, "What happened last night?"

"I don't know," said Roman. "Last I saw you were down and Chasseur was going to take you and there was nothing I could do about it. So I'm driving, just driving up and down the river until, you know, a better idea comes along, when Mom calls and says to come back and keep an eye on you. I go home, there you are. She isn't. Is she back yet?"

"No," said Peter.

"Well, looks like I won't be bringing you a change of socks." He rubbed his face and his hand came off blackened with soot.

"I watched you change back," he said. "This morning."

There was another pause. "Yeah?" said Peter.

"Yeah. It's actually . . . it's . . . beautiful."

"Okay," said Peter.

"I'm not a homo," said Roman. He hung up, noticing a black shape reflected in the driver's window, and turned to find the cat sitting a few paces off. It looked at him, flames licked the menisci of its eyes. Roman looked at the cat. It peered into his face hieratic and unknowable as the night. Roman stepped forward, scooped a hand under its belly, and tossed it into the car.

○

Peter hung up and regarded himself in the same mirror in which he had done the other night, pondering what it would reflect on this morning after the Snow Moon. It was equally useless, showing nothing but a face as grim and gray but one day older. A face without options. He had one option. Whose son was he? He slapped his bare stomach hard with both hands and went downstairs to the kitchen and rooted through the refrigerator. On the bottom shelf there was a twenty-two-ounce rib eye bulging red and wet against the wrapper. He put a cast-iron skillet on the stove and turned the burner on high and tore the meat from the package. He gave the skillet another minute to get hot before dropping the steak into a searing scream, that scream like it is just now dying. He let it sit for only a few seconds before pinching it between his fingers and flipping it. He extinguished the flame and lifted the skillet and slid the steak into his hand. The surface was brown but red juice welled in the striations and the trim of fat was still pink, and when he bit into it the center was an almost iridescent purple. Yes yes yes yes yes yes yes yes. He hardly chewed and swallowed before tearing another bite, and the next. The juice ran down his hands and his chin and the hair of his torso. He held it greedily with both hands and snapped his head back to tear the gristle. He saw Letha standing in the entryway.

Peter stood with his face glistening and the greasy trails running down his chest. Neither knew what to say. The mystery of what another person may be thinking at any given moment. Then, by nameless stimulus, he dropped the steak to the floor and they fell into each other and held.

"What do we do now?" she said eventually.

"I guess we just stand here like this until something happens next," Peter said.

She laid her face in the nook of his arm. He was clammy as though from a night of fever and smelled as bad as he looked and this sounded like a fine plan.

The front door was kicked in.

Peter seized Letha's arm and pulled her out the back door. Not thinking, but heedless obeisance to his most basic instinct, the foundation upon which all others were constructed. The woods, always run for the woods. They raced across the deck and through the yard, but before they reached the tree line there was the report of the back door banging the side of the house and along with it the Jehovan command *FREEZE*.

They froze. They turned slowly. Neck was standing in the doorframe. He was in jeans and a sweatshirt but he had a sidearm aimed at Peter. Peter had heard of the big bang theory and the idea of the whole of the universe squeezed into one little black dot but it was never something that made any sense to him until looking into the barrel of that gun pointed at him. Nose appeared, also in street clothes.

"Hands up," said Neck.

They raised their hands.

"You," said Neck, indicating Peter. "Down on the ground, you sick fucking animal."

Neck held the weapon on him as Peter lay flat on his stomach. The grass pricked his skin and it occurred to him now that it was a very cold day, how cold he was. The kind of cold like you feel you will never be warm again. Which Peter knew he would not. Nose came forward and roughly wrenched Peter's arms behind his back.

"Be careful," said Letha feebly.

Nose dug his knee between Peter's shoulder blades and pulled out a pair of handcuffs.

"Peter Rumancek," he said, "you have the right to remain fucked, you fucking deviant piece of shit."

He stood, pressing extra weight into the knee. Peter gasped.

"You have the right to fuck yourself," said Nose. "If you choose to waive this right, an ass-fucking will be provided for you in a court of law."

He kicked Peter. Letha screamed for him to stop. He ignored her. He was just getting into his element. He hauled Peter to his feet. The bolt of pain in his shoulder socket was an unwelcome distraction from the pain of the metal biting his wrists.

"You have the right," said Nose, almost singing, "to suck the hairy hose of whatever heathen god awaits you, buddy-boy— *goddammit!*"

Letha was trying to pry his hands from Peter. "I won't let you," she said.

"Stand away," said Neck.

"I won't let you." She sounded stupid like a child and gouged her fingernails into Nose's knuckles.

"Don't," said Peter. Her intervention before had saved him from a gang of boys, but these were men with guns and a mission and fighting it was only the difference between its happening here in front of her eyes or by the river somewhere, a bridge overhead like the underbelly of a snake. Assholes.

"Back off!" said Nose, shoving her. She fell to the ground and

Nose snaked a forearm hard around Peter's windpipe. Peter choked for air.

"Stay down or I break his goddamn neck."

He jerked Peter toward the house. Letha watched, sunken by her own powerlessness. A condition that seemed to give people named Godfrey so much trouble to understand.

Peter met her eye and he tried to say several important things with that look. When you have nothing else, have dignity, he tried to say. Nicolae had always told him that and he never knew how he himself would do in practice.

Tell Lynda when the time comes that with my last spit I will spit in their eye and with my last breath curse them so their dicks fall off, he said with his eyes. Tell Lynda when she feels the wind just before the first rain of spring it's me, that will be me checking to make sure she is still just as fat as she is today.

And Roman. Help Roman become a man on the path of light and love. Not the other way. Tell Roman . . . all the things I couldn't.

You are as full of light and love as anyone I know, his eyes said. I'm sorry I will never see the baby hanging off your tits. I'm sorry I will never see your tits again. They're good tits and I'll miss them.

Nose threw a fist into Peter's kidneys. "This one's sweating like a nigger trying to read," he said.

Behind the pain, this struck Peter as odd—didn't he realize how cold it was?

There was a creak and Shelley emerged onto the deck. Neck looked over and said, "Christ, fucking perfect."

"Go back inside," said Nose.

Shelley didn't move.

"Get back in the goddamn house," said Nose.

Shelley began swaying from side to side. She made a low keening noise like an anxious ruminant.

"Fucking wonderful," said Neck.

"Back in the fucking house!" said Nose.

"You don't need to yell at her," said Peter. He waited for the blow to follow and was obliged: the man's fist landed on the side of his head. The keen became a muted wail as Shelley covered her face and reeled.

"Will you deal with that fucking thing?" said Nose, shaking out his knuckles.

But there was a noise inside and Neck stood to the side of the door out of view of anyone else who might join this party.

"You don't have to do this," said Letha quietly, still sitting on the ground. "You think you do, but you don't."

Nose's face went red as a drunk's and the veins in his neck stood out. "One more word and buddy-boy gets gutted like a fucking fish right here!"

Shelley began to flash discordantly.

"What the Christ?" said Neck.

Roman emerged then from the house. Everyone but Shelley was silent. Roman surveyed the scene. He did not see Neck.

"There is," said Neck, "a gun pointed at the back of your head. Do not, repeat, *do not* turn around."

Roman turned.

"*Back off,*" said Neck.

Roman looked in his eyes. "Put the gun in your mouth," said Roman.

Neck put the gun in his mouth. Nose started to come at Roman, but Roman cast a finger at him without taking his eyes from Neck and said, "If he moves, pull the trigger."

Neck's eyes bulged and he grunted hoarsely and Nose stopped. Roman went to Shelley. He put his hands behind her head and pulled her to a crouch so his forehead touched hers and he breathed with her down to a gentle lull. He was calming because he was calm himself. He had made mistakes out of confusion but just now, when he had pulled up out front, he had heard the sound of his sister needing his help and this was all the focus he needed.

Letha stood by Peter. She did not understand what she had

just seen happen but did not need to. She reached for Peter's face and smoothed the bangs from his eyes and tucked them behind his ear. She needed to do that.

Roman addressed Nose. "Uncuff him."

Nose hesitated.

Roman looked at Neck. His face beaded sweat and he panted through his nostrils.

"If he's still handcuffed by the time I count to three, pull the trigger," said Roman.

"One," said Roman.

Nose freed Peter's hands. Peter rubbed the red rings on his wrists. Nose cast his eyes fierce and fearful to the ground, the mirror of an adolescent dealing with a hated cop.

Peter took Letha's hand. He saw Shelley observe this small intimacy and waved with a pinkie. No one's forgetting you.

"You will go to your car," Roman instructed Neck. "That faggot will take 19 to the Allegheny County line."

"There's no reason to call him a faggot," Letha said.

"That . . . knucklehead will take 79 to the West Virginia state line. At that point you can take the gun out of your mouth. And you"—addressing his partner—"punch yourself in the nose."

O

"Someone told her," said Nurse Kotar. "We were going to wait until you came to decide how to handle the . . . situation. But she knows."

Godfrey breathed deeply and tried to think of all the reasons not to put his fist through the drywall but the only one was habit. He didn't anyway.

"What's her condition?" he said.

"Catatonia. Not crying, not speaking. I had to double-check to make sure she was blinking. And Doctor. Her hair."

He went to Christina Wendall's room. She was in the arm-chair and her feet were flat on the floor and her hands were in her lap. Normally she was so full of nervous energy that in the moment he could not remember seeing anything sadder than her hands being still. Her hair had gone uniform white. Godfrey shivered, the window was open. But her arms were bare. She was wearing a spaghetti-strap shirt and her skinny arms and shoulders were indifferent in the chill.

"Christina," said Godfrey. She looked at him but he expected no response and she gave him none. His heart wasn't in it anyway. The thing between her and him right now was greater charity than any he might provide. He took the blanket from the bed and tucked it around her shoulders. This paternal reflex gave rise to another he probably should have curbed. But he was a father and a human, and he was tired. He brushed the hair from her face and kissed her cheek.

The door opened and Godfrey quickly straightened. Nurse Kotar stood in the threshold.

"Why is this window open?" said Godfrey, misdirecting his own impropriety.

"I'm sorry, Doctor, I don't know. But your daughter is on the line. She said it was an emergency."

Wisdom Is Where the Brain Meets the Heart

The chapel stood against the tree line under the gray of the sky, near enough in shade that it could have been an afterthought from the same brush. In the sanctuary, dusk light filled the chapel and cobwebs stretched between the crossbeams and the outside air sent small dust devils up the aisle as Dr. Godfrey shut the heavy oak doors. He assessed the situation and soon after took Roman back across the campus to the main facility on a supply run, Peter still needing clothes and Godfrey needing information that separating the suspects was more likely to provide. Godfrey put an arm around his nephew.

"Good to see you walking, kiddo. Now what the hell is going on?"

"Sometimes . . ." said Roman, and then he stopped, hesitating.

"Sometimes what?" said Godfrey.

"Sometimes a wolf goes crazy and doesn't eat what it kills."

Godfrey's first impulse was to consider this an evasion, but something older and deeper told him otherwise.

"When you say *a wolf*, what exactly do you mean?"

"I mean a werewolf."

Godfrey considered this. Any other day of his adult life and he would have been detaching himself and analyzing the cause of this shared delusion—plainly enough, it wasn't a lie. But he had resolved in the blue dawn, looking into his coffee and seeing the whorl of cream and knowing absolutely he was witness to the transmigration of two souls, knowing it had happened again and it hadn't happened to her and being as thankful as he was for anything, he had resolved to emerge from the world of shadow and come to a Rational Explanation for what was going on, and now in light of day it was necessary and impractical clarification he finally achieved. There was no such explanation. So, unfettering oneself of irreconcilables, where did this leave one? A werewolf loose in Hemlock Grove. How offensively obvious. And more striking than simple credulity was the realization that in a dark and hermetic corner of his mind he had of course known already.

He gestured to a bench and sat.

"Is it Peter?" he said, cringing inside.

"It's not Peter."

"Peter isn't a werewolf?"

"He is. But it's not him."

Godfrey was unsure how he felt about this.

"I was with him last night," said Roman.

Godfrey nodded. "And you've been trying to find this . . . bad werewolf?"

"He's not really bad, he's just sick," said Roman.

"But you didn't find him?"

"I was in a coma."

Godfrey chuckled. *Oh that.*

"Supposing," said Godfrey, "you were to sum up as much as you've actually learned that we can use."

Roman thought about it. He shrugged. Godfrey waited for something to follow but realized the shrug itself was his answer.

He patted Roman's knee and squeezed. "I believe," he said and nodded at the chapel, "they'll be able to keep themselves entertained long enough for us to step into my office and have a drink."

They stood and continued.

"So we have another month to find the bad wolf," said Godfrey.

"*Vargulf*," said Roman.

"*Gesundheit*," said Godfrey. "In the meantime keeping that one away from the torches and pitchforks?"

Roman nodded. *More or less.*

Godfrey flicked the edge of a withered holdout birch leaf. So, a goal. Or something. And compared with living day to day with your head in a lion's mouth of cloying and impenetrable nothing, what was there to say? Wisdom was where the brain met the heart and what he felt right now was the literal difference between life and death. He felt something that he hadn't felt since his aborted attempt to break things off with Olivia. He felt like drinking to be more and not less awake.

"Where's your mother?" he asked.

Roman looked off down the path.

"She's with Shelley."

○

It was nearly dark and the two of them were alone. Dr. Godfrey would return after nightfall to bring food and take her home. They lay on a pile of blankets on the altar, Peter wearing scrubs and Godfrey's sweater and Letha in his arms. Above them the stained glass was pelted by a light rain.

"They were in their beds," said Letha. "The sheriff was on a call. But he had a car outside, and they didn't see anything. Whatever it was got in without being seen and . . . did that. That's no wild animal. What kind of person has it in them to do that?"

The cat leaped onto the windowsill and sat; his dangling tail flicked, keeping time. Peter slipped his hand up under her shirt and ran his hand in slow hemispheres over her stomach. She toyed with the snake ring encircling her finger.

"Do you think plastic has a consciousness like stone or wood?" she said. "Do you think it remembers where it's been?"

She took his arm and pulled it over her snug and they lay

listening to the rain for a while. She thought about the life that grew inside her and the shadow of all this death. That if a thing is defined in contrast that's what life is, the shadow of death. So the mystery of death couldn't be the bad thing, because without it there wouldn't be life. The badness was life, just life happening, as essential a part of the good as the good. And what was there to do but to take it as it comes and to hope, to hope constantly and carnally and with no time to lose.

She pulled his hand over her breast.

"In . . . church?" he said.

Afterward they fell still, glowing and panting. She lay over him, unmoving, in routine feminine disregard for the man's body heat situation in such circumstances, but earlier in the day he had known he would never be warm again so he'd take it. Suddenly a black blur caught Peter's eye, the cat bolting from the window. And he looked over just in time to notice movement on the other side of the glass, a fleeting apparition disappearing before he could make anything out but the red-stained shock of white hair.

○

Shelley still seemed shaken when Roman got home so he tucked her in for a nap and said he would make dinner. The steak package was still on the kitchen counter, dried pink on the white diaper pad, and the meat on the floor had been stepped on. He cleaned up and was running hot water over the mop when Olivia said, "What happened to the front door?"

Roman turned. She wore a long white cardigan with the sleeves hanging girlishly past her thumbs and her hair was in a ponytail, and there was nothing in her demeanor to suggest she had been missing a night and a day or all the things that had happened in that time.

"Where have you been?" he said.

"The institute. I had a bit of a spell. But Johann says it's nothing to worry about."

They looked at each other.

"I feel much better now," she said.

Roman wrung out the mop.

○

At the other Godfrey household Marie was waiting for her husband and daughter to arrive. Dr. Godfrey had a sinking feeling, confronted with her in the foyer. She had known Letha was with him and even called twice to verify when they would be home. So what now?

"It was the soonest we could get away," he said, preempting his defense.

She did not respond. She came forward, that tension deliquescing like snow packed in a tight fist, and she seized Letha and held tightly. There was a tremor in her shoulders. She had not been angry, she just needed to hold her daughter.

Letha went upstairs and Godfrey sat in the armchair in the living room and exhaled. Long day. Long long day. Marie sat on the arm of the chair and rested a hand on the back of his neck and squeezed. They didn't look at each other, he just sat and felt the good pressure on his neck.

"Have you eaten?" said Marie.

Godfrey shook his head.

"I made you a mouse," said Marie, making her voice nasal in an impression of the actress Ruth Gordon. "A nice chocolate mouse."

Godfrey smiled and his shoulders shook and he began laughing. The explanation for why this was funny to them goes back a long way.

Godfrey said that he was going to grab a shower, and that that sounded perfect.

Godfrey showered, and parsed with the heedless lucidity of exhaustion the guilt he felt over the ugliness of his thoughts toward his wife, a woman whose greatest crime was giving her best years to a marriage with a man who was in love with an enemy she knew had the power to destroy her family. And he came to the second revelation of the day, and emphatically more immediate and inconvenient than the acceptance of men from time to time becoming wolves. He was ashamed. He was ashamed and so was Marie, ashamed over their years of complicity in never saying it: he was married to a woman he hadn't loved since the first time he saw Olivia.

He looked down and had a vision of the particles of dead flesh breaking from his torso and sluicing down the drain. Well, that was wrong. That was the wrong way to live.

He turned and cracked his spine. Six months, he decided. Six months was reasonable to acquit his obligations. After the birth. Twenty years ago, six months would have been an eternity. All those dinner parties, the slow, sweet poison of lingering glances, clinking glasses with her ringing through him for days after; ultimately the crisis as a doctor and a husband and a brother whether or not to take her on as a patient, the woman he'd contrived every opportunity to see if only to feel her fingers graze his arm as she laughed. Knowing before ever seeing it that her ass was like a stationary drop of water on a flower stem—twenty years ago, the six months it took before the first time he took possession of this remarkable ass were a torment.

Coming off a stretch of forty eventful waking hours, Godfrey felt something he had difficulty identifying at first. Something that in practical reality could hardly be less self-evident or inalienable. He felt free. Just imagine. After the passage and permutation of so much time, time a wheel always turning back on itself and yet moving forward all the while, he would in six months finally arrive at the destination of a long and by the day more astonishing journey. He would live right and have faith in love. He would become a grandfather, and he would marry Olivia.

Later, in bed, Dr. Godfrey finally fell into the most earned sleep of his life.

And then his phone rang to inform him Christina Wendall had disappeared.

The Price

With a troubling sense of déjà vu Peter was shaken awake by Roman the second day running.

"I ordered a redhead," said Peter.

Roman did not acknowledge the joke.

"What?" said Peter.

Roman walked to the pulpit and placed both hands flat. Hoping the pose might invest him with . . . he didn't know what. But it didn't do anything, so he just said what there was to say.

"Another one."

"Another what?"

"Last night. Another girl."

Peter was quiet for a moment.

"Who?" he said.

"They don't know. No head. But it wasn't her. I went there before I came here."

Peter was quiet. He put his fingertip to the floorboard and traced the words *thank you* in the old tongue and then blew the words away.

"It was the wrong moon," said Roman. "That's impossible, right?"

"Sure," said Peter agreeably.

The cat leaped onto the pulpit and raised his haunch pleasurably as Roman knuckled where his tail met his rear.

"Now what?" said Roman.

Peter lay back and closed his eyes.

"We need to talk to Destiny," he said. "Destiny knows more about the protocols than I do. She might have an idea."

He did not add that she better, because he was out of his own.

"If you go anywhere, you're going to get shot," said Roman. "Shot if you're lucky."

"You go. And hurry. You need to be with Letha by sundown. No chances tonight, she's on your watch. She's on your watch until this is over. That's your job now."

Roman looked at Peter. The motes in the light that fell between them went about their own affairs.

"I know," said Roman.

The cat splayed on his back and Roman rubbed his belly. He curled like a black velvet fist around his hand and bit him.

"Hey hey hey," said Roman, "we don't love with our teeth."

He cut through a trail not far from the chapel that ran from the campus between the hills. The opposite mouth of the trail opened on 443 and Dr. Godfrey had said to use it for their comings and goings. Little knowing this precaution failed in preventing Christina Wendall from spying uncle and nephew spiriting provisions to the chapel the previous afternoon. How little we all knew.

Roman drove to Destiny's apartment in Shadyside. While parking, he noticed in the street a crow picking at something flat and black on the pavement. Roadkill. Something off somehow. Roman got out and saw that the crow was feeding on the remains of another crow. A black feather tufted from the diner's beak. This was highly distressing to Roman.

"Hey!" he said in the admonishing tone of a counselor to a rowdy camper. "You—you stop that! No way, José!"

The crow looked at him, but when he didn't move any closer it resumed a disinterested pecking at its brethren as though nibbling more out of boredom than anything else and Roman felt a queasy impotence in chastising this abysmal augur. He shook it off as best he could and went upstairs and was admitted by Lynda, who seized him into a embrace that crushed an exhalation from his diaphragm.

"How is he? How's my baby?"

"He's safe," Roman said.

"What does he need?" said Destiny.

Roman brought her up to speed. Destiny pursed her lips and nodded mechanically for a while after he had stopped speaking.

"How is this happening?" said Roman.

She was uncomfortable. She picked up a shaker of salt from the table and shook some into her hand and threw it over her left shoulder. It was cold comfort.

"The laws of magic are like the laws of anything," she said. "They work because you obey them."

"You can just break them?" he said.

"Not for free," she said.

"How do we fight it?" he said.

She looked at him. "It's time for you to admit this isn't your fight."

"How does Peter fight it?" he said.

"How do wolves usually fight?" she said.

"Can Peter do the same thing? Turn when the moon is wrong?"

"Not for free," she said.

Lynda had been quiet but interjected now. "What's the price?" she said.

"I don't know," said Destiny. "The only person who can know the answer to that is Peter. I can give him what he needs to find the answer, but I have to tell you, I'm pessimistic, Lyn. I'm pessimistic there's any answer that isn't going to be a giant shit sandwich for him to eat."

Lynda considered this. "The brother of the man Nicolae killed found us years and years later," she said eventually. "Nicolae had to become a murderer twice in his life; these fires go out but the coals don't. If this isn't ended it will be just around the corner every day of his life. And if you don't let a boy become a man, it's no one's fault but your own when you're still wiping his ass when he should be making you grandchildren."

Destiny said nothing. She went to a shelving unit and began rummaging through drawers.

Lynda took both of Roman's hands in hers, and looking at her face he knew that what he was seeing was a person doing the hardest thing she was ever called to in her life. He knew that this was the face he would be forced to look into for all eternity if he fucked this up.

"I miss when he was a baby," she said. "If I could flip a switch, I'd just live in a whole world of babies."

Shortly after, Destiny gave him the provisions Peter would require but stopped him from leaving immediately. She stood in front of him and faced him, casting her eyes just over the top of his head and then closing them. After a moment she opened them again and said okay.

"What?" he said.

"Your Sahasrara," she said. She held a hand over her own crown, indicating. "Sometimes it glows."

○

They lit five beeswax candles and within this perimeter made a consecrate circle of chalk in the aisle, and Roman took a small satchel and emptied it in the center, making a pile of ash of willow bark and beggar's button and powdered greenfly, the still point in a turning world.

They held hands and the ganglia of their palms kindled discreetly as the frequency passed between them and Peter quietly said the old, old words as they walked three times the sinister path around the consecrate circle. This done, Roman did not know if he ought to be detecting any sort of shift in the balance of things, but he was not as sensitive as Peter.

"We . . . in business?" he said.

Peter didn't answer. Roman didn't speak, he didn't like the look that was now on Peter's face, and neither did Peter, wearing it. Peter walked down a pew and hunkered to his knees. Then straightened, returning with Fetchit in his arms. He knelt in the circle. The candle flicker spooked the cat and it attempted to worm free, but Peter held fast even as the struggle intensified with slashing claws and an unsettlingly human whine.

But . . . I trusted you, thought the cat.

"What are you doing?" Roman said.

"You might want to turn around," said Peter.

"What are you doing?" Roman said again.

Peter looked at him. Roman turned and looked up at the organ loft and the sounds of the cat's resistance ended with a popping sound like a shoulder dislocating. It was the worst thing he'd ever heard.

"It's over," said Peter.

But Roman didn't turn. He now hated the food in his stomach. He hated his relief that he had not been called, that this really was Peter's fight. He heard Peter open a penknife.

"I'm going to go outside for a minute," said Roman.

"Okay," said Peter. "That's okay."

Roman walked out and sat on the front steps. Storm clouds overhead as though someone had stood on the hills and run a roller of black paint over the sky. Roman wondered if someone was in a plane over the cloud cover at that moment, closing his window to block out the sun. Roman hoped his chair got kicked. He reached into his blazer and took out the tin mint container. Opened it and took out a Xanax and chewed it, the bitter lingering on his tongue. A little while after, the door opened behind him and Peter emerged.

"What are you doing?" said Roman. "You can't be out here."

But Peter did not look at him and Roman saw his eyes were like the eyes of the wolf, eyes with no regard for making conversation. He walked to the tree line and disappeared. Roman popped another Xanax and the cloud bank became a luminous bruise as lightning flickered without sound.

Roman waited on the steps.

"What the fuck," said Roman and his eyes were hot with water. "The fucking cat."

A few minutes later Peter emerged from the tree line and sat next to Roman on the steps. He didn't say anything. He stared off in the manner of a person who had just been handed one giant shit sandwich. Roman waited for him to say something.

"Bacon," said Peter eventually.

Roman waited for him to say more than that.

"I'm going to need bacon grease," said Peter.

"Is that how you fight it?" said Roman.

"Yeah," said Peter.

"Is there . . . a price?" said Roman.

Peter rubbed his face.

"It's my face," said Peter. "The price is my human face."

Roman rose and put his hands in his pockets as though to take the air. But he didn't go anywhere. He just stood there on the steps next to Peter with his hands in his pockets.

"Did Nicolae really walk across the ocean with lily pads on his feet?" said Roman.

"No," said Peter. "He stole a car at the nearest farm and sold it for airfare."

"Oh," said Roman.

"I'm going to need bacon grease," said Peter. "A lot of it."

"Sure," said Roman.

○

At Godfrey House, Roman stood over an iron skillet of a full pound of bacon spitting and cackling like perdition's coven when he felt a pair of hands massage his neck.

"I believe," said Olivia, "that's enough cholesterol to see you comfortably into your dotage."

Roman prodded at the skillet with a spatula.

"It's going to end tonight," he said. "Tonight we're going to kill it."

She squeezed. "Do turn the fan on. It will stink of pig to high heaven."

When it was finished Roman drained the grease into a Tupperware container and wrapped the strips in wax paper and set them aside for Shelley. He went out to his car and Olivia followed and placed a hand on his arm. He turned to her and took the shame over his softness in the chapel and made it hardness here. He was going to stand by Peter. Nothing was going to stop him from standing by Peter.

"If you may spare a moment for your mother," she said.

He studied her face, holding the hardness of his own. She was holding a thin black attaché case.

"Please, Roman," she said.

He set the container in the passenger side and she took his hand and led him to the back of the house, where he saw that she had moved the freestanding floor mirror from the guest room to the patio. On its oval face there was simple line drawing of a wolf made with white nail polish and within its chest a spot of red. Its heart. She handed him the attaché case and told him to open it. Inside was a small and ornate double-bladed axe. It was made of silver and the handle consisted of the bodies of two intertwining serpents, the heads flattening into the blade edges. It had the gleam of a recent polish but this was cosmetic: make no mistake, it was very very old. She drew him to the mirror and stood behind him. She placed her hands on his shoulders and told him to look into the glass and he did. She asked what he saw.

He didn't understand. "I see us," he said.

"Look closer," she said.

He met her eyes in the mirror and lids of his own fluttered and fingers came from the shadow place and closed around his field of vision and things went dark. But there was a sound. His ears were filled with the sound of a pulse, but it was not his own. He felt this pulse ringing in all of his nerve endings and he saw again, he saw through the pall of the shadow like the sun burning through cloud and he knew he was standing on a threshold and he knew what was real: the mirror, and in the mirror the heart of the wolf pumping and alive, and this was what his mother had wanted him to see.

It was his Kill.

Roman lifted the axe over his head and could feel with the back of his neck his mother's smile, and he brought the axe plunging down into the heart of it.

The breaking glass returned Roman to his senses and he backed away, panting and in a sweat in the cold air. Olivia pulled the axe from the splintered backboard and placed it back into the case and handed it to Roman.

"Try not to lose it," said Olivia, "it goes back rather a long way."

He did not know what to say. He did not have words for his gratitude. She put a hand to his face.

"We don't need words," she said.

You Moved

Sunset is at 4:55. You'll want to keep that in mind.

○

4:12 p.m.

Chasseur woke to the sight of angels' wings. They were spread on the wall above her, the color of rust and portent, whether rising or falling in the eye of the beholder. She attempted to move but found that both her wrists and feet were bound by her own ZipCuffs. She rolled to one side. The floor on which she lay was covered with paper and detritus, and several yards away was a door opening on the main floor of the mill building, the outline of the Bessemer visible over the rail of the stairs. She rolled to the other side. There was another pair of wings on the floor next to her, and more on the ceiling. It had to be admired, grudgingly: the artistic spirit in its purest incarnation, unintended for the eyes of the living. But more relevant to her reconnaissance: the artist herself was absent, leaving her for the moment alone, and there was a west-facing window jagged with broken glass like broken teeth through which the setting sun was visible, perfectly framed between the hilltop and cloud bank like God's eye peering through, as astonishing and unprecedented a sight as every sunset of her life. So another gift, the two crucial elements of an escape-and-evade scenario: time and opportunity.

She rolled to her belly and wended to the wall. It occurred to her that she no longer smelled of the urine she'd used to mask her own scent, or for that matter her own evacuation, which would have been an inevitable consequence of being unconscious for a day or more. She had been cleaned, her clothes laundered. And she felt between her legs a strange but familiar imposition: a feminine sanitary product, too long for her and ill-fitting, not her preferred brand. At least two days then, if it was that time of her cycle. She couldn't connect her last waking memory with her present circumstances but how she got here wasn't what mattered, getting out was. She shifted to a wobbling kneel, reached for the windowsill, and pulled herself to a standing position. From there she pivoted, bracing her elbow for increased stability, and brought the plastic of the ZipCuffs to a shard of glass and ran her hands back and forth in a sawing motion. Hands. Those unassuming appendages neither toothed nor clawed that had given that unlikely ape *Homo sapiens* dominion over all other carnivores. She pictured the hands that had cleaned and dressed her and stuck a tampon up her, the ones she was going to remove from their wrists and in a forgivably Protestant homage nail them to the front door. Take this sword: its brightness stands for faith . . .

The ZipCuff slipped suddenly and her arm plunged downward, the glass entering the flesh of her palm and snapping off as she fell on her back. It hurt but there wasn't enough time to hurt; she held the arm out in appraisal and blood issued unchaste down the jag of glass. She brought the glass between her teeth and pulled it free, clamping tight and bringing the ZipCuff to it and finally severing it. But the victory was short-lived: she nearly swallowed the glass at the sound above her of a turning flint wheel.

Chasseur looked up at Olivia, who regarded her from the doorway. She was wearing her sunglasses and lighting a cigarette and Chasseur was suddenly uncertain whether or not she had been standing there this entire time, if moments before she had simply looked right through her like a rainbow visible at only the precise angle.

Olivia said nothing, watching her, and despite the sunglasses Chasseur knew her sight line as well as if it had been drawn with a dotted line: she was looking at the wound. As a woman in the military Chasseur had thought she knew what this was like, but the reality was something else entirely: being looked at like . . . meat. Chasseur worked her hand under her shirt and out of view. She looked away from Olivia and up at the wings, disappointed. Not unintended for the eyes of the living, but set decoration for her own black box theater. Fucking actresses.

Chasseur fought for air, for the awareness of air going in and out. Of course Chasseur had imagined her own martyrdom; it had been part of her training. But when sleeping with a lover Chasseur could never lie face-to-face because anytime her own inhalations and exhalations married so closely with the inhalations and exhalations of another she became acutely convinced she was breathing in pure carbon dioxide. She had never imagined it feeling like this, like everything about it was somehow wrong.

The blood from Chasseur's hand spread out in her shirt in a blossom. She felt Olivia's eyes on it, they had never left. Chasseur closed her eyes.

"Hmmm," said Olivia. This recalled to her a fond memory. "When I was a young girl there was a game I used to play with my cousins, wicked little beasts of the first rank. The game was called Wolves in the Wood, and 'play *with*' perhaps misstates it, implying my consent as part of the proceeding. At any rate, after the moon had risen they would spirit me out to the forest, an enchanted place in the fullest sense of the word, filled with mysteries and nameless dangers prowling in the dark, and there would be hell to pay if we were caught. They would lay me down on a bed of moss—I can feel it to this day on the back of my neck—and I was to close my eyes and keep perfectly still as they circled through the trees on tiptoes, growling deep in their throats and warning me that there were *wolves* on the hunt with a taste for *little girls,* and that the slightest movement on my part would give me away and I'd be gobbled up in a blink. Of course I was terrified for life and limb and would do my utmost to escape this monstrous fate, but the harder I concentrated on not betraying myself, the more impossible it became not to smile. Fatal! A great cry would then go up—*you moved! you moved!*—and with yips and howls they would descend on me and cover my body head to toe with kisses."

Chasseur opened her eyes. "Write it on the bottom of your shoes for the devil to read," she said.

Olivia removed her sunglasses and placed them in her purse. She looked at Chasseur. There was no distinction between pupil and iris in her eyes, it was as though they had been overlaid with golden red rose petals and backlit by an opposing sun. She put her purse on the ground.

"Oh, Little Mouse," she said. "You moved."

○

4:39 p.m.
The last of the sun had disappeared and the hills had gone dark with pinpricks of light as though containing a single source of it inside when an institute van pulled alongside Olivia's truck, like opposing pieces of a game as old and esoteric as the totem overlooking it. Dr. Pryce exited carrying a plain canvas tote bag. There was a tar drum between the hot stoves and the river with an orange glow in its mouth and he went to it. Next to the drum was Olivia's purse and within what remained of what was formerly her outfit, streaked in crimson and engulfed in flame. He looked at the water. An unbelonging whiteness breached the surface as

though expelled from the river's unconscious. Olivia standing nude, waist deep, staring off at those lights dotting the hillside and gently disrupting the surface tension with a slow back-and-forth motion of her arms. Pryce's eye fell to the scar on the small of her back, all that demarcated her as an earthly body. He said nothing, the tableau too immaculate for her to be unaware of an audience. Eventually she turned and waded back, emerging on the bank and standing before him. She was covered with goose-flesh and her nipples were small and dark and black trails of mascara ran down from her eyes. Pryce handed over the bag and placed his hands on a broken length of rebar that stuck from the ground.

"In there," said Olivia, indicating the mill building. "Still warm, for whatever use that brings you."

"Lod isn't going to like this," said Pryce.

"If they want Norman's share they'll learn to," she said. "They knew where they were sending the little golliwog."

She shook her head. One did have to admire the ingenuity: recruiting women and homosexual military veterans with a background of sexual trauma likely to require the validation of an external patriarchal figure. But honestly: "The Order of the Dragon"—what utter poppycock.

"This was irresponsible," said Pryce. "And . . . uncalled-for."

He waited for her to react; in the history of their relationship he had never registered such direct insubordination.

She looked searchingly into his face and gave a sympathetic cluck. "You *liked* her."

Pryce was silent; nothing in the position of utilitarian ambivalence this arrangement forced him into was quite so galling as her ultimate trespass: knowing at any given moment what he was actually feeling.

Olivia removed from the bag a pair of surgical scrub bottoms and a sweatshirt. He watched her dress.

"Why is it that you're the only one who hasn't asked me what I'm really doing?" he said.

She gave him a why-do-you-think look. "Because I don't care," she said.

"Do you know who it is that's killing these girls?" said Pryce.

She took her wet hair in both hands and squeezed excess water from it.

"Of course I do, Johann," she said. "I'm a mother."

She knelt and picked up her purse. The hem of the sweatshirt rode up, revealing the pale of her back.

"You know I can fix you," he said. "Your scar."

She produced a compact mirror and regarded her reflection, wiping away streaks of mascara.

"The less you pursue this line of conversation," she said, "the more likely we are to remain friends."

Just then, somewhere in the valley, there was a rifle shot. Her head snapped, but not in surprise—he realized that behind the Olivia Show she had been steeling herself all along for its coming: the break. Several more shots followed, a flinch going through her body with each, and she made no attempt to conceal it, nor could she. How afraid she was.

Then it was quiet again and she replaced the compact and walked past Pryce, making her way delicately in bare feet.

"Clean it up," she said.

He did not turn, hearing the truck start up and pull away. The fire in the drum had burned down to embers, ash commingling with all the previous ash from all the previous fires, leaving only a dustbin for the next time Olivia decided to ruin a dress. Now he turned downriver, seeking the cap of the institute over the ridge.

"A lighthouse guiding a lone vessel through evil waters if ever there was one full stop," said Pryce. "He reminded himself comma again comma that whatever sacrifice of personal conscience comma even his humanity comma was required of him was ultimately of scant consequence in his penance full stop. A body comma he was making his best girl a body comma and until he had perfected the procedure for Shelley Godfrey's rebirth into a body to make the world love her as much as he did comma whatever was required of him to keep the lights on was a small price full stop."

And then the light of the White Tower went dark.

"What in blue blazes!" said Pryce.

○

Dr. Godfrey pulled into the drive of Godfrey House to find it empty of vehicles. He got out of the car and went to the porch and sat on the steps. The last thing he had to spare right now was a moment to call his own; it felt like stealing from the gods. His stop before this one had been to the hospital morgue to view the last girl; if it was who he thought it was this appointment was manifestly his. But to his surprise the body was too sexually mature to be Christina's, surprising because his wishing it on someone else continued to be granted and he knew he'd be paying for it somehow or other. It wouldn't hurt, he knew. Being consumed by a wild animal would not actually cause pain, fear triggering the release of naturally occurring opioids that would act as an analgesic. To die in that way wouldn't hurt, because you would be in a perfect euphoria of fear. And then he was scooped: a concerned roommate had called inquiring about a small burn scar on the inner left forearm and the latest had a name. Godfrey was left with a need to hold a woman's body, full of unruly life and lust and all the terrifically maddening things this beast ravened with love gone bad. And for this sudden carnal imperative what better archetype? But she wasn't here, nor had he had any contact in the last few days. Not that it mattered, really; he had spent so many years building a rational empire of words in a war against his own blood but now he couldn't give less of a shit what or wasn't spoken, he was possessed once more by something he actually *wanted*. He wanted to defeat the monster and save his family. He felt a light tickle on his wrist and looked down to find a daddy longlegs traversing it. He brought his arm to eye level and watched the spider move with a kind of startlement as though first encountering such an apparatus.

"Even if it is the world's most fucked-up family," he said.

There was a creak and he felt a dip in the boards under his posterior. He shook the spider free and slid to the side and patted the empty spot beside him. Shelley sat. They both looked out at the dip beyond the yard and the valley rolling out. It would soon be night and the lamppost at the end of the property came on. He reached and rubbed between her shoulders.

"It's almost over," he said.

He meant it as a comforting platitude but at the same time found it was true; like a sleeping body aware that the alarm would soon be going off he could feel it, the cusp of the end. Thankfully.

"Everyone's safe," he said. "Letha's home. The boys are at the chapel. Your mother . . ." He realized he hadn't the slightest idea where she might be, and that it would no more occur to either of them to be concerned for her safety than the sudden inversion of gravity, a cognitive unviability.

"Your mother and I are complicated," he said. "In the sense that a hadron collider is complicated. I'm sorry it meant lying to you. We've been lying about it so long I almost forgot there was anyone who still believed it. But that doesn't make it any less crummy."

He was quiet, then went on.

"You're a lamp," he said. "You shine on people and you're either going to show what's best in them or what's the most crummy. And you always got the best of me because there you were, lighting the way. So it's even worse how you had to learn about my shitheel side. But that's your tragedy, and nothing breaks my heart more: you're always going to be surrounded by people who don't deserve you."

Shelley turned to him. There was a glimmering in her eyes,

but not of water: it was a gossamer film of light. Godfrey looked away, a stone in his throat. Never in his lifelong quest for it had he encountered a purer promise of redemption, or felt less deserving.

His phone rang.

"I'm sorry," he said, voice faltering. "I . . . I have to get this."

He answered. It was Intake. He listened to the latest and then said he'd be there as soon as possible.

"Have him wait in my office," he said. "Try to keep it from going off in act three."

He hung up.

"I have to go," he said. "The sheriff is admitting himself, but he won't surrender his gun. The Fredericks family found him sitting in their driveway with his rifle in his lap, singing Patsy Cline. No good ever came out of possessing a firearm in a Patsy Cline–singing mood."

Shelley looked at him questioningly.

"Jennifer Fredericks," he said. "She was the last one."

She stared at him. The light in her eyes suddenly flared like looking directly into the noonday sun and he looked away, blinking.

"Are you okay?" he said. "Shelley . . ."

She rose. A noise escaped her, a low moan of bestial desolation: betrayal, in the way that all personal wounds are a kind of betrayal, and disbelief that such a thing had actually happened; *you*—the you and this is the kicker that has never really been there—let this happen.

"Sweetheart," said Godfrey, reaching out for her, but he grasped only air as suddenly she sprang forward, clearing the stairs and hitting the drive in a collision that caused the pavement to crack, and charged off with improbable speed, clearing car lengths at a bound. Godfrey watched helplessly as she crossed the boundary of the property, the lamppost's light extinguishing suddenly as she passed, and continued headlong down the hill; he heard the percussions of her footfalls after she passed from sight, and as those faded the rise of her cry into something horrific and wrathful, a thorn in the paw of the heavens.

Godfrey was at a loss. Nothing in his experience of his niece having provided him any indication she could move like that, or that that noise was contained inside her. Like the first time he'd seen the blow of the Bessemer as a child: a terrific vent of flame and fury from the mouth of a dragon, but that wasn't it at all— merely the latent potential of everyday iron, hiding in plain sight until given the pretext not to.

He took out his phone, but it was dead. He went to his car, but it would not turn over either. As, he suspected, would be the fate of any piece of electronics-based technology in Shelley's wake. He got out and stood under the blacked lamppost, his sense now not of impending climax but its initiation; whatever was happening was happening now and here he was, benched. The lone and useless rich man at the house on the hill, visible and still forgotten. He saw on the ground a single white feather, which he picked up and held on a flat palm and blew as hard as he could. It wheeled and tumbled back to earth, a victim of forces it could neither comprehend nor protest. He looked out on the valley and night fell around him. The moon was a broken ornament on the water and the White Tower became visible.

"Jesus H. Christ," he said.

Then in the distance there was a series of shots, followed by a silence of unequivocal authority. And there it was: over. Whatever that meant for everyone.

"Over," said Godfrey. Not in sorrow or relief or any speculation where it might fall between. He was just getting his head around the idea.

"It's over and nothing else is going to happen," he said.

Then the light of the White Tower went dark.

○

On Roman's return to Hemlock Acres there was a news bulletin: "The search continues for Hemlock Grove teenager Peter Rumancek, suspected of involvement in a series of local slayings previously attributed to some kind of animal. The third victim in last night's carnage has been positively identified as area woman Jennifer Fredericks . . ."

Something stirred in Roman, that niggling sort of something that lodges in the back of your teeth but you can't get it out.

"It is now theorized that the killer may have trained one or more wolves for use in these terrible crimes. Francis Pullman, deceased, claimed to have witnessed the first victim, Brooke Bluebell, attacked by a black quote demon dog, while last night there were multiple reported sightings of a large white wolf . . ."

Roman turned off the radio. Could there have been more than one all along? One black, one white . . .

And then he swerved into the nearest driveway and swiped the mailbox, knocking the passenger-side mirror so it hung dispirited like a mostly severed limb. He reversed and made a 180-degree turn and put the pedal to the floor and brown leaves did rejoicing somersaults in his wake.

○

3:43 p.m.

"This is fun!" said Letha. "Can you believe I've never had a tea party before? Doesn't it make you want to refer to yourself in the royal *we*? Here, give us your cup and we'll just refresh you then."

Outside there was the noise of a car coming down the street at an aggressive speed. The tires screeched and it stopped out front. Letha gingerly took the cup from her guest's quaking hand and went to the window, parting the curtains.

"Oh, it's fine," she said. She looked at the pale and cringing figure on her bed. "Don't be scared. It's fine."

Downstairs there was the sound of the door being thrown open and footsteps taking the stairs two at a time.

"Okay," said Letha. "Okay, if you want to, you just wait in here, okay?"

The sound of Roman calling her name as the footsteps approached her door.

"One minute," said Letha. "Just wait in here," she whispered.

She went and opened her door partway.

"Are you okay?" said Roman.

"I'm fine," she said. "I was about to sneak out and meet you guys like you said. What's up?"

"You're okay?" said Roman. "Everything is cool?"

"I'm fine. Don't worry, I'm fine."

They both looked at each other suspiciously. It was then he noticed over her shoulder the teakettle on her dresser. Two cups.

"Who's here?" he said.

"Okay, don't freak out," she said.

"Who's. Here," he said.

"Okay, I need you to not freak out. I need you to wait right here, okay?"

She tried to close the door but he held out his hand and stopped it gently but implacably with his fingertips and she didn't press it. She walked to the closet.

"Hey," she said. "Hey, it's just my cousin, and he's going take us where we're going to be safe, okay? No one is going to hurt you. We're not going to let anyone hurt you, okay? I'm opening the door now."

Letha opened the door and Roman stood fixed where he was and Christina Wendall emerged. She looked at him and he looked at her.

We looked at each other.

Black Run

Remi stretched her gleaming neck
Like a rush-imbedded swan,
Like a lily from the beck,
Like a moonlit poplar branch,
Like a vessel at the launch
When its last restraint is gone.

It wasn't until she was eleven that the mill came to haunt her dreams. Although it had frightened her at the time, and every time after that she saw it, it was with the knowledge of the way the smallest noises became large in those walls, or how it was to feel the dark on the outside and the inside of your skin; she wasn't any more afraid of it than her grandparents' attic or the caverns she had visited at summer camp, or any place where it took no real strength of imagination to conjure all the things that might happen to little girls in there. She thought no more of the mill except the odd day shiver in passing.

Until the dreams, but the dreams didn't start until after the poem. She came across the poem through Debbie, her baby-sitter, a senior. The twins made fun of her for still having a baby-sitter, but she didn't mind, really—she read her grandmother's thrillers, she knew the kinds of things that happened to little girls. Debbie was reading the poem for an English class. She finished it and raised her eyebrows and said, "Well, the boys are sure going to get a kick out of this one." Naturally, Christina had to see.

She couldn't even read it all the way through the first time. The first time her heart pounded and her hands shook and the act of breathing felt like swallowing rocks. Debbie asked if she was all right and she said it was just a dizzy spell. She gave the book back to Debbie and said she was going to lie down. In her room she found a copy on the Internet and now read it through and through and through. Words are thermal energies. These energies were introduced into her system to become kinetic in her thighs and her fingertips and behind her eyelids. States of matter changed. Her heart became a liquid that pooled under her feet and she was a water bug racing on molecules.

> *She clipped a precious golden lock,*
> *She dropped a tear more rare than pearl,*
> *Then sucked their fruit globes fair or red:*
> *Sweeter than honey from the rock,*
> *Stronger than man-rejoicing wine,*
> *Clearer than water flowed that juice;*
> *She never tasted such before,*
> *How should it cloy with length of use?*

She doesn't know what it will want if she faces it. She is paralyzed. She doesn't know whether to turn and face it or Go Down the Hole.

> *She sucked and sucked and sucked the more*
> *Fruits which that unknown orchard bore;*
> *She sucked until her lips were sore;*
> *Then flung the emptied rinds away*
> *But gathered up one kernel-stone,*
> *And knew not was it night or day*
> *As she turned home alone.*

There were things no one knew about her. You wouldn't know she'd had her first kiss but she had, in secret. It had been the previous summer, one day at twilight she went up the lane to Peter's and found him asleep on the hammock. She liked Peter better than other boys because he was just easy to be around, you didn't have to worry about coming off as weird because he was the weirdest person you had ever met. And he had poked her in the pit of her stomach and told her it's where she knew the unwritten universal histories of the terrible and ecstatic, numbnuts, and went and overturned her head and her heels. She said his name but he didn't wake up so she bent close to him and sniffed and he smelled like bad beer. Then he snored one of those half snores like a piglet and there he was this funny sleeping goon who had opened up a world of infinite possibilities and what else was she supposed to do?

But the twins were less chaste. They had both gone all the way that same summer, Alyssa with Ben Novak and then Alexa with Mark Smoot. This was incredible to her. It was enough putting her lips on this boy's because it was just the perfect thing to do in the moment, but to think of the whole of him on top of her and the rest of it, nature's final puzzle, what was between his legs and what was between hers.

> Golden head by golden head,
> Like two pigeons in one nest
> Folded in each other's wings,
> They lay down in their curtained bed:
> Like two blossoms on one stem,
> Like two flakes of new-fallen snow,
> Like two wands of ivory
> Tipped with gold for awful kings.

She was not simply incredulous that Alyssa had lost her virginity, and Alexa on her heels to keep up. It wasn't just the how of the act itself, opening your legs and letting it into you, wanting it all up in you. But an incredulity no different than if they had slipped a poison into her drink that was a thousand needles in her heart and delivered this information to her with a blushing glee she—*she*—was expected to take part in.

How they could do that to her.

Moon and stars gazed in at them,
Wind sang to them lullaby,
Lumbering owls forbore to fly,
Not a bat flapped to and fro
Round their rest:
Cheek to cheek and breast to breast
Locked together in one nest.

Identical. Are you kidding! She could have told them apart with her eyes closed.

She looked it up and found there was another way, a way to become a werewolf without being bitten. But it's not like one had anything to do with the other. Not in her head. It wasn't that she was hurt and the next day she went about looking into becoming a monster. Life isn't as clean as all that. Life isn't clean. This was weeks after the fact and she was over it, basically. The heart is an absorbent muscle, basically. Why, then, become a wolf person? The same reason as kissing one. Peripeteia. An important writer of her time needs Material. But how was she supposed to know? How was she supposed to know it would actually work?

Early in the morning after the Corn Moon when she knew there was no danger of Peter being awake she searched the ground around the trailer until she found what she was looking for. Tracks. Tracks tell the story of who this animal is and what it wants and how this is interwoven with the fabric of its ecosystem. As long as the animal believes in itself.

She got down on her knees and poured water from a bottle into the deepest impression and got to all fours and drank. But the water was quickly absorbed and she ended up less drinking from the track of a werewolf than lapping up mud. This was what her inquisitive temperament had brought her to, on her hands and knees with mud on her lips. She was not optimistic.

But the next cycle she had the mill dream again, though now it didn't end as it had before, without resolution. This time the thing was behind her in all its unknown immensity and the hole in front of her and she made her choice. She could not turn around. She could not look at its face. And so, not knowing what she did, on the night of the Harvest Moon she Went Down the Hole.

> *Tears once again*
> *Refreshed her shrunken eyes,*
> *Dropping like rain*
> *After long sultry drouth;*
> *Shaking with anguish fear, and pain,*
> *She kissed and kissed her with a hungry mouth.*

What happens when the head is not removed from a werewolf after its death? It is doomed to tell its story. The forever howl.

Christina was a girl both young and old for her years; she had never shed the breathless curiosity of a child assembling its universe: What is that? Where did that come from? Why is that like that and not another way and what is its orientation with every other thing?

Why?

Why?

Why?

She is her own Greek chorus now, and she's very very sorry for everything that happened.

Peripeteia, Redux

"Baby on board," said Letha, chastising.

Roman flicked his cigarette out the window.

"We're going back to the clinic now," said Letha. She was sitting in the backseat with Christina. "Don't freak out, there's another place there that's safe."

The girl had said she did not want to go back to her room. She said her room was cold and full of ghosts. Letha made Roman promise not to tell her dad. Roman promised readily enough; he had no intention of bringing Norman into this. Where this fell exactly vis-à-vis the Hippocratic oath was thorny but moot. This was werewolf law; Peter would know what to do.

Roman really hoped Peter would know what to do.

"The chapel," said Christina.

Letha said, "Yes."

"Will . . . he be there?"

"Peter?" said Letha. "Yes, he will. But he's not going to hurt you, I promise. You know I'm not going to let anyone hurt you, right?"

"I know," said Christina.

Letha's breastbone oppressed her heart at the girl's bravery after all that had happened to her, to her friends . . . Letha's eyes welled but she could hardly let herself cry if the girl did not. She put an arm around Christina and said, "You know it's going to be okay now, right?"

Christina cuddled into her and put a hand on Letha's belly with a wondering look: a little person lived in there!

"It's weird that *impossible* is even a word," said Christina.

Roman's hands tightened on the wheel. The sky was black and the sun was a blood yolk. Roman made a detour, turning off toward the Wal-Mart.

"What are you doing?" said Letha.

"Peter needs some things," said Roman.

"What things?" said Letha.

"An extension cord."

"What does he need an extension cord for?"

"I didn't ask."

"Why didn't you just grab one from the house?"

"Slipped my mind."

"How did that slip your mind?" she said, nagging.

Ahead, on the side of the road in their lane of traffic but trundling down the opposing direction, was an old person in a motorized wheelchair. This person was hunched forward in a bulky sexless sweat suit pinned at the knee stumps, grizzled sexless face, eyes dim and indifferent, watching an old rerun on television.

"Someone must have dropped a banana peel," said Roman listlessly.

"That's *silly*," said Christina.

"He's silly sometimes," said Letha.

Roman wondered what it would be like to have the brain of a girl for just one day, how much more sense things would make.

In the parking lot Roman pulled into a space and crept over the white line to be nose forward but suddenly a yellow pickup swung aggressively into the same space from the opposite direction and both braked to avoid collision. The pickup honked and Roman backed up.

"Careful," said Letha.

The other driver stepped out. He was a skinny but at the same time paunchy young man in a Penguins jersey with a crew cut and one of those birthmarks overtaking half his face like he had been spewed on with pale pink dye. He leered at Roman and grabbed his crotch with an obscene thrust.

Roman turned to Letha. "Will you come in with me?" he said.

"I'll wait with her," said Letha.

Christina looked at him with a dreamy expression.

"Leave the keys so we can listen to the radio," said Letha.

Roman went inside and paced, deliberating whether or not to simply make Sporting Goods give him a gun while she was still a girl. But he decided against it because he wasn't sure that was what Peter would want. Not really. The reason he decided not to was that he needed the decision to be Peter's.

He passed a dressing room as a boy of ten or eleven exited. The boy was plump and mildly retarded and wearing only a pair of girl's panties with strawberries imprinted on them and he started mincing around, swishing his rear from side to side in an exaggerated catwalk strut. Roman tried not to stare, but honestly. "No! No! No!" said the boy's mother with an unmistakable not-again inflection as she swooped in and wrenched him back into the dressing room and gave Roman a dirty look, but honestly, lady.

Roman turned and nearly collided with another person, a small Asian woman with the precise and fragile beauty of a ceramic figure. They looked at each other with the kind of mutual astonishment of finding oneself suddenly and intimately in eye contact with a complete stranger and Roman had the impulse to take her delicate hand and place it against his face just for one moment and say, *She's just a fucking little girl, a little girl like all the rest of them, this isn't how it was supposed to be*—not that he expected this person to have a satisfactory answer to that, or that one existed, but at least for one moment she could touch his face with soft, sensuous Oriental understanding. But before Roman had the opportunity to act on this impulse or for that matter mumble an apology, the woman abruptly turned away and hastened down the aisle and Roman got a fleeting view of her profile, discovering that the side of her head was dominated principally by a burn scar about the dimension of a palm laid flat, no hair growing within its perimeter and the skin like butter melted and congealed once more, and in place of an ear a hole you could look into like a key slot.

"Well okay," said Roman. He went to the men's room with the intention of being sick but both stalls were occupied and the air hale with defecation and he leaned over a urinal only to be greeted by a fat pustule of blood on the pink urinal cake as though someone had leaned over much like himself and rocketed a nosebleed.

"Well okay!" said Roman, finding his distaste to have the perverse effect of repulsing his nausea. He straightened and smoothed his lapels and proceeded to Hardware for his original goal. Up front he purchased a twenty-five-foot length of extension cord, paying cash as a precaution to prevent leaving a paper trail. But though the total was just over $22 the cashier gave him an even $3 in change. Roman paled.

"Oh no," he said.

The cashier began ringing the next customer's purchases, though Roman had not moved.

"I need my change," he said.

"Excuse me?" said the cashier.

"My change," said Roman, handing back the third bill with shaking fingers.

The cashier looked at him, wondering if he was serious. Roman blinked back tears of desperation. He held the dollar out in one hand and the receipt in the other.

"I need the exact change right here," said Roman.

"Why?" said the cashier, who was a gaunt gray young girl possessed of the spirit of reverse charity that overtakes some when seeing another in clear need.

"Because I can't go," Roman pleaded heedlessly. "I need you

to give me the amount of money that's here on the receipt before I can go."

"Sir, I'm assisting another customer."

Roman commanded his feet to lift from where they stood, but it would have taken a claw hammer. He felt distantly like he was forgetting something and he started breathing again. But the fact remained, blank and pitiless: the numbers didn't add up and he could not go before they did, the fact of it crushing him like the handshake of a small-dicked god.

The old woman after him gave Roman a nervous look as she handed over her money.

"I'm . . . I'm not normal," he said apologetically, then suddenly muscled between her and the checkout counter and snaked his arm into the register as it opened and helped himself to a handful of coins and sprinted to the exit as commotion rose behind him, counting out his exact change and flinging the excess behind him, the weight of the heavens from his shoulders.

O

At the copse along 443 where the trailhead breached, Roman parked.

"We're going through the woods?" said Letha.

"Sunset isn't till four fifty-five," said Roman.

Letha looked uneasily at the lengthening shadows beyond the tree line. She looked at Christina.

"To grandmother's house we go," said Christina.

They got out and Roman gathered the supplies. Christina took Letha's hand and they entered the trailhead.

"Do you want me to carry anything?" said Christina.

"I got it," said Roman.

"What's in the case?" said Christina.

"Papers," said Roman.

"What papers?" said Christina.

"My Christmas list," said Roman.

"That's not what it is," said Christina. "We peeked while you were inside."

They were on a path. At the end of this path was a destination. Roman decided that any other details were extraneous.

"Are you going to use that to cut out its heart?" said Christina.

"Okay, shush," said Letha indulgently.

They went down the path. Dry leaves crackling underfoot, the reverent twilit hush. They passed a lone Cat digger, its belly consumed by rust and the shovel end disappeared within the undergrowth. Up ahead was a hill bisected with a gully down which a load of old tires had been discarded as though disgorged by a dyspeptic Earth and there was a sheer rockface along the path with a carving of the Dragon on it. Christina stopped.

"Hey, we need to keep moving," said Roman. This was not their destination.

Christina ran her fingertip down the curve of the Dragon's back and her fingertip came away dusted with chalk powder. She looked at Roman earnestly and said, "Would you like to know a secret?"

This was not their destination!

"Let's get moving," said Roman.

Christina nodded and took Letha's hand once more and then Roman's and walked between them. Her hand was cool and dry like crepe paper.

"I think your sister is a good person," said Christina.

"Yes, she is," said Roman.

"She just gives you a good feeling," said Christina.

He nodded, not seeing the thorny tip of a low branch that scratched his eyebrow. He sucked in his breath and refrained from swearing loudly. In this of all circumstances he would succeed in watching his language.

"Ooh," said Christina. She stopped and touched the scratch by his eyebrow.

He looked at her face and it occurred to him he could just do it. Here and now. They did not have to get where they were going, Peter did not have to be the one to decide. Roman could just give her the blade and tell her to cut her own wrists and inside of her legs and her neck and anywhere else that would bleed fast and comprehensive into the dirt. Maybe he could even tell Letha to forget. For all he knew he could do that too. He looked at her. He tried to summon the intention and warrior's focus he had felt so recently looking into the mirror, but this was not a picture, it was a person. A little fucking girl. Roman did not feel like much of a warrior.

They went on and when the trail broke Roman said he would go up ahead to make sure everything was all right and jogged up to the chapel and entered carefully. He imagined being spoken to by the affirming mechanized voice of his GPS. *You have arrived.* Peter was waiting. Roman held his finger to his lips before Peter could speak. Peter did not need him to explain. It was here. Roman had brought it here while there was still sun in the sky. He looked at Roman.

"Good," he said. "You did a good job."

Roman said nothing. He handed Peter the bag with the cord. From the steps, Letha asked if it was okay.

Peter became rigid. "What is she doing here?" he said.

"It's complicated," said Roman.

He called that it was okay and Letha led Christina in, and Christina's and Peter's eyes met, and Letha looked from one to the other and did not know just how but knew she had made a bad mistake; the look on her face the instant you realize the car is no longer obeying the steering wheel.

"I'm sorry for telling everyone you were a werewolf," said Christina.

Peter walked up to her. He pulled the cord free of the packaging. She looked at him with those dreamy eyes. He knotted a loop in the cord.

Letha asked what was going on. Peter did not answer her.

"Get her out of here," Peter said to Roman.

Roman went to Letha and put a hand on her arm but she was fixed where she stood. She could only dumbly spectate. Roman gently told her, "Come on," but she did not and he did not force her, and could not himself. No one was going anywhere now, any more than a moth flies away from the light; it would have broken the law of attraction.

"Get on your knees," Peter told Christina.

Letha felt a wave of nausea and Christina obeyed. Peter slipped the cord over her head and fastened it tightly around her neck. She stayed there on her knees, docile, as he went and knotted the other end to where the nearest pew was bolted to the floor. He went back to her and stood over her.

"Can you control it?" he said.

She looked at him sleepily.

"Last night was it just something that happened or did you make it happen?" he said.

She did not answer him.

"Did you make yourself turn, or did you hear it? Did you hear your other name?" said Peter.

She did not answer. It was like she was actually asleep with open eyes. He took the cord and yanked it and she collapsed into a sprawl.

Letha's nausea intensified into a kind of vertigo. Roman was afraid she might faint and guided her to a pew and she allowed him to sit her down. Standing was doing her no favors in coming to terms with the mistake.

"If you don't answer me," said Peter, "I will choke the life from you right here."

Christina got back to her knees.

"I decided to," she said. "I wanted to."

"Okay," said Peter, nodding; now they were getting somewhere, and he said it again. "Okay."

He crouched so they were level. "If you decide to turn tonight, you are going to die."

"Are you going to kill me, Peter?"

"Yes," he said.

"Do you hate me?" she said.

"No. I don't hate you," he said.

She beamed.

"Why her?" said Peter. "Why did you go to her?"

Christina looked at Letha. Yesterday, seeing Roman and the doctor slipping food and blankets into the chapel, she knew that Peter was in there. It was no more in question than the location of her own heart. Peter had made her, he was part of her now. There was no hiding from yourself, not in the end.

"Because when I saw you in here with your ugly little thing in that whore I wanted more than anything to feel her fear on my tongue and her bones crunch between my teeth and her blood run down the fur of my neck."

She looked at him hopefully. "We can eat her together," she said. "I always left you the bigger piece."

Letha was ambivalent now. It was sinking in that her initial impression of the mistake she was watching unfold was not entirely on target, but this brought her no relief.

The color drained from Peter and he got to one knee to support himself. Christina smiled with a wistful melancholy.

"It's okay," she said. "You can kill me as long you don't hate me. You should do it now, while you still have me like you want me. It's already happening, you haven't got a lot of time. I can't turn it around any more than you can turn around night and day. Do what you have to while it's still day. You made me. I'm yours."

She put her hands to the floor and crawled forward on all fours and brought her face inches from his.

"You're my master, you can do anything you want to me."

Peter kneeled there in the last of the light peering back into eyes that now hardly seemed a thing of the sublunary world.

"Oh God," he said. "Please forgive me."

She smiled again. "I've never heard my name," she said, though it was not the voice of a girl that spoke, it was a sound like the hinge on hell's gate, the sound of a thing that most dangerously of all things didn't know its name.

And then she turned.

Letha's mouth formed the shape to allow the release of a very loud sound that did not emerge. Roman seized her arm and pulled her up and to the altar. Peter wheeled back behind a pew. Christina quivered and howled and the thing in her was so much bigger and meaner than she, it simply burst forth in a clap detonation of efficient violence. The transformation was instantaneous and irrevocable. Now the beast. The killer. Standing, the dimensions of a starved horse, flesh and clothing hanging in wet tatters from white fur. Every hair a killer. It looked at Peter. Enough has been made of its eyes. Matchstick legs crouching and then the spring-release of coiled rage and the beast, drunk on the fear in the room, pounced to kill.

But in what might have been a great comic effect in other circumstances, the cord yanked it back in midair with a clipped yelp, its entire body snapping in a whiplash and falling to the ground. It scrabbled forward, now on foot and the cord pulling taut as it struggled. Foam sprayed from its snapping jaws, white flecks of it hitting Peter's face as he emerged from the pew. Peter's face calm and understanding. Understanding this beast. Its name, its not-so-secret name, was Pain.

Roman kept himself in front of Letha and fumbled with the case and pulled out the axe and hoped Peter really had something up his sleeve because holding it now in his hands and faced with the primeval fury that had been let out of its cage he knew he held no weapon against this beast. But it was no great comfort when Peter stood there placidly watching as the white wolf snarled and frothed, straining so hard it was choking, and no way that cord would hold it back for very long, Peter just standing there like watching a barn burner of a storm or any other natural phenomenon that happens on occasion.

"Do something!" said Roman. He had no better suggestion.

Peter turned from the white wolf and Roman saw now he was holding something in his hands, picked up from behind the pew. The Tupperware container. Deliberately, Peter wiped the dog slobber from his face. He then opened the container and dipped his hand inside. This was not what Roman had in mind. The white wolf reared back and attempted another vain pounce, pratfalling to its side, the cord entangling one of its slashing legs. Like an actor applying stage makeup, Peter rubbed the grease on his face. He turned back to the white wolf. Roman realized.

"Peter! No!"

But Peter ignored him as the white wolf took the cord in its jaws and brought them together with an earsplitting *SNAP* and rose with the severed cord around its neck. It walked forward and stopped in front of Peter. Letha screamed now, finally joining the party, and she clawed at Roman's shoulders trying to struggle past him, but he held her in check, remembering that he had a job and he was doing it. To be between this and her.

The white wolf sniffed Peter's face and experimentally licked. Peter stood there. He shut his eyes. He might have been better appreciating a scent or waiting for a kiss. But what he was doing was remembering. This was the first wolf he had encountered since Nicolae and he was remembering with sudden vividness the feel of Nicolae's tongue. The memory a good one, fine for the last behind his human face.

The white wolf snapped and tore the face from his body.

Letha continued to scream but Roman could not be sure if it was right at his ear or somewhere far, far off. Peter crumpled and the white wolf lowered her head and lapped at the remaining grease. It was not a good sight, this beast with its muzzle licking his friend's face away, and Roman's eyes floated up the nave to the quote Jacob Godfrey had seen fit to have inscribed over the tympanum: OUR LOVE MUST NOT BE A THING OF WORDS AND FINE TALK. IT MUST BE A THING OF ACTION AND SINCERITY. Roman nodded. So his moment after all. This beast wouldn't want him, it would want her, and this was not a thing that would happen. It would come for her and he would throw himself at it and maybe he would kill it or more probably it would kill him, but either way she would make it through this. He saw the beating heart in the mirror earlier, his Kill, and he knew that the heart was his own, as were all hearts, there was no hiding from it. But she would make it, because maybe he wasn't much of a warrior but if there was one thing that he was cut out for it was an epic and retarded act of love.

The white wolf finished finally and lifted its head, leaving something gleaming, and looked up at them. Roman took Letha's wrist and said, "When I say so, run. Run for the acute unit and lock yourself in as deep as you can. Will you do that?"

She did not answer him and he saw in her terror and grief right now that whatever she did, she would do it wrong. The *vargulf* took a gingerly first step over Peter toward them.

Roman looked her in the eye. "Live through this," he said.

But then there was a startled yelp and the white wolf listed to the side. The brown wolf's jaws were clamped around its throat. The *vargulf* thrashed wildly, pulling the brown wolf fully formed from the grisly chrysalis of what had been moments before a boy called Peter. The white wolf shook frantically but the brown wolf's fangs only closed with greater implacability, so it was forced to change tack, turning inward and its fangs working for purchase in the flesh of its enemy. The fangs of a werewolf the end of the story.

Roman watched the two beasts rip and rend at each other with a ferocity that knocked them back and forth against the wall and through the pews and to the floor; the white wolf larger by threefold but no smell of fear to the brown, only resolution, the resolution to hold and hold and beyond any reasonable measure to hold. A resolution breakable only by death. And as they rolled and sprawled and clawed, ears flat and muzzles pulled taut revealing white teeth and black gums and undercoats matting red, yet both of them silent all the while—once the fight has begun, werewolves do not make a sound—it was apparent that that was exactly where this was going. Death. In the warring silence that was the one clear thing: neither of them was going to survive this battle.

The white wolf ripped off half the brown wolf's ear and its rear claws hooked into its stomach and tore, but in all its savage power it could not hurt the brown wolf enough to make its release. So the primal intercourse. Good versus evil at its most raw and elemental. But standing beholden to the full catharsis of what had seemed so necessary to Roman now just seemed tiring. Tiring because he felt prematurely the weight of carrying how stupidly fucking sad this was for the rest of his days.

He noticed a low murmuring by his ear. It was Letha. She was praying. She was praying for her angel. *You crazy-ass fucking bitch*, thought Roman. He started praying too.

Just then the darkening light outside took on a queerish blue cast and with it a low and distant thunder. But the light did not diminish as it would have with a lightning strike. The light grew brighter. Whatever it was, it was moving. Getting closer. And Roman felt a tremble in his shins and realized that the rumble was not thunder but the ground itself moving. The dogfight continuing heedless. Letha fell silent and Roman himself wondered if such a ludicrous deus ex machina was actually happening. Had their prayer been answered?

The light grew brighter still, spilling from the crack under the doors, and disruptions of dust fell from the beams, the foundations of the church quaking. And in that moment a connection that had failed earlier clicked suddenly in Roman's mind: Jennifer Fredericks. Jenny.

"Oh," said Roman, and he tackled Letha, throwing his body

over hers just as the doors exploded from their hinges and shattered stained glass rained on his back and the room was filled with a blinding light that was visible to planes in the sky and the bellow of a giant's rage. There followed the sounds of a vengeance nasty, brutish, short. The thud of one body being unceremoniously cast from the fight, the crack and howl of another breaking.

And just as suddenly it was done with. Roman blinked the color from his eyes as though snowblind to see the aftermath. The doors splintered and upended in the pews. The brown wolf bleeding and motionless against the wall. Kneeling in profile against the dusk his baby sister, chest heaving and cradled in her arms the nude body of one more dead girl, her back curved and a fragment of spine protruding. Shelley looked at her brother. Her eyes fathomless, the magnitude of it. The first time in her life she had ever made the choice to hurt another living thing.

He stood, carefully brushing the dust and debris from his sleeves. He went to her.

"Put her down," he said. "Put her down, Shelley."

He lay a hand on her back. Her face sagged against him. He braced himself to bear the weight of it. He told her it was okay. He told her again to put her down. And that was when he saw it was not over yet. And that was when he saw the man.

The man was standing outside. He had in fact come to Hemlock Acres with the intention of admitting himself, realizing that the tenor of his own thoughts was no honor to anyone, least of all those lost. But the man had been drawn to the commotion of the chapel and he stood now outside it with hate in his heart and a Mossberg 500 in his hands and there was nothing for him to see but the murderer of one more dead girl.

The women of the audience may want to close their eyes now.

Roman's cries were drowned out by the ring of the sheriff's first shot. Shelley seized from the bullet's impact but she did not fall, and Christina Wendall slid from her arms to the floor. Roman made an unthinking dash, arms waving, for the sheriff, but Shelley took him by the scruff of the neck and tossed him aside. Roman splayed backwards and out of harm's way as the next shot buried in her chest.

Roman continued crying out and struggled to his feet but Shelley had begun to move. She lumbered down the steps and let out a low of pain as Sheriff Sworn shot her a third time, but she reached the ground and loped past him, and he pivoted and chambered another round but as he was siting there was the clash and spark of metal on metal and the rifle dropped from his hands and Roman looked into his eyes and said, "Don't hurt her. Please don't hurt her," and raced after Shelley, yelling her name. But she would not stop, she could not stop, she was an engine building steam that could only power faster and faster into the forest and up a single track, and Roman followed the sound of her crashing as she hurtled to the summit of the hillside, beginning once more to fluoresce, each bound building more power and momentum, propelling her farther into the air, branches and even full trees snapping as that juggernaut steamed inexorably for the only destination, all that was left, and far behind her Roman crested the hill to see her blue light; from this height it might have been a firefly as it approached the institute, the place of her creation, coming closer and closer before, as he knew it would in the moment just cusping the actual event, winking out as though swallowed by the very earth.

Roman stopped and caught his breath. The front of his jeans was cold. Apparently his bladder had released at some point, but he had not noticed. He saw snagged in the snarl of a hemlock a torn skein of thread from Shelley's shirt and he wiped his hands dry and pulled it free. Roman had a series of protocols that was supposed to maintain order and balance in the world. He had an alliance with the virtuous and harmonic number four and multiples thereof and was an enemy of primes; primes the emissaries of the dark place. He would reset his alarm a fixed number of times depending on the hour it was supposed to go off, would sooner step on a nail than a crack, could not fall asleep unless he was certain every drawer and cupboard in the house was securely shut, always entered water with his left foot, and *always* untied knots. But as he worked with trembling fingers, freeing one fiber and another and another, frantically loosing individual and innocuous strands by the light of the institute, it occurred to him for the first time in his life that what he was doing was completely pointless. That there was no protocol that could undo the things that had been done this night in the naming of what is good and evil. He dropped the thread to the ground, his work unfinished. He had never performed such a breach before. Could never have imagined such a thing. He felt empty. He had never imagined such an emptiness.

And then the light of the White Tower went dark.

○

Letha approached the wolf. It lay on its side, unconscious and wheezing and its fur stickied red. She lay behind it and pulled its body into hers and looked into its eyes. The wolf looked back and they were Peter's eyes. She was the only one to learn Peter's true secret: that there is no "it," only him, always him. She buried her face into his coat and she inhaled this smell of dog as the wise wolf died. She lay with his body in her arms and closed her eyes.

When she opened them some time later her cheek did not lie on fur but on flesh, pink and wet and warm. A man. Her arm rising and falling on his chest with his breathing. She sat up bemused and looked at Peter. Peter in one pink and wet piece. She was not sure what to make of this beyond some occult understanding that it ran over any sensible order of things, that receiving yet another miracle was not simply tackily excessive but quite possibly made her the most selfish person alive.

"I'll take it," she said.

Peter groaned and shifted but did not awaken. She leaned forward, her lips not quite touching his face. She did not understand this thing that had happened, nor intended to. As it had been said: Death is fucking magical. And with a tenderness like no kiss, she licked him.

You Must Make Your Heart Steel

The winter was cold, but then the spring. It was now six months since the incident at Godfrey Chapel and though only questions remained about that night, they were rhetorical. Because the killing had stopped. How and why was catching a ghost by the tail; the killing had stopped and life in Hemlock Grove went on. The White Tower was light again as ever, but gone was the controlling share of Norman Godfrey. The principal holders are now Olivia Godfrey in trust for her son until his fast-approaching eighteenth birthday and Lod LLC. From time to time Olivia, Dr. Pryce, and a man of imperious girth and military bearing with, on close inspection, a signet ring of a serpent and a cross can be seen strolling the nautilus trail around the institute, on what business beyond enjoying the weather's pleasant turn is anyone's guess. For Dr. Godfrey only questions remained, but they were rhetorical. A question is a door and an unopened door is just part of the wall and as long as it's standing it's doing its job. The killing had stopped. Upon the lump receipt of Lod's improbable payment from a Luxembourg account, he put it all into the Godfrey Foundation, stipulating to his wife that whatever it was used to build bear any name but his. Plans were also under way to convert the mill into an interactive industrial museum and learning center, the central attraction an exhibit visit inside an authentic

Bessemer converter. (There are rumors it's haunted.) There were cardinals and goldfinches in the trees and greedy mud on the ground that would suction off a shoe and finally, on the thirteenth of April, after the very last of the long chill, Peter was making up for lost hammock time when a warmth suffused his Swadisthana. He listened to the sound of the wind like the roar of a distant crowd.

"Well I'll be," he said.

Moments later the phone rang and he went inside. The latest stray raced through the open door into the trailer, a double-wide. He answered the phone to receive a glad piece of news. It was expected; she was due at any moment, but some things can never be expected no matter how much they are.

Peter said nothing; being philosophical made him quiet. Fetchit jumped on the kitchen table and mewled. The black ones had a way of finding the Rumanceks' door. Peter nooked the phone with his shoulder and went to the cupboard and took out a can of tuna.

"Well!" said Letha, on the other end of the line.

"Sorry, I'm feeding the cat," said Peter.

"Good to hear you have your priorities straight."

"Babies have to be born, and cats have to be fed," said Peter equitably.

Now there was a quiet on the other end suggesting he might want to reconsider his response.

"Baby," said Peter, "my heart has no words. Your smile makes flowers grow and your tits could knock a rhino sideways. I love your ass to pieces and anything that pops out of you. This is the best news I've had all day."

"Oh, my chariot arriveth. Catch you on the flip side."

She hung up. It had been agreed that he would not be present for the labor: she felt it was important to be on her own. Peter did not object—he had seen a video of childbirth in biology once and just didn't have the stomach for it.

Later in the afternoon Peter met Roman at Kilderry Park. A few undergraduates were throwing a Frisbee. Peter and Roman sat on a picnic bench at the pavilion. Roman was wearing the vintage Italian sunglasses that were his latest affectation and produced two cigars. Peter nodded. *Nice touch.*

"Uncle Roman," said Roman.

"Hail Mary, full of grace," said Peter.

Roman handed a cigar to Peter. Peter asked him if he'd made any headway with the Cat Lady and Roman shook his head.

Since the abrupt termination of Project Ouroboros in November, Roman had maintained hope of finding some kind of trail to his sister, of whom no sign had been found. No tracks. The latest was a medium to whom Destiny had referred him who operated a cougar sanctuary in West Virginia.

Roman pursed his lips. The Cat Lady had induced a trance in an attempt to communicate with Shelley but wound up falling to the floor in a sort of seizure, whispering incoherently about fate lines and heart lines and unholy communion and the headaches, the headaches, and the cottage was surrounded by low hisses and snarls as her agitation spread among her brood. Roman stuck a pen between her teeth and rolled her into the recovery position and waited for her to come to and escort him to his car without being eviscerated. In parting she apologized that she would not be able to help him—though did not refuse her fee—but instead offered these words: "Still. What she is trying to say is 'still.'" Roman would have written off the entire expedition as a fool and his money, except that he had been experiencing headaches of increasing severity lately. A heightened photosensitivity of the eyes that forced him to keep his sunglasses on more or less continuously before dusk.

"Dead end," said Roman.

Peter nodded. Both rationally and instinctively he believed Roman's search to be futile. Shelley was gone. And wherever it was she had gone, there was no looking for her. But he never voiced his pessimism to Roman, nor for that matter was there cause. He doubted Roman himself believed his quest to be anything but quixotic, and on balance it was simply better for him to have something keeping him busy.

Roman looked off into the sky at a lance of sun penetrating cloud and was quiet a moment.

"I see her sometimes," he said. "In dreams."

Peter looked at him. Why was he lying?

"Not in dreams," Roman admitted. "I've been . . . trying it on myself."

Peter didn't understand, then he did. The thing they didn't talk about, because when one friend has this power, not talking about it is a lot easier than talking about it; the paths it can lead down that one virtue of the male sex is an unparalleled lack of curiosity to see where they go. The power behind his eyes, and the meaning of this power.

"I look into the mirror, and I tell myself to see her," said Roman. "I feel her all the time, but I tell myself to see her. And things go dark, and I can feel myself on a threshold, and I don't know what's on the other side, where the shadows are. But there's a light way off. And I know the light is an angel, and the angel is her.

"It's her," he repeated, as though this had been contested. "She's out there, and I want to get closer but I can't. I'm afraid of what will happen if I go too far. Then she starts calling out to me, but she's so far away and I can only just hear her. What she's saying is, 'You must make your heart steel.'"

He sat and looked at Peter. Peter fidgeted, uncomfortable. He could sense when Roman was going to bring up that night at the chapel, and though he didn't mind providing an ear he was himself loath to volunteer anything. In truth he had almost no memory of what happened, and he didn't want it otherwise. The thing about coming back from the dead was that your life went on, and he didn't like dwelling on it. The presentiment of an unpaid debt that he didn't like dwelling on at all.

"When you did what you did," said Roman, "how were you not afraid?"

But this was not a question Peter was expecting. At first he was bemused, then he chuckled and shook his head as though at a foreigner's comical malapropism.

Roman was as baffled as a Chinaman. "What?" he said.

"I've never been more scared of anything in my life. I could never have done it if I didn't know you were there too."

They were quiet. Roman looked out at the hills, seven shades of ever flusher and more life-giving green. He shook his head.

"Fucking angels," he said.

○

Outside, the moon was a boar's tusk and the owls gave their two cents while in the bedroom there was only the whir of the projector's motor. There was a white sheet tacked to the wall for a screen and the movie being projected was from the silent era and was black-and-white with a tint of green, as was the fashion of the time to create a sense of mood and mystery. The setting was a soundstage that was not really a soundstage but an expressionistic representation thereof where the shadows cast by the arc light of even the straightest lines fell like a maze of thorn brush. The facsimile of the thing constructed within the thing itself, dream within the feedback loop of the brain. Or vice versa. And within the soundstage a lone player, a woman. She had on the exaggerated eye makeup that was the fashion of the time and nothing else. And alone within this cathedral of ingenuity and infinity she danced. The dancer aching, grieving for the mist-covered mountains of the home she was so far away from, and so far away from returning to, and this dance inelegantly rendered by a shutter speed sixteen frames per second due to the technological limitations of the time, causing a simultaneously increased and halting speed. But the inelegance of the motion only contributing to the poetry of it. Essential truths gained by loss in translation. The essence of beauty not perfection, but the doomed aspiration.

Olivia lay in bed and watched, savoring like wine the shared age-old ache in her own bones as on-screen the woman danced the grief of her slow, slow journey home and in turning from the camera revealed her own imperfection. There was on the dancer's spine above the coccyx, like the mountain range of a relief map, a pale pinkie-length scar—the remnant of some crude surgery.

○

In his room Peter was awakened by a pang in his groin of such pressing acuity he mistook it initially for the need of a beastly piss, but he had gotten as far as the toilet before he realized it was not his own bladder he had felt but a different plane of signal altogether. He stood there dumbly, appurtenance in hand, waiting for a flash flood or a meteor or whatever it was that could have caused so profound an agitation within his Swadisthana. But then he realized, and then the phone rang. He did not go to answer it. He stood there knowing. It continued to ring until eventually Lynda picked up. He heard her answer and then she just listened. Her end of the conversation simply a hushed "Oh no oh no no no oh no." He tucked himself in his boxer shorts and gathered up his ponytail in one hand and with the other opened the cupboard and reached for a pair of scissors. He put the toilet seat down and sat, releasing the fistful of hair so it scattered to the floor as footsteps approached the door and he waited for the gentle, gentle knock.

○

Pryce received a call informing him of the disturbance in the OR and gave the order not to get in the way. He turned and stood at his office window and looked up at the night and stars.

"Where are you?" he said.

He pressed his fingertips against the window, the cool of the glass.

"Why did you leave us all to her?" he said.

Soon there was a sound at his office door not of knocking but a brute and insistent kicking. He opened the door and in the hall stood Dr. Godfrey. In his arms was a sheeted bundle. His eyes were stained as red as the sheet in his arms.

"Do it," said Godfrey.

Pryce said nothing.

"Bring her back, Johann," said Godfrey.

"Norman, come in and sit down," said Pryce.

"You need to bring her back," said Godfrey. "Do whatever you need to. Just bring her back."

"Norman, what say we sit down and talk about this?"

"She's getting cold! Bring her back. You think I'm being irrational but I'm not. I will write you a check for any amount you can imagine. Bring her back to me."

"Norman," said Pryce. He stepped into the hall and reached to take the bundle from his arms. Godfrey jerked away with hot feral eyes.

"Norman, give her to me," said Pryce.

"You'll do it?" said Godfrey.

"Norman, let me have her," said Pryce.

Godfrey was reluctant, but complied.

"You'll do it now," said Godfrey.

Pryce waited until his hold was secure before answering.

"No," he said.

Godfrey was quiet. The crazed inspiration that had sent him on this mission was suddenly and completely extinguished. Other fires went out now too. He eased himself against the wall and slid to the floor.

"She's too old, Norman," said Pryce. "What about the baby? I may have a chance with the baby."

Godfrey addressed his knees. The square fluorescents reflected off the floor down the hall, a long row of molars.

"Fuck the baby," he said.

Pryce took the bundle into his office and laid it on the floor. He pulled aside the sheet and looked into the face, which had contracted into a mask of the mocking ugliness of death. He called Hemlock Acres and told them to send a car, then came into the hall, locking the door behind him, and sat on the floor next to Godfrey. He inhaled the smell of disinfectant. He had never understood before why people didn't like that, the way hospitals smell. He had never known before how comfortless it could be.

"I'm sorry, Norman," said Pryce. "I'm not God."

○

Olivia insisted she drive although Roman was what is called holding up. But she knew it was not only deceptive but more dangerous. She knew about holding up. He had at least gotten sleep—she had doctored the vodka with several tablets of Ambien—and she had sat at his bedside like she had months ago during that god-awful business with the little dead lesbian. When he woke she asked where he would like to go and was relieved when he simply said "Peter." Pryce had phoned her the night before and she had enough on her hands; she wasn't ready yet for Norman. She had priorities.

As they drove in silence, Olivia debated whether or not to warn him but decided against it. He could only hate the messenger regardless of how much more the messenger loved him than anyone else ever could. There was nothing that could make this easier on him, no matter how much it harrowed her heart to be reduced for the present to chauffeur, bearing him to a destination where he had no suspicion what he would find, what he wouldn't. He sat next to her, holding up. She reached and touched his face. He flinched; the one thing his inner heart did not want now was to be touched, but she did not remove her hand. A mother has certain rights, and when a person can't be consoled, sometimes irritation will have to suffice to remind him that you're here, you are right here. They passed the park and turned down the lane.

As Olivia predicted, when they reached the Rumanceks' plot the car was gone and the trailer door hung open; they had not bothered to shut the door behind them. They stepped out and Roman looked mildly befuddled as though searching for a puzzle piece that was not in the box. Then his eyes overfilled with sudden awful knowing. The obvious she could not prepare him for: that a Gypsy was a Gypsy was a Gypsy. They will steal the rings off your fingers or the love right out of your heart and leave no more to show for it than a trail of smoke in the night. But she said nothing as the full weight of it came on in, taking admittedly small satisfaction in being, naturally, right. But only very small. How ill matched the boy was for this enemy!—death was one thing, quite involuntary for the most part. But desertion. There was no destroyer of worlds quite to match it. She reached to the small of her back and lightly traced the ridge of her scar through her blouse.

Many years ago Olivia had been a young girl in the land beyond the forests and the uglier of two sisters. Hers was not the kind of lack of beauty that suggested the promise of something unrealized but a drab androgyny that when placed beside her sister's loveliness was a perverse joke. And the punch line, at the base of her spine and extending about the length of a long thumb: her tail. But she had always been a happy child nonetheless, a gentle spirit who could lose entire afternoons wandering through a valley of sunflowers singing to herself, and much protected by her father and elder sister who believed the heart of the world could not extend charity to so simple and homely a girl.

But their great love could not prevent their fear from coming to pass, and in her thirteenth year Olivia had her first taste of the suffering from which she had been shielded for so long. His name was Dimitri and he was a slave. It was standard at the time for the aristocracy, and no name was older or more vaunted than her father's, to possess numerous Gypsy slaves, and it was something she had never put any more thought into than their horses or pigs. For it to occur to even so gentle and sensitive a spirit to hold an opinion on the thought of owning people like horses or pigs would have required it to occur to her that Gypsies were in fact people—a notion not even a child could take seriously. But then Dimitri. Which is not to say that the purchase of this slave suddenly clarified the issue of taxonomy but rather complicated it infinitely. Not so much that she realized that Dimitri was a man no different from her father or his friends, but that he was a creature quite unlike any other man or Gypsy she had ever encountered.

Olivia's father bought Dimitri for the unthinkable sum of two oxen, for which entire families might be purchased. But he was indeed an unparalleled specimen: it was not as if his shoulders or his thighs were near as stalwart as the ruminants for which he was traded, or his mind or beauty of any remark; it was a particular talent famed throughout the mountains that commanded him such a price. For being a member of a race of dance and song, Dimitri had a way with the fiddle to make the devil stomp his feet.

This is a story older than stories. From the first time the little girl who loved songs witnessed the Gypsy slave give a demonstration of his instrument, her tail wagged. Olivia, who along with her sister possessed the finest things of any girl in the land, had never felt the jealous pain in her soul of wanting a thing all her own until seeing through her own watered eyes the fingers on that wooden swan neck. But Dimitri, inconveniently, was no gift for her, nor an extravagance on her father's behalf for aesthetics as its own justification. Dimitri was her sister's dowry.

Olivia's heart was like a hand towel wrung by a strongman. She was devoted to her family and would never have ranked her own happiness of greater import, but with Dimitri it was not a question of happiness so much as the unique breed of misery that is first love, which she no more could have voluntarily abdicated than ceased her own heart through force of will. And so the girl whose gentle spirit had always been as dull as her face did the unprecedented. She defied the law of the land and her blood and she stole him.

Dimitri, who was a genius of young girls' hearts the same way even the most doltish of musicians are, needed no explanation when his new master's daughter unlocked his quarters and led him silently through an ancient catacomb that let out in the mountainside with two horses she had left in waiting. They rode all the day and all the night, not resting until they came to a river far away enough that there was no danger of a search party catching up. Dimitri took his unlikely deliverer into his arms and petted her hair on the riverbed. They had hardly exchanged two words except necessarily conveyed instructions the entire flight, but he told her they would have to sleep; much running still awaited them. But sleep was unthinkable! Now that they were here, of course, the process must be commenced of him learning every last little thing about her; no time could be lost in so urgent and comprehensive an undertaking. However, as the toll of the last two nights caught up with her and the Gypsy's magical hand stroked her she was lulled into the peaceful realization that time in fact stretched ahead of them in an endless meadow full of sunflowers now that she possessed him all to herself.

When she awoke at daybreak to the tittering of tree creepers, Dimitri, both horses, and the rings on her fingers were gone.

Olivia searched the riverbed until she found a piece of slate with an edge like a clamshell. She hitched up her skirt. She looked up and opened her mouth to join the tree creepers with her favorite song but fuck it, fuck songs and where they came from.

When the search party came across her the following day, she lay face forward and unmoving. Her skirt, bunched at her waist, had soaked so much blood it looked from a distance like a bunch of rose petals. One hand was outstretched and in its limp fingers what may have been a pale pickle.

Time passed. And something happened to the girl—the light of innocence in her eyes was lost as the face of unpromising homeliness around it rearranged into one of unpleasant beauty. It took nine months for this transformation to be complete, and at the end of it she looked at the newborn girl-child in her father's arms through a mask of cruel perfection.

"We will say she is your sister's," he said. She was then married, and it would bring dishonor to no one.

"The blood of a slave makes a slave," said Olivia. "Give it to the swineherd."

So the child was taken to the swineherd, the old Rumancek, whose low name the tainted bloodline would forever bear, and Olivia informed her father she would be going to the academy in the city, to learn the dramatic arts.

Presently, she stood by as Roman walked shakily to the front door and entered. She waited. There was a hum not far from her ear. Her arm darted and snatched a fat, ambling bumblebee from the air and she mashed it in her palm, dropping it to her feet. She regarded the small pink weal it had left and dug her nail in, scraping the stinger out. She waited. Then it came: from within the trailer the cry of the left-behind. She stood where she was as the cry rose at the immensity and grandeur of this desolation; she waited as the boy's pathetic howl went on, and on, and her heart howled right along with it.

She was here, she was right here.

○

A,

For a week he hardly left his room. The silence down the hall, I will always hear it echo. What a trial for even this battleworn heart! Could anything be more selfish than a mother's love? But how can they be strong if we are not? A satisfactory answer eludes . . .

He was apathetic to Norman's release into our custody, or at least the shell that vaguely responds to Norman's name. Such a pity. I loved the man, make no mistake about that. That sublime bitch of an irony that in the conquest of one heir to the Godfrey dynasty I would fall in love with the other. Unthinkable! So I finally share a roof with father and son. At least what is left of the father. Perhaps in time he will recover; he isn't made of sugar candy. But at any rate my nights will be less cold. To think, after all this fuss and bother over the years his defection aroused not so much as a moo from his old cow (her late defeat a not insignificant consolation prize; I have had the unique privilege of being around long enough to see all my rivals get ruined or get fat, but I can't name a single instance more satisfying). And scarcely more reaction from our child than if I'd acquired a new houseplant.

I did not interfere; I sat with his grief with brutal compassion but purpose held. We come from a motherland that has never conquered another, or repelled an invader from either direction, and yet here we stand. We do what is necessary. And it was only a week until his birthday. After all this time, no time at all. A bit arbitrary I suppose to wait until that exact date, but things must have a proper sense of proportion; I have no greater contempt than for those mothers who submit to having the stockings raided on Christmas Eve. And finally the night in question!—I had such butterflies I wouldn't have been surprised to find my feet lifted from the ground, but as Papa was sure we learned, haste is of the devil, and dutifully I placed Norman in the extaz for fear that the program of the evening would physically kill him. (How old were we before mastering the extaz? And Roman an adept by seventeen? My hair tingles.) I then knocked on Roman's door and requested he join me in the attic in several minutes.

Imagine the mise-en-scène! He had not noticed the renovation: the room now bare of furnishing after going untouched all those months, the flicker of ninety-nine black candles in a circle around the altar stone, and atop the stone: the bassinet. The incomprehension in the boy's eyes, the old—are we possibly so old?—wisdom in his mother's.

He stood in speechless soliloquy. I held his face in my hands and his eyes with mine and released him, by *extaz* released him from the unknowing it had been necessary to hold him in until this moment. All those secrets, whispers of a dream, now revealed. Finally!—no more secrets: it was time for us to be whole again and I gave him everything at once. How horrendous had been my ordeal—so many years and tears, so many hopes and frustrations for one womb, wasted efforts disposed of with a disconsolate shake—until finally he came! My miracle, swaddled in that luminous red caul that I peeled from his wrinkled skin myself and consumed in one swallow with humblest gratitude. How I could not believe my luck when Shelley too was born with the caul, but in intoxication over my prosperity sautéed with wine and wild mushrooms—only for the child to pay the price for my license. How all those times Roman found me unkind, the wearying old cunt I found myself playing, it was only, always, out of a mother's love of her most precious treasure (well, perhaps on occasion because of what a little shit he could be). How there was not nor ever had been an "angel," the fanciful by-product of a terminally birdbrained imagination, nor for that matter had he ever in fact had a cousin—how the Godfrey who supplied his name was not the same who supplied his blood, and that nine months ago Letha Godfrey was visited by her own brother, incapable of managing the dark tides within him.

(Boys will be boys!) And here the product of that impetuous union, far from stillborn, lying asleep not ten paces away.

I continued looking into his eyes, smiling in the hope that he would know that no matter how bitter the medicine his mother would be there with a spoonful of sugar to follow. But I'm afraid he rather had the countenance of the cartoon coyote who has just realized he has stepped off a precipitous cliff. In silence, he turned his back to me and sat on the top stair with a creak, listlessly allowing his weight to fall into me and resting his face on my thigh.

Just then the baby woke and began to cry as a tremble ran through Roman's body. You and I both know how hard it is, just as he knew in the heat of his blood what came next. He encircled my legs with his arms and clung closer, shaking now through and through, and brace your heart, he fought. He was a handful of iron shavings flung at a magnet. He felt the pull, but he fought it. This culmination, there was not a stray moment in his life that was not a step on the path to right here. All the time I was bringing him here. He squeezed the hem of my dress and began to whisper to himself. The same words over and over but I could not hear what they were. I waited and his pain flowed through me, but I knew that this was a necessary passage and that he would be overtaken soon enough, as we all are.

Suddenly he stood and stumbled to the window. A tad disheartening, I must profess—I had thought there would be more fight than all that. How I underestimated him! He braced himself with both hands and looking into his own eyes summoned the hardest stuff in him, repeating more loudly now what he had been telling himself: You must make your heart steel. I realized: he was trying use the extaz on himself! My prodigy! I glowed with pride even as the precocious failure of this strategy set into his posture and at last he turned to me. He asked why I was doing this.

But he knew. *The heart's compass finds its true north. The blood is the life.*

"All I want in the world is what's best for my baby," I said.

He looked at me and scraped from the bottom of his resolve.

"You don't win," he said.

He reached into his breast pocket and took out a small tin container. He opened the container and took out a small razor blade. He pressed the blade into the vein of one forearm and slashed it from elbow to wrist, and then repeated this with the other arm. He slumped against the wall and looked down at himself as the life pulsed out of him. It did not find its way to the floor but rather climbed the wall around him to form the most excellent incandescent wings.

My baby was flying!

Finally his head fell and I went to him. I pulled him to my lap and closed his eyes and held my fingers to his lifeless neck. I sang to him, the same way I would sing to our sunflowers to make them blossom. And so it happened: life thundered in my fingers and those eyes opened anew and my own precious sunflower blossomed. He looked up at me. All ambivalence and abhorrence now gone from his eyes. He knew. I held out my hand and he rose. Hand in hand we stood before the bassinet. The child now peaceful as he looked up at his father. Blood of blood. I released Roman's hand and stood back as the flesh of my arms rose. I could hear it in his veins. It was happening. I stood witness to the most delicate miracle of creation. Never in my life had I better earned a cry. So I bawled and he Became, forged as is needful for our kind in the furnace of incommunicable loss, at last at last at last his virgin fangs descending—such fangs! as white and perfect as an angel's, and he lowered his head into the bassinet to drink.

To think!—how those bleating chattel refer to us in epithet: the tragic absurdity one could be in a more perfect condition and happier with God unalive than undead!

Soon,

    O

O

Still. You must make your heart still.

The Boy Who Made Water of Ribbons

They are still driving. She said they would drive until he said stop and he hasn't said stop yet. She reaches to reflexively run her fingers through his hair, forgetting that it is now gone, and she massages his rough scalp, knobbed red with razor burn, the flesh pitifully white compared with the rest of him. She asks if he's hungry and he says maybe a little later. That is the hardest of all to countenance. In her own school days skinny as a willow, she learned it was light that fed the leaves and the grass and in turn everything that fed on leaves and grass and had since she held as firm a belief as any that turning away from the world of food was turning away from the world of light. But even in the remotest provinces of night the dawn will still come and a little later he would be hungry.

They approach a tollbooth. There is a bank of sand and strawlike grass to the left and Lynda's window admits salty air. A pit bull's head hangs out of the truck ahead of them, tongue lolling from its death grin like an unspooling red ribbon. Nicolae had said to her while she was pregnant that he had had a vision of holding the baby and the baby peeing on him and the pee coming out as one red silk ribbon after the other, and that was how he knew Peter would have a heightened receptivity in his Swadisthana.

"I knew that life for this little pisser would be long and full of great adventures," he said. "And it made me hurt inside of my bones with sadness. Because in a life that is long and well lived there are sorrows and darkest doldrums that cannot be understood by those who live day to day like it could be any other. And I knew that the lump inside that great big belly would grow one day into a fine man with fine shoulders and a big heart and he would need both in his adventures, which would take him many times through the Rivers of Woe and Lamentation. But even as these bones were sad for him there was O Beng's grin on my face because still this boy who had made water of a red ribbon was a Rumancek and this is America, and who knows, who knows!"

Somewhere close by there is a siren. The dog ahead of them lifts its nose into the air and closes its eyes. Peter closes his eyes too. He does not open his mouth, but the message is clear.

Yes, says Peter.

The message is clear.

Yes, I say, and so do you. Yes.

"A-ROOOOOOOOOOOOOOOOOOOOOOOOOOO," says the dog.

"A-ROOOOOOOOOOOOOOOOOOOOOOOOOOO . . ."

Acknowledgments

Sean McDonald and Emily Bell, for alchemy.

Lydia Wills, for being a champion.

Lee Shipman and Philipp Meyer, good medicine.

Michael Connolly, walking down that hill.

The memory of Patrick McGreevy, for the Dorothy Parker line (among others).

And for their generosity: Jim Magnuson, Michael Adams, and the gang at the Michener Center for Writers; the Reverend George Hickok and Avalanche; Kate Bolick; Adrian N. Roe and Gilbert Vasile; Smaranda Luna; Carolyn Hughes, Dr. Robert Hudak, Dr. Roy Chengappa, and the University of Pittsburgh Medical Center; the Austin State Hospital; Maja D'Aoust; Ron Baraff and the Rivers of Steel National Heritage Area; the Wolf Sanctuary of PA; the Waverly Presbyterian Church; and Lei-Lei.

Also, God.